To Kea

Many the

All the b

Robert

15/9/10

INVADING DARKNESS

Awakening

Robert Parker-Bowen

authorHOUSE®

AuthorHouse™ UK Ltd.
500 Avebury Boulevard
Central Milton Keynes, MK9 2BE
www.authorhouse.co.uk
Phone: 08001974150

First published by AuthorHouse 8/12/2010

ISBN: 978-1-4490-9642-7 (sc)

This book is printed on acid-free paper.

*To my lovely Wife, Family, Friends
and all the loved ones we have lost.*

*Thank you for always supporting me in
everything I do
(including the really daft things).*

*I love you all.
Robert*

Prologue:

Five hundred years ago the Dark God of Chaos attempted to invade the world of Vishante. He projected his consciousness out into space from his own Dark Realm. Not bound by the laws of time and space he surveyed Vishante searching for a suitable host to be his 'Key of Darkness'. The 'Key of Darkness' would be the physical presence of the Dark God's will on Vishante. Eventually after spending many years probing and testing the different races that exist on Vishante he found a susceptible mind... that of a small boy.

Using his vast power he forced his influence into the young boy's mind. The strain of trying to shut out the constant whispers and visions in his head sent the boy mad. While he was committed in jail he carved strange symbols all over his cell, as the whispers slowly took control of his mind. Then one day he escaped from jail by killing a guard and using his uniform to disguise himself as he fled.

The boy spent many years wandering the different lands of Vishante speaking the Dark God's words to the outcasts of society. He promised that a new world order was approaching. Slowly as his power and influence grew he built a large gathering of cultists all over Vishante.

After several years he commanded his cultist followers on Vishante to build strange devices called 'Dark Gateways'. Dark Gates were built in all the towns and cities where he held influence. No one knew The Dark Gateways would serve as conduits between the Dark God's Realm and Vishante until it was too late.

As each of the gates was completed, the Orcish minions of the Chaos God poured through the Dark Gateways situated in the towns and cities. The invasion of Vishante had begun. The Orcs quickly took control over the small towns in mere hours, while some cities took several days to be brought fully under the Dark God's control.

Under the guidance of General Fabiou Scar, the Dark God's champion, and The Key of Darkness, the Dark Army spread across the land slaughtering all resistance that stood in its way.

Using enslaved prisoners from the different races of Vishante, the Dark Army started to build The Gate of Darkness, a gateway large enough for the Dark God himself to travel through into Vishante. Once that happened nothing on the planet would be able to prevent the destruction of the remaining free races of Vishante.

The Gate of Darkness was constructed inside a massive fortress built into the side of Mount Demota, an active volcano, in the Western Mountains of Vishante.

Steam vents from the bowels of the volcano provided power for the fortress, while molten lava provided the heat to fire the massive foundry, and forges that produced the weapons and armour that powered the Dark Army's campaign across the planet.

Vishante was on the verge of becoming a true dark world, one of a large number ruled by the Dark God. Vishante was saved from the Dark God, by three brothers and an army called 'The Amassing of Light'.

The three brothers Anot, Bashir and the eldest brother Sanon escaped from their hometown just before it was totally destroyed. Their escape took them to the north where they found themselves in the kingdom of the Dragonlord and his brood of dragons.

The Dragonlord never usually got involved with the affairs of what he called 'the lesser races' but even he had to acknowledge the danger the Dark God posed to Vishante. During their time spent amongst the dragons the brothers learned one of the oldest legends of the dragons of Vishante. The legend told of an ancient and powerful dragon that lived somewhere in the Ice Desert to the very south of Vishante.

The brothers were informed that this dragon, if it existed, might hold the key to Vishante's survival. The brothers decided to try and find the ancient dragon so they journeyed far into the south of Vishante. They did not set out alone however. To help them on their journey Fara, the Dragonlord's own daughter accompanied the group. Fara was a golden coloured female dragon and had taken an interest in the human world much to her father's disapproval. Protected by Fara, the brothers set out to find one of the last remaining Ancient Stella Dragons.

Stella Dragons would travel from world to world seeking out safe places to nest. They were also bitter enemies of the Dark God who had destroyed their home world and forced upon them their nomadic wandering of the stars.

The brothers and Fara travelled across Vishante helping those who were trying to resist the Dark Army and making many allies who aided them in their travels. Finally after many adventures and a long journey they finally found the Ancient Stella Dragon of Vishante nesting in the Ice Desert to the far south of Vishante as the Dragonlord had said. At first the Ancient Dragon was reluctant to help the group, fearing any involvement would reveal her presence on Vishante and put her nesting ground in danger. However the Dark God was already aware of her presence and had dispatched General Scar and his troops to destroy the nesting grounds. A fierce battle to protect the nesting grounds broke out between the group and Scar's troops. The battle nearly cost Sanon his life. He tried to fight Scar but was easily beaten by the general; but before Scar could deliver a fatal blow, the ground erupted as the Ancient Stella Dragon sacrificed her nesting grounds to seal the group safely underground. Scar, believing them dead and his work done, returned north to continue the conquest of Vishante.

The Ancient Dragon had sealed the group, along with herself, underground in a pocket of time using the magic from her sacrificed young in the nesting grounds. She vowed that the Dark God would not have Vishante

Over the course of a year inside the pocket (or only seven days outside of the pocket) the Ancient Stella Dragon taught the brothers about special crystals found on Vishante and other worlds. She taught them how to harness the elemental properties of the different crystals to gain special powers to use against the Dark Army and help her to get her vengeance.

Armed with this new knowledge and skills the brothers returned north with Fara and started to gather the remaining bands of resisting survivors together during a period known as 'The Rising Sun'. During this period the brothers began to fight back against the Dark Army and built up a network of hidden bases over Vishante. Some bases would mine the special crystals needed for Vishante's resistance, others produced weapons while some were dedicated to the training of others to use the special abilities of the crystals. Soon the brothers had called together an army to combat and drive back the Dark Army. This army was known as the 'Amassing of Light'.

The brothers divided the 'Amassing of light' into three separate armies. Anot led the Western Amassing, Bashir the Eastern Amassing and Sanon with the aid of Fara led the Central army, later known as the Spearhead.

The goal was to stop the flow of the Dark Army resources into Vishante from the Dark realm. The three armies headed north, west and east destroying or burying any Dark Gates they encountered and freeing as many slaves as they could to bolster their own ranks. By almost constantly moving and using the established hidden bases the three armies avoided engaging the superior main force of the Dark Army.

The final battle for Vishante took place at the Dark Fortress itself. The three armies attacked the fortress from different sides drawing out a majority of the Army stationed inside. As the battle raged on the side of the volcano, the brothers reunited and led a small contingent of men inside the Dark Fortress.

Once inside they managed to reach the Foundries. Diverting the flow of the molten lava they set the foundries to explode destroying the foundations and sinking the Dark Fortress into the volcano.

As they made there way out of the Dark Fortress they encountered General Scar and his own group of elite soldiers. Fighting their way out of the Dark Fortress the two brothers escaped. Sanon and one other man remained behind to face the general and his elites. They hoped to allow Anot, Bashir and their men time to escape.

The two great warriors fought on the battlements of the fortress surrounded by the dark elite and in the presence of the Key of Darkness himself. The two were evenly matched until the foundries finally erupted ripping through the Dark Fortress. Sanon barely managed to escape after an explosion blew him from the battlements of the fortress as it erupted. He was caught as he fell by Fara who managed to carry him to safety.

The Dark Fortress sank into the volcano which erupted destroying all trace of the Dark Fortress and the Gate of Darkness. It was never known what happened to Fabiou Scar or the other man. It is assumed that they both died in the explosion that destroyed the fortress along with the Key of Darkness.

Though the Gate of Darkness and Fortress were now reduced to rubble there was still a large Dark presence on Vishante. Though it now lacked the coordination and tactics of the General or the guiding control of the Key of Darkness it still posed a major danger to the free world. The remaining force could potentially rebuild or reopen the existing Dark Gates allowing reinforcements back to Vishante.

The brothers separated again with their armies to remove the remaining Dark presence from Vishante. The brothers formed the first three main kingdoms of Vishante as bases to strike against the Dark forces still in the world. Gias, the western kingdom, founded by Anot. Bashir formed Kilyus, the eastern kingdom, and Arlieana, the central kingdom, was formed by Sanon.

After 50 years, the Dark Army was reduced to a mere memory, a story told to frighten the next generations. Songs of victory were sung each year on the anniversary of the great battle, to honour those who had fallen in the battle for the planet. In that time the brothers had established cities and started to rebuild the world.

In Arlieana it was decided to set-up a college that would pass on the knowledge of the crystals and teachings that the Ancient Stella Dragon had taught the brothers. Over the five centuries each of the kingdoms developed and grew to fill Vishante. Peace reigned and Vishante slowly recovered.

Darkness had been beaten and driven back, but across the black void of space dark eyes still watched and patiently waited.

Invading Darkness:
Book 1 – Awakening

Robert Parker-Bowen

A man slept uneasily, tossing and turning in his bed.

Images flashed in front of his sleeping eyes, the view of the darkened room as seen from under a bed. Tattered boots are walking into another room. A woman screams. The scream is suddenly cut off by a heavy thud.

A woman is dragged out of another room, pulled across the floor by her foot. Her arms are outstretched in front of her.

Blood flows from her head leaving a large red trail across the floor. The footsteps continue past the bed then pause. The woman's face is turned toward the bed, her face frozen in terror and her eyes wide open. The bed is lifted and thrown aside...

His eyes snap open and blink away the sweat that stings his eyes. The room is lit by the moonlight shining through the open window. Sitting up he swings his legs out of bed and wiped the sweat from his face with his hand. Outside the clock tower on the Library gently chimes twice.

"An hour this time" He muttered to himself as he turned and looked out of the window at the clock tower.

Sleep was becoming harder to do these days. He stood up and walked over to the desk on the other side of the room. Clothes had been laid out on its wooden surface. He dressed and walked over to the door. The light from the corridor filled the room briefly as he opened the door and stepped through. Darkness returned as the door shut.

Several hours later in the morning light, a knock sounded out on the Craftmaster's office door. The Craftmaster looked up from the papers on his desk and took the pipe out of his mouth.

"Come" He shouted at the door.

The door opened and a face appeared around the side of it.

"Excuse me Craftmaster have you seen Malik?" The face said.

"Ah Charleston" replied the Craftmaster leaning back into his chair.

"He was here this morning before I got here"

The Craftmaster puffed on his pipe sending a wisp of smoke into the air.

"He was working on something in the forge again"

"He's not there Sir, it was the first place I checked"

The Craftmaster scratched his head.

"Hmm, now I think about it I thought I saw him out of the window about twenty minutes ago. I think he might have been heading over to the training grounds if that's any help?"

"Thank you Sir" Charleston said and disappeared from view, a few seconds later he then reappeared.

"Oh, if I miss him and he comes back could you tell him the Captain wants to see him in his office"

"Certainly Charleston" Replied the Craftmaster.

Charleston nodded and shut the door while the Craftmaster took a pencil from behind his ear and made a note in a book and went back to reading the papers on his desk.

Charleston walked along the corridor that led the way out of the workshops. Daylight now shone brightly through the open doorway at the end.

The sounds of the city filtered into the courtyard as he stepped out of the doorway and into the open air.

At one end of the courtyard was the entrance to the Crimson Guardian training grounds. Attached to the entrance there was a little office and a guard inside who sat by the open hatch marking people in and out.

Charleston waved at the guard as he made his way toward the entrance. As he approached the guard inside came out to greet him.

"Morning Brent, has Malik been past here?" Charleston asked as Brent approached.

"Yes he signed into the Clay Golem Arena"

"Great thanks!"

Charleston rushed off into the training grounds. He paused and shouted back.

"Beers are on me and May tonight, Malik won the bet so we're meeting at the Brewers Maid"

He turned and set off toward a large dome shaped building while Brent waved and turned back toward his office.

A man stands at the top of a set of stone steps. At the bottom of the steps in the centre of the room there was a set of circle patterns engraved into the floor.

Four deep lines ran from the outside into the middle where it formed another circle pattern. In the centre of that circle there was a bubbling pool of dark brown coloured liquid.

Directly above the inner circle attached to the ceiling by four large ornamental claw shaped supports was a large dark green sphere. The four grooves ran up the walls to each of the supports.

The man drew a sword from his belt and examined it. He ran his fingers along the blade as if searching for any imperfections it the metal.

"Begin Minotaur training" He commanded and started to walk down the steps toward the circle.

Bright green light flicked and sparked around the sphere's surface. The sphere slowly began to glow brightly and the sparking across the surface became more intense.

The light flowed from the sphere into the supports that held the sphere in place. It continued along the supports and into the four grooves and ran down the walls to the circles on the floor. The circles glowed as they were filled with the unnatural green light. The light seemed to be flowing into the bubbling pool of liquid.

The liquid in the inner circle bubbled vigorously then a shape began to form and rise up from the liquids surface. The shape continued to rise and began to form a humanoid shape. Arms and legs developed from the shape. A bull's head took shape. The figure spread its arms wide and tilted its head back and let out an unnatural roar.

The light swirled up and around the figure, then exploded in a blinding green flash, and revealed standing before him was a clay beast with the head of a bull, the body of a man, and its massive legs were that of a goat. The eyes flared bright green.

The Minotaur reached behind its back and withdrew a huge hammer that it held with both hands. The man changed his stance and held up his sword while the clay beast raised the hammer behind its head and stepped forward bringing it down at the man.

The man dived forward as the hammer hit the floor with enough force to smash the stone slabs and bury the hammers head deep into the ground.

The man hit the floor and rolled over his shoulder past the Minotaur's leg. As he rose to his feet he turned and brought his sword up and round at the Minotaur's left leg. The blade sliced through the Minotaur's leg causing it to loose its balance and fall sideways hitting the floor with a hollow thud before rolling onto its back. The man jumped on the clay chest and raised his sword to thrust it down toward the clay chest.

The Minotaur caught the blade in its left hand, wrenched the sword from his grip then flung the sword into the closest wall. The sword entered the wall blade first and buried itself up to the hilt.

A large clay hand grabbed the man around the shoulder and with no apparent effort flung him over arm to the other side of the room.

The man hit a wall side on before he landed heavily on his back. He staggered to his feet clutching his chest trying to catch a breath of air before he fell over again. He shook his head to try and stop the world from spinning and gathered himself.

Gasping for breath, he tried to reclaim the air that the fall had knocked out of him. Looking up he saw the Minotaur grip the severed leg and put it back on to the stump that was its leg.

Getting to its hooves the Minotaur grasped the hammer shaft and pulled the hammer free from the floor with one hand. The man unsteadily stood up and leaned with his back against the wall still gasping for air.

The Minotaur charged at the man, as it gained speed it held the hammer outstretched in front of it like a large battering ram.

At the last possible second the man spun out of the hammers path, which smashed into the wall causing cracks to appear on the walls surface. He pulled a smaller sword from behind his back. When he gripped the hilt the blade extended to twice the original length.

He brought the blade down on the shaft of the hammer cutting the shaft behind the hammers head.

The Minotaur held the hammer's shaft up to look at it, then turned and hit the man with a right back fist sending him into the air again and across the room.

The man rolled as he landed on the floor then steadied himself on one knee and spat out some blood. Wiping the remaining blood from his mouth he scrambled to his feet and ran to his original sword still buried in the wall.

Grasping the sword he started to try and pull the sword free from the wall. Behind him the Minotaur turned toward him and grasping the broken hammer shaft like a spear started to charge again at the man.

Hearing the sound of the approaching hooves the man braced a foot against the wall trying to pull harder on the sword. Even with the extra leverage from his foot he was still unable to pull his sword free.

Time seemed to slow as the sweat on his brow begun to sting his eyes. The sound of the hooves on the stone slabs slowed to a steady slow thumping.

"You had to test the sword didn't you? You had to see if it would respond" He muttered to himself and grunted.

He closed his eyes and concentrated as the Minotaur closed the distance on the man. The broken hammer shaft still aimed at his exposed back.

Around the hilt where the blade was buried in the wall a faint red glow appeared through the cracks. As he continued to concentrate the red glow intensified. He lowered his foot back down to the ground as the blade started to loosen itself from the wall.

The Minotaur lunged forward with the broken hammer shaft aimed at his back.

Time seemed to stop.

Several things suddenly happened at once, the sword came free from the wall its blade covered in brightly glowing red symbols. The sword edge glowed brightly as if it was red hot.

The man moved incredibly fast, turning away from the wall bringing the blade round with him.

The hammer shaft grazed his stomach and pierced the wall while the red glowing blade sliced through the air leaving a faint red trail behind it. The blade met no resistance as it connected with the Minotaur's head slicing the top half clean off. There was silence.

The top half of the Minotaur's head made a hollow clunking sound as it bounced around on the floor before finally rolling to a halt. The body remained standing upright in the position it had been before the blade connected.

The man lowered the sword and wiped his brow with his sleeve. He examined both sides of the blade as the symbols faded away.

"Well that seemed to work well" He chuckled.

He turned and walked toward the steps leading back out of the room.

As he reached the bottom step he looked down and noticed a shadow moving up behind him on the floor. He ducked and felt the rush of air pass over his head as the broken hammer shaft was swung across where his head had momentarily been.

Turning around he saw the Minotaur's body was still moving without the top half of its head. The Minotaur swung the shaft around and brought it down at the man. There was a ringing sound as the man blocked the attack with his sword.

The Minotaur lifted the broken shaft to strike again and as it did the man thrust the sword into the Minotaur's chest.

"Put this back together" He growled through his gritted teeth at the Minotaur.

The sword flared bright red.

Cracks formed where the sword was embedded into the Minotaur's chest. Red light shone through the cracks as they continually spread across the whole of the Minotaur's body.

The man pulled his sword from the chest and walked up the steps. When he reached the top step he held his sword with the tip pointing down and tapped the sword against the stone floor three times.

On the third tap the Minotaur exploded in a ball of bright red light.

When the red light died away the man lowered his hand that he had used to shield his eyes.

"Malik!" A voice shouted from outside the chamber.

The man turned as Charleston entered the room.

"What's the matter Charleston? I'm not letting you or May back out of paying up on the bet!" Said the man called Malik as he wiped the sweat from his face with his hand. He looked down at the sword again and smiled before he then sheathed it back into his belt.

"No no, the Captain wants to see you. That's if you've finished playing with the pottery of course"

Charleston looked at the room as the pieces of shattered Minotaur turned back into a liquid and flowed back into the pool at the centre of the room. The damage on the floor and walls repaired itself. After a few seconds the room looked as if nothing had ever happened.

"What the hell were you fighting in here anyway Malik?"

"Minotaur"

"What? On your own! Bloody hell that's a team training exercise" Said Charleston looking worried.

"Oh I forgot to tell you, I finished your short sword" Malik said and patted Charleston on the shoulder as he walked past.

"Great! Where is it?" Replied Charleston worries temporarily forgotten.

"Still in there"

Malik motioned with his thumb over his shoulder as he walked past.

"It works really well if I do say so myself! Oh and thank you for the message" Malik called back as he walked outside into the sunshine.

Charleston walked down the steps into the training area looking around until he finally spotted the sword stuck into the ceiling

"How in the hells am I supposed to get that!?" He shouted at the door.

12

A girl runs through dark woods following a small path, ahead she can see faint lights shining in the distance. Thorns and branches whip at her bare legs as she sprints past.

Jumping over a log lying across the path she lands in a puddle of mud and slides to a halt. As she gasps for breath something howls behind her, the howl echoes out into the distance. She scrambles in the mud trying to get back to her feet.

Managing to get her breath back she grips a branch with a numb hand and pulls herself out of the mud. She staggers to her feet as another much closer howl echoes into the night. The sound causes the hairs to stand up on the back of her neck as she begins to run along the path again.

As she runs she becomes aware that something large is breaking the bushes and branches beside the path she is running on.

What is worse is that it is quickly gaining ground on her. Up ahead she sees a broken tree has fallen down against another, forming a small opening at the bottom. She runs for the tree and dives through the small gap.

There is a roar of annoyance and something very large hits the tree shaking it. The girl turns and looks back briefly at the tree as she desperately fights for breath. She scrambles on the muddy ground and starts to run with all of what remains of her strength toward the town.

Several yards ahead another howl causes her to pause. She looks back in terror at the tree. As she does the tree is lifted and thrown aside where it smashes into several other trees knocking them down.

Panic fills her mind and she starts to sprint toward town this time propelled by sheer terror until she reaches the outskirts of the town. Running from door to door she bangs on them shouting and screaming for someone to let her in.

She continues to run along the street toward the town centre. The street lanterns that illuminate the dark streets stream past her as she runs. She reaches a large house with light streaming out of the windows and around the edges of the double doors. She ran up the steps to the double doors and pressed her back up against them and looked around at the dark town. She continued to bang on the doors with the palms of her hands.

The lanterns that light the streets began to blink out one at a time. Darkness slowly starts to close in around her until the only light left was that of the house. She started to beat frantically on the door with her hand.

Inside the house the people huddled together as a scream echoed out from behind the barred doors. The screaming suddenly stopped and all that remained was a deafening silence.

The Captain's office was on the top floor of the Crimson Guard headquarters. Malik climbed up the stairs to the top floor stopping once or twice to let people past. There was usually always a lot of activity around the headquarters day or night.

Malik made his way down a corridor to the Captain's outer office. There sitting at a large desk piled high with papers was the Chief Administrator, May. Along with Charleston, May was one of Malik's closest friends. The three had grown up together, after Malik had been brought to the city by the Captain.

She looked up from the pile of papers on her desktop. She had a worried face but managed to smile at Malik as he approached.

"He's expecting you, go right in"

"Thank you, what's the matter? Worried about having to pay out for beer later on?"

"No!" She said hotly "We've been getting horrible reports from the northeast of Arlieana"

She picked up a sheet of paper and read a few lines.

"People have been disappearing at night, livestock has been found mutilated. Whole towns are being found deserted"

May put down the sheet of paper again and pinched the bridge of her nose with her thumb and forefinger.

"We're being stretched thin at present. Every able Guardian is being deployed, anyway you had better go in" She said waving a hand at the door leading to the Captain's office.

Malik nodded and patted her on the shoulder as he walked past.

The Captain was standing looking out of the window his hands were behind his back. Malik entered and stood to attention in front of the Captain's desk.

"How are you Malik?"

The Captain turned and walked over to his desk and sat in the chair.

Malik said nothing he just stared straight ahead.

"Please sit down Malik you are starting to make me nervous"

"Thank you sir" Malik said and sat down in the chair.

"First let me congratulate you Malik, you have been commended for your last mission. The Baron was most pleased by the way you single-handedly rescued his daughter from the bandits"

"Thank you Sir"

"May I ask what your strategy was since you were outnumbered? I believe there were twenty five bandits?"

"Well Sir, have you heard that the Baron's mines were haunted?"

"No?"

"The bandits didn't at first but when they started to disappear into thin air and they heard a strange moaning they soon did"

"Moaning?"

"Yes Sir, I did feel like a bit of a pillock at the time but it was all I could come up with on the spur of the moment. After a night of that most of them ran out of the mine leaving just the ring leader and the Baron's daughter behind and he wasn't much of a challenge by that point"

"I see, I see, well I'm impressed well done"

"Thank you Sir"

"The Craftmaster has again requested you join the Armourers he believes you have a natural talent"

"I would prefer to stay with the Guardians Sir"

"Why is that, may I ask?"

"The Armourers make the best weapons in Arlieana, but the Guardians use them"

The Captain smiled and crossed his legs as he sat back in his chair.

"It seems that the Craftmaster is very excited about a recent project you finished. He has just finished reading your notes" The Captain said and glanced at Malik's sword.

Malik looked at the Captain then drew his sword and carefully placed it on the Captain's desk.

"May I?" The Captain asked.

Malik nodded and the Captain picked up the sword.

"By the Gods it's light" He swung the sword around a few times then looked down the length of the blade. "Perfectly balanced, mind you I'm not surprised given your talents. And you shattered a Clay Golem Minotaur with this?"

Malik looked surprised.

"How did you know that? Err Sir?" He added remembering himself.

The Captain looked up from his examination of the sword.

"When a lone trainee gets the stupid idea to try and complete a three man team exercise on his own. Then manages to actually complete the exercise, it does tend to cause comment among the trainers, even when you cannot see them"

"Have you been watching me Sir? I told you I'm fine"

The Captain watched Malik for a moment, smiled then handed the sword back, Malik took it and put it back in its sheath on his belt.

"Excellent craftsmanship Malik, The spirit trigger for the red spirit stone I see mounted to the blade is set to your blood only I imagine?"

"Err not quite, I can add other people if I want too" Said Malik slightly taken aback.

"I've not seen a Spirit stone that colour before usually they are purple, strange I wonder..." He said quietly to himself.

"Err how did you know about the spirit trigger? May I ask?" Malik spoke up.

The Captain snapped out of whatever he was thinking about and pressed a single ornamental jewel on his desk. The jewel glowed red and a secret drawer extended from the side of the desk. The drawer barely made any sound at all as it opened on well-oiled runners.

Inside the drawer was a sword and set into the hilt was a purple jewel.

The Captain took the sword out of the drawer and held it at arms length.

The jewel in the hilt began to glow with a red light. The light got brighter and patterns shone along the blade.

The blade edge glowed as brightly as the spirit stone set in the hilt.

"The same way you did Malik. By reading the texts in the library your father wrote. You are not the only one to fuse a spirit stone to a blade" The Captain said and looked at his sword. "Mine is fused to the hilt of my father's sword. Yours is the red jewel fused directly into the blade am I right?"

Malik looked stunned and said nothing as the Captain smiled and continued.

"I know how hard it is to do and I did it twice, it nearly drove me mad the amount of effort I had to put in to get it right"

The red glow faded from the Captain's sword. He lowered it and placed it back into the drawer and pressed the jewel on the desk again making the drawer slide shut again.

"You fused spirit stones in two swords!" said Malik.

"Gods no that would have killed me"

The Captain sat back down in his chair again and crossed his legs.

"No I fused my sword and a silver pendent from a single split stone"

"So it is true about the Princess Pendent" Malik gasped.

"Yes and I said that in confidence, understood" The Captain said while glaring at Malik.

"Yes Sir"

Malik had heard stories about the Captain, they all had. When Crimson Guardian training first started, gate duty was part of the training. The older Guardians would tell the trainees stories about the Captain.

The story went that the Captain in his youth had saved Princess Tia of Arlieana while they had been on a diplomatic visit to the Kingdom of Gias that bordered Arlieana to the west.

The Kingdom of Kilyus in the east had sent a team of assassins to Gias to kill the Princess and frame Gias for the crime. It was an attempt to damage the recently agreed cessation of hostility treaty between Arlieana and Gias and the reopening of trade routes between the two kingdoms.

The Royal Carriage was ambushed while it was travelling through the open countryside that led to Nelvin the capital of Gias. The assassins had planted an explosive device on the road which they detonated as the coach passed. The explosion killed the advance guard and blocked the road. The assassins then attacked the coach in the confusion.

The initial attack killed nearly all the carriage's guards except for one who was only wounded. The wounded guard managed to get the coach out of the ambush and away but was later forced to abandon the coach a short distance afterwards due to the damage it had sustained in the initial ambush.

After having his wound treated, the last surviving guard led the Princess through the wilderness back to Arlieana while being hunted by the Kilyus assassins hell bent on killing them both.

During one confrontation the guard and the Princess managed to capture one of the assassins and learned the details of the plot against Arlieana. It was never revealed how they actually managed to extract the information from the assassin, as they both never spoke of it to anybody. All that the guard reported is that the assassin died afterwards in a failed attempt to escape from their custody.

As the pair crossed the Western Mountains to get back into Arlieana they sheltered from a snowstorm in a cave. It was here that they found a rare Elemental Spirit Stone. The Princess took the stone and gave it to the guard when they finally returned to Arlieana.

Upon their return to Arlieana the guard was honoured by the King himself and promoted to the position of Captain and set the task of forming the Crimson Guardians, a group of elite guards charged with the protection of the Royal Family and Arlieana.

What wasn't widely known is that the Captain took the Spirit Stone he and the Princess had found and split it in half. One half he forged into the hilt of his family sword. The Spirit Stone when forged with a weapon grants the wielder boosted physical abilities when activated making them a most sought after accessory for any warrior.

The other half of the Spirit Stone he used to create a small silver pendent which he gave to the Princess. She has never been seen without the pendent since and the two of them have shared a close bond ever since.

Whenever the Princess is to be sent away on diplomatic matters the Captain always insists on going as her personal bodyguard. It is rumoured that he can sense where she is and if she's in any danger.

"Sir can I just ask, why are you showing and well... telling me this?"

"Malik I have known you for going on fourteen years now. You are the son of two of my closest friends, may the Gods smile on there souls. I trust you, and along with May and Charleston you are the most promising of the new generation Crimson Guardians. No trainee has ever fused a Spirit Stone, which shows me you have your father's talents. You have demonstrated exceptional skill with weapons and crafting, you have proficient knowledge of healing and survival techniques, the list goes on and on"

The Captain picked up some papers and read a few lines then looked up again.

"Tomorrow I will give you your next assignment. I suggest you prepare your equipment"

"Yes Sir"

Malik stood up as he went to open the door when the Captain called out.

"It would also seem that you don't sleep any more Malik"

"I try not to these days" said Malik quite honestly.

The Captain stared at him over the top of his sheet of paper.

"It's just bad dreams Sir that's all"

The Captain continued to stare for a few more seconds. Malik shifted uneasily.

"I see" The Captain made a note on a piece of paper before continuing "Go and see the Healers, in any case you are due an examination before your assignment"

"Yes Sir"

"And Malik, I'll be watching"

Malik saluted at the Captain who nodded, Malik opened the door and stepped out into the corridor. He shut the door and leaned against it before taking a deep breath.

The Healers Guild was located east of the Crimson Guardians Headquarters. Malik wandered toward the Healers Guild House, people filled the streets going about their daily lives. Carts clattered by as Malik glided through the crowds. It was one of the lesser known perks of being a Crimson Guardian, people tended to get out of your way. No Crimson Guardian would injure a civilian intentionally, after all they were their protectors – but no one wanted to put it to the test just in case.

The clock tower on the Library roof sounded noon as Malik passed by and crossed the street to reach the Healers Guild. Opposite the Healers Guild House down the next street the Elemental Mages College shimmered in the sunlight. The outer wall of the college was made of ice and was maintained by the Elemental Mages within the college. It never melted even in the hottest of summers. The other strange thing is that the ice wall wasn't cold to the touch. Malik personally thought that they were just showing off.

He climbed the steps to the main doors of the Healers Guild and wandered inside. The doors were always left open as ordered by the Master Healer. Above the door was a large brass plaque. It had a quote from the current Master Healer engraved on it. It read 'People hurt themselves no matter what time of day it is' which pretty much summed up the Master Healers view of people. It always cheered Malik up no matter how many times he saw it.

Passing through the open doors Malik entered the main reception chamber and walked to the main desk in the centre of the room. Sunlight shone into the room through the large glass dome that formed part of the roof up above.

Under the dome there was a large lush garden inside the Healers Guild. It was full of various brightly coloured plants of all different types and species. Placed around the garden were large comfortable padded benches providing seating for the different people who were waiting to be seen. A small ornamental waterfall ran out from one of garden walls and gathered in a small pond filled with a few small fish. A man in a white robe was carefully watering the plants.

The garden was well maintained as it not only provided a relaxing seating area but also provided some rare medicinal herbs that the healers used in their treatments.

Malik smelled the floral aroma as he walked past, he remembered when he had been badly hurt once while training and had to be brought to the Healers Guild. He had spent most of his recovery time in the garden talking to the Chief Gardener about the uses of the different plants.

As Malik approached the desk the receptionist looked up from her paper work and smiled.

"Can I help you Guardian?"

"Err, yes I have a Crimson Guardian pre-assignment examination"

"Ahh yes, Malik Owen is it? The Master will see you in his office"

She turned and pointed at a large set of stairs that led up to the first floor of the Guild.

"If you head up the stairs behind me his office is straight down the corridor, please knock before entering"

"Thank you very much" Malik replied and set off toward the stairs.

The stairs were large and ornate. They were also tapered so they were wider at the bottom. As Malik reached the top of the stairs he saw the main corridor in front of him and two other side corridors on the left and right.

He walked down the main corridor heading for the very end where the Master Healer's office was. There were many doors on either side of the main corridor, each one had a brass nameplate on identifying which examination room or office it was.

The sunlight shone brightly through the high glass windows casting shadow patterns on the floor. Malik felt the warmth from the sunlight on the back of his neck and was oddly cheered by it.

Malik finally reached the Master Healer's office and knocked on the door.

"Enter!" He heard the Master Healer's voice sound out from behind the door.

Malik took a deep breath again before opening the door and walking in.

Inside, the Master Healer's office was well lit, large and roomy. On the right hand side shelves covered most of the office wall space. They were adorned with books and various vials of different coloured liquids. There was a curved desk sat by a large set of windows. It was positioned so as much natural light as possible would shine onto the desktop.

Lining the left side of the office wall were bookcases, shelves and a set of medicine cupboards. There was also another door leading to the Master Healer's own examination room. The Master Healer was just replacing a book onto a bookshelf and turned as Malik entered.

"Ahh, Malik how have you been hmm? That injured arm of your's back to normal?"

"Yes thank you Master Healer it's as good as new"

"Well that's good to know, Captain Heald always takes an interest in your health"

"Does he really? Anyway I've been told to report to you for a pre-assignment examination"

"Splendid, He did tell me to expect you. Please come this way"

The Master Healer beckoned Malik to follow him into the examination room. Inside the examination room there was a large padded table in the middle of the room and suspended from the ceiling above was a machine with many frightening mechanical arms.

Attached on the end of each arm was a shaped crystal each one a different colour.

"Please lay down on the table this won't take long" The Master Healer said cheerfully.

Malik lay down on the table and the Master Healer disappeared behind a large glass screen where he started to pull leavers and flick switches. The arms on the machine sprang into life and extended out from the centre. They stopped briefly then started to spin quickly.

"Are you sure this is safe?" Malik shouted at the Master Healer.

"Oh yes don't worry I'm quite well protected, oh yes please don't make any sudden movements"

"Oh that's very reassuring thank you!"

The spinning arms slowed and then finally stopped spinning. An arm equipped with a gently glowing red crystal extended and stopped roughly twelve inches above Malik. The arm then moved horizontally from Malik's head down to his feet.

"Very good" The voice of the Master Healer could be heard from behind the screen. "The break has healed far better than I ever expected"

The red crystal arm retracted back to the middle and a yellow crystal arm extended out and repeated the motion of the first arm.

"Good good" The Master Healer's voice sounded out again.

The yellow crystal arm retracted and the Master Healer appeared from behind the screen.

"The Captain tells me you suffer from insomnia?"

"No, well not really I can go to sleep but it's the nightmares that keep on waking me up" Malik said as he sat up on the bench.

"Nightmares, hmm" The Master Healer looked thoughtful and pulled a device from his pocket. It looked like a gold magnifying lens with a purple crystal attached in front of the lens.

He walked over to Malik and held the device with the crystal close to Malik's head. The Master Healer moved it around Malik's head while looking through the lens.

"Is it always the same nightmare?" He asked.

"Yes"

"For how long has it been going on?"

"About four months now"

The Master Healer removed the purple crystal and replaced it with a green one. He looked through the lens again with the new crystal in place and ran it slowly over Malik's head again.

"Well it isn't a result of any physical damage or if it is its nothing that I can detect. I suppose I could run a series of deep cranial scans to be sure"

"Err, lets not" Malik replied looking nervously at the mechanical arms again.

"Are you sure? Oh very well then" The Master Healer said disappointedly lowering the lens. "I believe that it is possibly a suppressed memory, probably a very old one, you must have been very young at the time"

"I don't remember?"

"Your mind shut out the trauma to protect itself. At least that is the best way I can explain it. As to why it has started to recur recently I really cannot say"

"What can I do?"

The Master Healer walked back into his office with Malik in tow and opened the medicine cabinet and started looking through the contents.

"Well I can give you some pills that will put you to sleep without dreaming, they may help you in the short term"

The Master Healer reached into the cabinet and removed a small bottle of tablets and gave it to Malik.

"For the long term I don't think there is anything I can really do to help you Malik. The only thing that may stop the dreams is to totally remember everything and come to terms with whatever happened or just suppress it again. The trouble is suppressed memories may just come back again and again"

"Can I still go on assignment?" Malik asked.

"Physically there is nothing wrong with you apart from the lack of sleep. I'll tell you what, go back to your quarters now and take two of those pills and I'll give you clearance to go on assignment tomorrow"

"I will, thank you Master Healer" Malik said as he put the bottle of pills into his pocket.

He nodded at the Master Healer then set off back to the Crimson Guardian Headquarters and his room.

There was a series of knocks on the door. The Captain looked up from his desk recognising the knock. It was May's 'You've got an official visitor' knock.

"Come in May" He called out.

The door opened and May entered the room and shut the door behind her.

"Father, Marcus is here to see you I have him in the waiting room, shall I send him in"

"Thank you May, please bring him in"

May opened the door and stepped out. She returned shortly followed by a man in a long brown robe. The Arch Mage carried a long wooden staff, which he used to help himself walk.

"Marcus my friend it's good to see you again!" The Captain said rising from behind his desk and walking over to the Arch Mage and giving him a hug.

"It is good to see you to James" The Arch Mage replied.

"May, would you fetch some wine for us please" The Captain asked.

"Certainly" She said and opened the door again.

May left the room and the Captain ushered the Arch Mage to the seat in front of his desk.

"How are Helena and the children?" The Captain asked.

"She is still overjoyed at finally being a grandmother. She sends her love by the way"

The Arch Mage sat down and leaned his staff against the chair.

"May has certainly grown since I last saw her, how long has it been now?" The Arch Mage asked.

"Almost two years now. I still cannot believe it has been twenty years since she was born and her mother died"

The Arch Mage raised an eyebrow at the Captain. There was a knock at the door.

"Come in" The Captain called out while shifting uneasily under the Arch Mage's steady gaze.

May entered the office carrying a tray with two glasses and a tall jug. She walked over to the desk and placed the tray on the Captain's desk.

"Thank you May, finish up and you are free for today. There is something going on at the Brewers Maid Tavern why don't you go join the lads? Charleston probably has something to do with it, so I need someone to keep an eye on him. Gods know I don't want to have to go through all that apologising again with that twit Baron Richardson"

"In Charleston's defence father, the Baron did start it"

"Yes and Charleston and Malik finished it" The Captain sighed. "Richardson is a pompous arse I know, but I have things to discuss with Marcus so go on"

"Alright, but don't stay here all night again, please father"

"I won't, now go on have some fun let your hair down for a little while"

May smiled and turned to leave.

"Hold on a second May" The Arch Mage called out to her. "I have something for you my dear"

The Arch Mage reached out his hand and closed his fist. He muttered a few words under his breath and light shone out from his clenched fist. When the light died away the Arch Mage turned his hand palm up and opened his fingers.

Sat in his hand was a broach made of ice.

"Oh that's beautiful. Thank you!"

May gave the Arch Mage a hug followed a kiss on the cheek.

"Well I haven't seen you for so long my dear, it's the least I could do" The Arch Mage said pinning the broach onto May's jacket. "Go on now, and have a good time, the broach won't melt at all"

The Arch Mage leaned back into the chair and grinned at the Captain.

May still smiling bowed her head and left the room. As the door closed the Arch Mage went back to his intense staring at the Captain and raised his eyebrow again.

"What?" The Captain said looking sheepishly at the Arch Mage.

"My friend you cannot lie to me, she has Tia's smile, eyes and blonde hair. If I am also not mistaken she also has her mother's charm in abundance"

"Alright, alright so her mother isn't dead but I'll have to kill you if you breathe a word to anybody"

The Captain pointed a finger at the Arch Mage who raised both his hands in a submissive gesture.

"James I had guessed as much a long, long time ago, you don't have to worry about me you know that"

The Captain relaxed and lay back in his chair.

"Does May know who her mother is?"

"We decided not to tell her until she is older, both for her own safety as well as Tia's but she suspects I'm lying to her. She is just like her mother in that respect"

"I see, James far be it from me to interfere but don't you think she is old enough now?" The Arch Mage paused and looked thoughtful for a moment then added. "Hold on you actually let her go out drinking with a bunch of men well into the night and it doesn't worry you in the slightest?"

The Captain smiled.

"You mean why do I let her out surrounded by some of the most highly trained men in Arlieana who treat her as a little sister? Those men would rather cut off there own hand than let anyone even remotely harm or lay a finger on her"

"Ah I see your point" Said the Arch Mage.

"All things considered May is one of the most well protected individuals in Founders Rock and besides, she is my daughter and she can look after herself"

"She does have your strength that is true" The Arch Mage said nodding to himself. "She might need it, I fear dark days may be upon us soon my friend" The Arch Mage said as he reached over and poured wine into the glasses.

He handed one to the Captain and took a sip from his own.

"You sense it as well then" The Captain replied.

"We've all been sensing a growing dark presence in the kingdom these past few months"

"That fits with my information, People have been disappearing from towns and villages close to one of the old recorded Dark Gate sites" The Captain replied.

"That is troubling news indeed. Let me guess, have you had a lot of reports from the Torkle region in the northeast?"

"Yes and we have had no direct reports from Lord Vindrel which worries me. We have only been getting reports from Stonewall and Falstaff the Mayor of Torkle. Something bad is going on out there. As a matter of fact I am planning on sending Malik there to investigate"

"James, how good is he really? Is he as strong as Tiber was?"

"He fused the Spirit Stone to his sword and then shattered a Clay Golem Minotaur by himself"

"Impressive, Tiber was the only other Crimson Guardian stupid enough to do that without awakening"

"He is capable enough without the stone or awakening. He is one of the best I have in the Crimson Guardians"

"I agree, but I would like to request that a Specialist go with him"

"Oh really, might I enquire as to why?"

"I've been looking through the surviving archives from the Dark Age. Torkle was one of the larger Dark Gateways into Arlieana. I want to send our Dark Gate expert in to make sure it stays closed"

"Who is your Specialist?" The Captain said as a large grin began forming on his face.

"Aris"

"Aris, it will be dangerous you do know that!"

"Yes I do" The Arch Mage sighed.

"But she knows more about the Dark Gates than anyone else and she is a powerful Elemental Mage"

"Much like her father then" The Captain said taking a drink of wine.

"She will be an asset to him and besides you know about the spell. I think it's time to reunite them. The poor boy has gone through a lot and deserves some happiness"

"Why doesn't he remember anything Marcus?" The Captain asked as he poured more wine.

"I don't know Aris has been patiently waiting for him. Her trust is unbreakable, all part of the spell I suspect but something should have triggered a response by now. Something is very wrong and until I know what it is he would be safer if she is with him"

"Alright I know better than to argue with you when you get that look on your face. She can go with Malik anyway if it might bring him some peace then that is fine by me we owe Tiber and Darcy that much at least"

"Thank you"

"I'll ask Malik to keep her safe for you"

"And I'll ask Aris to watch over Malik, I sense something evil is at work"

"Agreed"

Malik entered his room and shut the door behind him. He walked over to his bed and placed the bottle of pills on his bedside table.

He reached under the bed and pulled out a roll of black leather, which he unrolled on his table. Inside there was a selection of weapons of Malik's crafting.

He removed six throwing knives from the roll and examined each one before replacing it back in the leather roll. He took a sword from the roll and replaced it with his new sword from his belt that he had finished that morning.

Malik got up and opened his small wardrobe. He reached in and took out a crossbow and a length of black cord. The crossbow was another of Malik's designs. It had a loading slot under the crossbow, which he could load several arrows into. It also had a cocking mechanism allowing the crossbow to be quickly reloaded.

He examined the cocking mechanism and moved the lever built into the grip that cocked the crossbow. The mechanism made a satisfying clunk as the built in tensioners moved into position. He pulled the trigger and it clicked as the trigger hook released.

He reached back inside and removed a quiver of arrows from the wardrobe, then as an after thought took some more arrows and slotted them into the leather roll. Malik looked at his sword in the roll of leather, the Spirit Stone shone brightly for a moment as he touched it.

"I'll have to think of a name for you at some point" He said to the sword.

He folded the leather roll over and re rolled it up before tying the leather fasteners shut and putting it back on the table.

Malik went back to his bed, this time he pulled a travelling pack out from under it and sat down at his desk. He took a leather strap out of the bag and attached it to the crossbow so it could be slung over his shoulder. Next he took the leather roll and securely tied it to the side of his travel pack. When he was satisfied with the travel pack Malik undressed and got into his bed.

He reached for the bottle of pills and shook two pills out onto his open hand.

"Ah well, here goes nothing" He said and swallowed the pills, he lay back and was asleep as soon as his head hit the pillow.

The Brewers Maid Tavern had become the unofficial second Crimson Guardian Headquarters in Founders Rock. Guy Redleaf the owner didn't mind though. Spending weeks, sometimes months on assignment meant most Crimson Guardians returned home with new tales to tell, a deep desire to have a very large drink and best of all, pockets full of back pay!

The regular custom of the Crimson Guardians had made The Brewers Maid Tavern one of the most successful taverns in Founders Rock. So much so that in return Guy had set aside a wall upon which were mounted silver plaques with the names of those who hadn't returned home. The Crimson Guardians affectionately called it the 'Wall of the Lost' any Crimson Guardian lost while on assignment would always be remembered here. The tavern was filled with both male and female Crimson Guardians all talking and laughing. In one corner a group of Crimson Guardians were playing darts and drinking happily.

Charleston sat at table with some other Guardians playing cards.

"Where in the nine hells is Malik?" One of them said.

"Last I saw him he was heading to the Healers Guild" One of the other Guardians replied. "Charleston? Hey are you alright? Charleston!" The Guardian snapped his fingers by Charleston's ear.

Charleston's head was turned away, he was watching May enter the tavern and walk to the bar. She looked over at him and smiled as she passed.

The other Guardians around the table began laughing and sniggering.

"What?" Charleston said coming back from wherever he had been.

"Nothing, nothing we were admiring your death wish. You know her old man would go nuts and beat the living snot out of you if he knew you looked at her like that" A female Guardian said as she slapped Charleston on the shoulder.

"Yeah, well she would be worth it" Charleston said hotly.

"Hey hey we're all friends here right?" Another Guardian said holding up his hands.

"Sorry, I'll see you guys later" Charleston said standing up.

"Don't do anything stupid now!" One shouted at Charleston as he walked away.

May was leaning against the bar with a tankard in her hand as Charleston approached. She held it out to him as he stood by her.

"Since little brother isn't here that just leaves you and me to drink his winnings" She said.

"Shouldn't be too hard he is a lightweight after all"

May laughed and picked up her tankard from the bar.

"Too little brother, may he finally wake up and learn to drink properly!" She said holding up her tankard.

"Too Malik" Charleston replied and clinked his tankard against May's and downed the contents.

May stared at the silver plaques on the Wall of the Lost.

"Do you ever worry your name might end up on there?" She asked.

"Nope never"

"Why?"

"I would always come back to you"

May turned and smiled at him.

"You really are a charmer aren't you Crimson Guardian King?"

"That I am Crimson Guardian Heald"

"You know no one else has dared to make a move on me because of the sheer terror that is my father"

"Yes, you said that the last time I kissed you if you remember"

"He'll go up the wall"

"I know! You said that as well" He said leaning closer to her.

The room was suddenly very quiet Charleston turned around and discovered he had the entire tavern's attention.

"Don't you lot of drunken buggers have some drinking to do?" He shouted.

"We do indeed Charleston!" Brent shouted down from the Tavern's upper level. "But first give us reason to celebrate!"

A chorus started low and grew until the whole tavern was chanting as one.

"Kiss her!"

Charleston turned back to face May and shrugged his shoulders.

"Who am I to argue with that?" He said and gently took her hand pulling her away from the bar.

The tavern was silent as he put his arms around her and kissed her, the tavern erupted in a chorus of cheers and clapping.

"That boy is as good as dead" Brent said.

"Yup but at least he'll die happy!" The Craftmaster replied putting his pipe in his mouth and clapping.

The following morning Malik awoke and blinked in the morning sunshine that shone through his window. He stretched, got out of bed and dressed. For the first time in several weeks he felt really hungry and went down to the kitchen hall for something to eat.

While Malik was eating his breakfast, Charleston appeared with a mug of tea in his hand.

"Where were you last night little brother?" Charleston said sitting down in front of him.

"Believe it or not I was asleep and I really, really wish you wouldn't call me that, it's bad enough May calls me that"

"You were asleep? Bloody hellfire that hasn't happened for a while" Charleston said taking a drink of his tea.

"The Master Healer gave me some pills to take before he would let me go on assignment"

"Did they work?"

"Sure did, best sleep I've had for months"

"Any idea what your assignment will be?" Charleston asked taking another swig from his mug and pinching one of Malik's sausages from his plate.

"Not yet, I'm going to see the Captain in an hour to find out" Malik took the sausage back and began to eat it.

"By the way between you and me, how did you know the Captain wouldn't find out about me kissing May the other week?"

Malik looked up at Charleston and thought for a moment before he answered.

"Easy you're not suicidal!"

"Err I think I might have buggered that good and proper now!"

Malik stopped eating and stared at Charleston.

"Oh Gods, Charleston what did you do?"

"I kissed her in front of everyone in the Brewers Tavern"

Malik choked on his half eaten sausage as Charleston frantically slapped him on the back.

May opened the Captain's door and let Malik into the office. She closed the door behind him as the Captain looked up from his desk.

"Crimson Guardian Owen reporting for duty Sir"

"At ease, Malik let me fill you in on our situation. Please be seated"

Malik sat down in the chair in front of the Captain's desk while the Captain continued.

"As you know the Crimson Guardians are currently spread all over Arlieana. Something is happening in the world. Reports are coming in every hour of strange disturbances in the outer borders. So far we have managed to cope and keep order but what is disturbing me are the reports that I'm getting from returning Crimson Guardians"

The Captain picked up a piece of paper on his desk read a few lines then added.

"Monsters and beasts we thought extinct have been encountered roaming the land again. Some have not been seen since the Dark Age some five hundred years ago"

The Captain rose from his chair and returned to the window where he stared out at the palace.

"I think that someone is trying to reopen the Dark Gates again"

"Can that be done? I thought they were destroyed or buried?"

"They were, but it is possible that they may be repaired with the right knowledge"

"Who would want to do that?"

"Well the Dark God himself for one" The Captain turned around and placed both hands on the back of his chair. "I'm sending you to Torkle in the north-eastern borders. I have received requests for help from Mayor Falstaff of Torkle. People have been disappearing from the local towns and villages"

"What is the link with the Dark Gates Sir?" Malik asked.

"That is what you are going to find out. I've learned from the Arch Mage himself that Torkle was one of the larger Dark Gates in operation during the Dark Age"

The Captain sat down at his desk and leaned back in his chair.

"Go to Torkle, investigate the missing people and if someone is trying to reopen the Torkle Dark Gate stop them by any means"

"What if the gate is opened before I get there?" Malik asked.

"I'm sending a specialist Elemental Mage with you just in case"

"A specialist?"

"Yes her name is Aris Calgar"

"Aris?" Malik said with a puzzled look on his face.

The Captain noticed that Malik absentmindedly rubbed his right shoulder. That was a good sign he thought.

"She knows more about the Dark Gates than anyone else at the college. If the gate is open then she can shut it again, permanently"

"Very well sir. If those are your orders"

"There is one other order I must ask of you Malik, a personal one"

"Sir"

"Aris, the specialist I'm sending with you has not had much experience outside of the Elemental Mages College. As I know her parents very well and owe her father much I must ask you to watch over and protect her on your assignment"

"Sir if I am going into combat she could be a fatal distraction"

"Be that as it may she is the only one who could possibly go, besides I happen to know she is a powerful Elemental Mage and she will prove useful"

The Captain leaned over his desk closer to Malik.

"Besides that was a direct order Crimson Guardian"

"Sorry Sir" Malik said uncertainly.

The Captain sat back into his chair again.

"Good, meet her at bay fifty three on the east dock at four o'clock, I've arranged a River Runner to take you both to Stonewall from there you will travel by road to Torkle. Your contact in Stonewall will be Sheriff Killdare"

"Yes Sir, bay fifty three"

"Go and see the Craftmaster to collect your armour before you go"

"I'll go directly now Sir"

"Very good, the best of luck Malik and come back safely"

"Thank you Sir" Malik stood up and saluted to the Captain then turned and headed out of the office.

Outside May was sat at her desk going over some papers.

"Make sure you come back little brother. I don't want to have to add you to the Wall of the Lost" She said as he went past.

"It's not me I'm worried about, I'll see you later May, Oh and look after Charleston for me while I'm gone, and don't tire him out with all the kissing!"

"Shut up you stupid sod! If my father hears you..." May hissed at him under her breath.

Malik grinned and ducked just as a pencil thrown with extreme accuracy bounced off of the wall where his head had been. Smiling he walked down the corridor to the stairs. He suddenly felt a lot better. That was for the little brother crack he thought to himself and grinned.

Malik walked across the courtyard from the main offices back to the workshops. He climbed down the steps that led into main corridor and continued past the workshops until he reached the Craftmaster's office at the far end of the corridor.

He knocked on the door and the Craftmaster's voice sounded out from inside.

"Yes who is it?"

"It's Malik Sir, I've been told to collect some armour from you"

"Oh yes, please come in Malik"

Malik opened the door and went inside. The Craftmaster got up from his desk and walked over to a large cabinet situated in the corner of his office.

He opened the cabinet and took a set of armour out of it. The armour breastplate was made of studded leather.

"Leather armour?" Malik said looking at it.

"This is my latest achievement Malik!" The Craftmaster said handing it to Malik.

"It is as strong as steel but is really only marginally heavier than ordinary leather"

"Really! That's impressive how did you manage that?" Asked Malik as he took the armour and inspected it.

"I've devised a new tanning process based on some of that work we did for the Royal Guard. This is the only prototype, I'd like you to field test it for me"

Malik put the armour on and twisted left and right feeling how the armour moved.

"I can move so freely in it! How much protection does it give?"

"Glad you asked! Just stand still for a second would you"

The Craftmaster wandered over to his desk and opened a draw.

"Err Craftmaster what are you doing Sir?"

"Right, Malik just face me please"

"Pardon!?"

Malik did so and the Craftmaster nodded reached below his desk, pulled out a crossbow and shot Malik in the chest.

As the arrow hit Malik it exploded in a ball of flame that threw Malik into the wall behind him. He slid to the floor with books landing around him.

All was silent until the Craftmaster said.

"That was more energetic than I thought!"

There was a groan from under the pile of books then after several seconds a few books fell from the top of the pile as Malik sat up.

"What in the nine hells did you do that for?" He shouted at the Craftmaster as he rubbed the back of his head.

"Look down" The Craftmaster smugly replied.

Malik did so he saw a red glow on the armour where the arrow had struck him.

"That was a fire shard arrow" The Craftmaster said putting the crossbow back into the desk drawer. "If you had been wearing standard armour you would now have a large hole where your chest once was"

Malik groaned again as he climbed to his feet and rubbed the armour. It was cool to the touch and had no mark on it where the arrowhead had hit it.

"Why did you have to shoot me though?" Malik said walking over to the desk and slumped into the chair sat in front of it.

"Practical application, the best way to show you!" The Craftmaster replied as he handed Malik a cigar before picked up his pipe and lighting it. "I wanted you to be totally confident in the armour's ability to protect you"

The Craftmaster blew out a smoke ring and leaned back into his chair with a smug expression on his face.

"Yes but you still didn't have to shoot me!" Malik protested lighting the cigar.

Twenty minutes later Malik had collected his equipment and had left the Crimson Guardian compound. Walking out of the Master Gateway he headed toward the East Gate, which led through to the outer rim of Founders Rock.

He passed by one of the city's many foundries. He stopped to let a cart full of metal ore be pulled through the large open double doors by two horses. Next door to the foundry a metal workshop also had it's large doors open. The sound of the steam driven hammers pounding metal into shape echoed out from the metal workshop into the street.

Feeling hungry again Malik stopped and sniffed as a tempting aroma caught his attention. Just across the street from the foundry Malik spotted a little bakery. He wandered across the street following his nose and after a few minutes of waiting patiently in line he bought a pastry slice. Leaning against a pillar by the bakery's serving hatch he watched the street with mild interest as he took a large bite.

Across the street he observed a young woman dressed in a white cloak strolling quickly toward the East Gate. Curiosity took hold and as he watched he saw the reason for her haste. Following her quickly was a man dressed in an expensive looking red velvet outfit. He carried a walking stick with a large red jewel mounted on the tip and was closely followed by four other large men.

"Probably more hired thugs, I wonder where he gets them?" Malik thought to himself as he recognised the man.

"Who is that arse?" The Baker asked Malik as the man dressed in red knocked several people to the ground as he passed.

"Baron Richardson" Malik sighed as he watched the man. "Looks like he's bought himself some new friends"

Malik took his pack from his shoulder and put it on the ground.

"Would you keep an eye on my pack for me please?" Malik asked the Baker.

"Sure"

"Thanks"

The Baron finally caught up with the woman and grabbed her arm stopping her. Malik sighed again and wandered across the street, he heard the woman shouting.

"Please let me go. Baron I've already told you I'm not interested"

"Of course you are you just don't know it yet"

"I said no!" The woman brought the end of her staff down on the Baron's foot. The Baron yelped and grabbed her again.

"Why you little…" He shouted and raised the stick to strike the woman.

"Baron, when will you learn when a woman say's no she means it!" Malik shouted from the middle of the street.

The Baron stopped and cringed before slowly turned around.

"Well well if it isn't the whore's little brother"

"Actually we're not related and if you call May that again I'll break your jaw" Malik said very calmly. He slowly took another bite from his pastry and watched the Baron.

The Baron laughed.

"Whore, there! What are you going to do? You don't have your friend with you this time, but I have my four bodyguards who are going to break you in two"

The Baron let go of the woman and clapped his hands.

A man grabbed Malik from behind and lifted him off the ground causing him to drop his pastry. One appeared in front of Malik and met Malik's boot coming up which connected with his head and knocked him to the ground.

Malik tilted his head forward then brought it back sharply so he hit the man holding him from behind on the nose with the back of his head. There was a crack and Malik was released as the man screamed and clutched at his nose that was now gushing blood. Malik turned around and hit him across the head knocking him unconscious.

Malik spun around again and faced the remaining three bodyguards.

"I'm a Crimson Guardian gentlemen I suggest you leave now while you are still able to walk" Malik said.

One of the bodyguards produced a knife and charged at Malik. Malik knocked the man's wrist aside with his left hand, caught it with his right hand then hit the man across the chin with the palm of his left hand. There was a crack as most of the man's teeth were broken by the impact. The force of the impact also caused him to bite off part of his tongue as his jaws were smashed together. Malik swapped hands and took the knife from the man's grip and drove it into the bodyguard's thigh. The man screamed spitting out blood and fragments of teeth as he collapsed onto the ground.

The last two bodyguards looked at one another decided on their chances then turned and ran down the street.

Malik walked over to the Baron who was stood defiantly holding his walking stick like a club. He swung it a Malik who caught the walking stick in a single hand and pulled it from the Baron's grasp.

"You know you can't touch me, you're a Crimson Guardian there are rules for your inferior kind" The Baron said smugly.

Malik grinned. Several people nearby who were watching with interest suddenly took a step back as they saw Malik's grin.

"So my Captain keeps telling me" Malik said and punched the Baron across the jaw with the hand holding the walking stick.

There was a satisfyingly loud crack and the Baron dropped to the ground clutching at his jaw spluttering as he tried to speak.

"I warned you, next time you will not get one" Malik said and snapped the walking stick in half and dropped the two halves.

He stepped over the Baron and strode back over to the bakery the crowd of people who had been watching events parted to let him pass. He took a gold coin out of his pocket and gave it to the Baker who had been watching events. He grinned at Malik.

"Can I have another one of those meat and potato slices please? I seem to have lost the last one" Malik asked.

"Here, on the house" The Baker said winking and flicked Malik's coin back to him.

"Thanks! Say you didn't see where that woman went did you?" Malik said as he looked around trying to spot her.

"No sorry, she must have run off when the arse let her go, can't say I blame her"

"Ah well" Malik shrugged, nodded at the Baker and picked up his pack then strolled on toward the East Gate happily eating as he went.

As he approached the East Gate, Malik saw two trainee Guardians on ground level standing on either side of the gateway. He stopped and stared remembering the days when he had done gate duty before he was fully integrated into the Crimson Guardians.

All of the current Crimson Guardians when they first started their training had to spend two years training with the City Guard before being accepted into the Crimson Guardians as trainees.

Malik had learned a lot from Old Tom his assigned instructor. Old Tom was one of the most experienced of all the City Guards.

He remembered when he and Old Tom had stopped a smuggler trying to escape through the South Gate. The man had been twice the size of Old Tom and Malik.

The smuggler knocked Malik clean off his feet with a massive hammer he had been hiding in his cart. Malik would have been killed if Old Tom hadn't tackled the smuggler before he could crush Malik.

Old Tom wrestled the hammer from the smuggler. Malik then watched in dazed amazement as Old Tom faced the smuggler single-handed and knocked the man unconscious with no trouble whatsoever.

Malik had been Old Tom's last trainee as he retired to the coast shortly after Malik's acceptance into the Crimson Guardians.

Malik had heard from the Captain that he was enjoying his retirement on a plot of land by the south coast that the King himself had given to Old Tom in recognition for many years of faithful service.

Malik sighed at the memory then strolled under the East Gate and entered the dock area of Founders Rock the outer most part of the city.

The docks ran all around the very outside of Founders Rock. Bays were spread out periodically around the docks. The bays were identified by number and were the main way for people to embark or disembark from the different vessels that came to the city.

There were ten special large bays that were designed for the very large transport ships to dock and unload their cargo.

Each bay usually had a crane for loading and unloading goods. The cranes were powered by steam generated in huge boilers. The boilers were fired by fire crystal energy and produced so much steam that it allowed them to lift and move huge weights.

Malik watched as a large create was lifted out from the cargo hold of the nearest docked ship. A worker on the dockside was giving hand signals to the crane operator who gently placed it onto a waiting cart.

Malik continued along the docks down toward bay fifty-three, he weaved in and out of the dock traffic that flowed between each of the four main gates that lead into the city itself.

Malik eventually managed to reach bay fifty-three and looked up at a nearby clock tower. The time was exactly four o'clock as he dodged a cart and walked down the set of stairs that led to the jetty of bay fifty-three.

A River Runner was docked next to the jetty. Malik read the name on the side of the River Runner.

"Hmm the Red Devil, well that sounds friendly!" He said to himself.

The bay crane up above on the dockside was lowering a pallet full of boxes and barrels into the hold of the Red Devil through a large open hatch on the deck.

Malik noticed a figure cloaked in white robes standing at the end of the jetty looking out at the ships sailing on the

Junction. The figure held a staff that it was idly bouncing up and down on it's foot.

The staff was covered in strange markings and Malik could see crystals embedded up and down the shaft. He walked over to the figure and dropped his bags and crossbow against the jetty wall.

"Excuse me are you Aris?" Malik asked.

The figure turned toward Malik and leaned on the staff. He couldn't see a face because it was hidden from view by the cloak's large white hood.

"Yes that's me and I presume that you are Crimson Guardian Owen" Aris replied.

"Yes Ma'am, I've been ordered to keep you alive while on this assignment to Torkle"

"Really I was told to keep you out of trouble" Aris said. "Don't worry about me Crimson Guardian, I am quite capable of looking after myself without any help from you!"

She strode past him.

"Really? Well let's hope we don't have to find out. Oh by the way the Baron won't be talking to anyone for a while" He said.

Aris stopped for a moment before she carried on.

"I'm sorry?" She asked.

"Ah, my mistake sorry. I thought you were someone else"

Aris turned and looked at the River Runner with uncertainty.

"Have you been on a River Runner before?" Malik asked her.

"This is my first time on one this small"

"Well we should have a smooth ride out of the Junction. The wind is calm and judging by the skies we should have clear sailing for the next few days" Malik said.

He looked out into the Junction at the ships that were sailing around the outer skirts of Founders Rock.

"To be accurate we will have two days of sun before a storm will hit us from the west"

"You are definitely an Elemental Mage. Well they do teach us good manners in the Guardians so here let me help you onboard"

"I can manage myself thank you" She said and climbed unsteadily onto the gangplank. "But you could bring my bags onboard please"

"I can see we are really going to get on" Malik muttered as she slowly crossed the gangplank.

When she reached the end of the gangplank he picked up his bags and tossed them onto the deck of the Red Devil.

He picked up Aris's bags and grunted in surprise at the weight. He crossed the gangplank onto the River Runner's deck then carefully put her bag's down on the deck and looked up at her.

"What on Vishante have you got in here? Half of the Arcane Library?"

"Just one or two select tomes of knowledge that may be useful" Aris said looking around the Red Devil's deck.

"Yes if we get attacked we could kill someone by throwing one of these books at their head or possibly build a small barricade to repel invaders!" Malik said more or less to himself.

Aris flashed a glance at him but ignored the comment. Malik though he saw the brief outline of a smile from under the white hood.

Above them another pallet of supplies was now being lowered inside the open hold of the Red Devil, there was a faint thud as the pallet landed on the cargo hold floor. A whistle echoed from inside the hold and the crane hook emerged up out of the hold and disappeared skyward.

"Welcome aboard the RR Red Devil"

Malik and Aris both turned to look at a man who had appeared out of the cabin. He was dressed in loose black clothing and wore a long coat.

"I am Captain Worthington I've been expecting you"

"Captain" Malik said and bowed his head. "I am Crimson Guardian Malik Owen and this is Elemental Mage Aris Calgar"

Malik held out his hand indicating Aris.

"Pleased to meet you Captain" She said also bowing. "Thank you for allowing us passage on your ship"

"Such polite manners" The Captain remarked. "If you would follow me young lady I'll gladly show you to your quarters"

The Captain climbed down a set of ladders onto the deck. He picked up Aris's bags, grunted with surprise and hindered by the weight of the pack led her awkwardly toward a door that led inside the Red Devil.

Malik watched them walk away shrugged his shoulders then grabbed his bags and followed them.

The door led to a little corridor underneath the ship's bridge the Captain stopped halfway down the corridor at two doors. He opened one and went inside.

"My lady this will be your cabin" He said putting down Aris's bags inside the doorway with much relief.

"Thank you Captain" She said following him inside.

The Captain turned to Malik and motioned with his thumb.

"Your's is across the corridor"

"Thank you" Malik muttered and opened the door and went in.

Inside the cabin there was a small bunk bed under a porthole and a chest bolted to the wall and nothing else.

"Cosy" Malik said to himself and shut the door with his foot.

Malik put his bags down inside the chest and locked it again. He wandered back out onto the deck to look for Captain Worthington. When he couldn't find him on the deck or down in the cargo hold, he climbed the ladder that led up to the bridge of the Red Devil. At the top he found a door that led into the bridge of the River Runner.

The bridge had large windows on each side to allow maximum visibility of all areas around the River Runner. Malik saw Captain Worthington through the glass window. The Red Devil's Captain was standing in front of a table looking at some charts and plotting points on a large map.

Malik gently knocked on the bridge door's glass window and the Captain looked up and beckoned with his hand for Malik to enter.

As he entered the cabin Malik realised he was always amazed how different each River Runner was. It was almost as if they took on the personalities of the Captains that commanded them.

The bridge of the Red Devil was no exception. On the rear wall a selection of fishing rods hung on a special rack. The helm was situated at the front of the cabin and comprised of a comfortable looking padded seat mounted on a raised platform with the steering wheel attached to an arm arrangement above the seat.

In front of the seat were two pedals and on the left side a lever housed in a console with some other switches and coloured crystals.

Spread around the outside of the cabin there were various cupboards and drawers used for storing charts and other useful items. Captain Worthington was standing at the navigation table that was behind the helm on the right hand side of the bridge.

"Captain, when can we depart?" Malik asked.

"We are all set, I'm just waiting on clearance from the Harbour Master" Captain Worthington pointing through the window to a signal box mounted on the side of bay fifty-three. It was glowing bright red at present.

"A cargo ship is passing by here on it's way into one of the big bays further down the docks" The Captain explained.

"If we leave port now we might well either get hit by it or be smashed into the dock by its wake as it passes by"

"How long before we can go do you think?" Malik asked.

A siren wailed out and the red light in the box started to flash rapidly.

"Not long now" The Captain said and walked over to the helm and sat down in the seat.

"You might want to sit down in that chair over there and hold on to something, this could be a little rough"

The Captain pulled a strap from the seat and clicked it into place securing himself into the seat. He then casually pulled a cigar out of a coat pocket and lit it.

Malik quickly walked over to the chair behind the helm and sat down before he also secured himself in place with a strap and held on to the arms of the chair.

In front of the bay the large cargo ship passed by at a deceptively fast speed given it's huge size. From where he was sat Malik could see the three massive steam vents on the rear of the ship and the large plumes of steam that were being expelled from them by the ships powerful engines.

He could also see the people on deck wandering about doing their tasks as the ship prepared to dock.

As it passed by the cargo ship started to raise cranes from it's own deck that would unload cargo from the bowels of the cargo ship to the deck ready for the dock cranes to unload to dry land.

The Red Devil gently rocked from side to side.

"That wasn't so bad Captain" Malik said as he went to undo his strap.

"Wait for it!" The Captain quickly replied and held up a finger.

The Red Devil suddenly started to violently bob up and down as the wake from the passing cargo ship entered into the bay. The waves bounced off of one another causing turbulence in the bay making the Red Devil dance on the water even though it was securely clamped to the bay's sturdy moorings.

"You have to be careful even if you are on the jetty when one of those things goes past" The Captain said casually putting his feet up on a console as the ship violently rocked.

"Sometimes you get a surprise wave that can knock you into the water and the rip current will drag you right out into the Junction"

"Really I didn't know that" Malik gripped the arms on his chair. "Has it happened to you?"

The Red Devil continued to rock violently from side to side. Malik thought he heard a crash from the deck below them.

"Once. Before the warning beacons were put in place" The Captain replied as he blew out a puff of smoke from his cigar. "I was fixing a mooring cleat on the portside. While I was standing on the jetty one of those big buggers went past. Two wake waves hit in the right spot and made one large wave that swept me clean off my feet and into the water. Luckily I'd tied the mooring line round my waist to keep hold of it while I was screwing the new cleat into the hull. If not I would have been dragged right into the Junction shipping lanes"

"I bet that hurt"

"Yeah it hurt like hell, it broke a couple of ribs and I had internal bleeding. I spent several months in the Healers Guild after that" The Captain said as he scratched his cheek.

The Red Devil began to steady itself in the water as the waves gradually subsided.

"Ahh there we go, that's the last of it" The Captain said undoing the straps on the helm seat.

"What's that sound?" Malik asked.

The pair listened, there was a frantic scrambling sound coming from below. The sound subsided for a second then there was the sound of someone climbing the ladders outside. The door to the cabin was thrown open and Aris flung herself inside and slammed the door shut.

"What in the nine bloody hells is going on!" She screamed. Her hood was not covering her face anymore and revealed a tangle of long red hair and it suddenly occurred to Malik that even in her current state she was quite pretty.

He scratched his right shoulder again. It felt like something had bitten him.

"What happened to you?" He asked, getting up from his chair and walking over to steady her as she stood swaying slightly.

"I was standing on the bed putting my tomes on the shelf when everything went sideways"

"Ah sorry I should have warned you about that" Said the Captain.

"Should have, should have, I'll bloody well give you should have!" She said with a nasty glint in her eye. The Captain cleared his throat.

"Yes well, perhaps we should get underway. If you would both please strap yourselves in we shall depart"

The Captain pulled the steering wheel down into place in front of the seat. He flipped some switches on the console to the left of the helm and a gentle hum started from the back of the River Runner.

The beacon light on the bay wall changed from red to green. Malik carefully sat Aris down in another chair and returned to his own.

"Everyone set? Good" The Captain asked looking back over his shoulder.

The Captain moved the lever forward and pressed down on the right hand foot pedal. The Red Devil started to slowly move forward.

The Captain hit another switch on the steering wheel and the arms that moored the Red Devil to the bay jetty disengaged and retracted into the hull.

The Red Devil slowly moved out of bay fifty-three and moved away from Founders Rock.

"When we pass the yellow markers you can move about and I can get us to cruising speed" The Captain said throwing his finished cigar out of the window.

Out in the Junction the Red Devil moved alongside a host of other boats and ships that were all moving in the same direction away from Founders Rock. They were all heading toward the open waterways in the north of the Junction.

The Red Devil passed a set of yellow flags that were floating in a spaced out line that ran in a large circle around Founders Rock.

As it passed the markers the Red Devil accelerated away from the rest of the ships. The outriggers lowered themselves into place and the Red Devil turned to the northeast and headed for a large river mouth that was the beginning of the Great Serpent River.

"Alright you can get up now we are out of the restricted zone"

"How long will it take to get to Torkle Captain?" Aris asked as she got out of the chair and walked over to the helm seat.

"About four days travel up this river will bring us to the town of Stonewall, Torkle is then one or two days travel on foot across the plains and forests up to the base of the mountains"

"Where are we stopping tonight Captain?" Malik asked.

"There is a place we can stop for the night about three hours upstream, we can eat and rest there safely until morning"

"Captain, may I use one of your fishing rods please? I'll see if I can catch us something to eat"

"Be my guest, it'll save time later on. Try the red rod. It has one of my special lures on it"

"Thank you, do you have a keep net anywhere?"

"In the cupboard underneath the fishing rods I think, it fixes into the slot on the stern of the hull"

"What are you doing?" Aris asked Malik as he walked past her to the back wall and opened the cupboard underneath the rack of fishing rods.

"I'm going to do some fishing for dinner, would you hold this for a second please"

Malik pulled several rings covered in netting out of the cupboard and handed it to Aris. He then closed the cupboard and took a long red fishing rod out of the rack.

"Thank you" He said as he took the net from Aris and headed for the door.

"Wait a second, I have to brief you about the Dark Gates before we get to Torkle" Aris protested as Malik was just about to shut the cabin door.

"We have plenty of time, you brief while I fish" He said holding the door open for her to follow. Aris stalked out of the bridge cabin.

"I can not believe that they would send someone as unprofessional as you on an assignment as important as this!" She said waving her finger under Malik's nose as she walked past him.

"It's going to be a long, long journey" Malik muttered to himself as he shut the cabin door.

Ten minutes later and Malik couldn't have cared less. He was sitting on a seat attached to the deck of the Red Devil. The lazy afternoon sun shone down and glinted off of the water's surface. He casually cast the fishing line out behind the River Runner and let it trawl behind the Red Devil as it moved upstream.

Aris was sitting on the deck opposite him with one of her tomes open on her knees.

"As far as I understand the mechanics of how the Dark Gates work, they fold the space between each gate causing a sort of shortcut hole between them, yes?" He said reeling in the line and recasting it out behind the Red Devil again.

"In very basic terms yes"

"So how did they get here in the first place then? Don't you need two gates to make a shortcut hole?" He asked.

Aris looked up at him and raised her eyebrows in mild surprise at this display of intelligence.

"Very true, I believe that the Dark Gates were built here on Vishante"

"How can that be? I thought there is no one on Vishante who knew exactly how they worked?"

He cast the line again and started to slowly wind it back.

"Again very true, but the Dark God of Chaos does. I think that he can project his will from the Dark Realm to other worlds including ours"

"Project his will?" Malik cast the line out again.

"Yes basically take over a susceptible persons mind and influence them to do things, for instance build a Dark Gate"

"Alright so the Dark God influences susceptible people on a planet. He then instructs them to build a Dark Gate. When the Gate is complete the Dark Army comes through and wipes out everything"

"Yes quite right" Aris said closing the book and laying it down beside her on the deck.

"Five hundred years ago the Amassing of Light couldn't destroy all the Dark Gates as they simply didn't have the resources available. So they did the next best thing and bury or hide the Dark Gates. One of them we know for a fact was buried in the Torkle region"

"And now people are disappearing from around Torkle. I have a feeling they are being used to unearth your gate" Malik turned and looked sidelong at Aris.

"Why do you say that?" She said cocking her head to one side.

"My Captain briefed me that other Crimson Guardians have had encounters with creatures that have not be seen since the Dark Ages some five hundred years ago"

Malik wound in the fishing line and cast it again.

"Now either they have been in hiding for five hundred years or at least one gate has already been reopened. What the hells happened to all the fish?" he muttered to himself.

"That sounds logical" Aris agreed, again she raised her eyebrows at this display. "They would take their time and gather strength before they tried another invasion"

"Right gather a small force and try to reopen a Dark Gate to let more reinforcements through. Torkle is quite a remote region"

"And it was one of the larger Dark Gates to be buried" Aris said standing up and stretching.

She walked to the stern of the Red Devil and looked out across the water. A shadow moved under the surface and caught her eye.

"What was that?" She said turning to Malik.

"What was what?"

At that moment the reel on the rod screamed and the rod jerked in Malik's hands.

"About time I hooked something!"

He lifted the rod high and started to reel in the fishing line. The end of the rod dipped toward the water. The line went slack and a large fish jumped out of the water. Light shone off of it's scales and it entered the water again with a splash.

"That's a good size trout a couple more of those and we'll be ready to cook" Malik said heaving on the rod.

He continued to reel in the line bringing the fish closer to the Red Devil.

As the fish was pulled closer to the River Runner there was an explosion of water moving straight at the fish. Something large had suddenly accelerated under the water's surface.

Malik was yanked forward and was nearly pulled over the stern of the Red Devil. He managed to put a foot against the hull of the Red Devil and brace himself against the pull on the fishing rod.

The fishing line snapped and Malik was flung backwards onto the deck. He sat upright.

"Captain, stop the engine!" He shouted at the bridge.

"What?" The Captain's voice shouted down.

"Cut the bloody engines!"

The engines ceased and the Red Devil slowed in the water.

"Aris get away from the side!" Malik shouted quickly getting back on to his feet.

Aris slowly backed away from the stern of the Red Devil looking at the water.

"What's going on?" Captain Worthington shouted as he came out of the bridge door and leaned over the railing looked down.

The water exploded again and a large creature landed on the deck. It had a long body and a single arm on each side of its body. Each arm had a long curved claw on the end of the limb.

It opened a large mouth full of more teeth than was natural. The mouth opened wide and snapped shut a couple of times in rapid succession making a horrible chattering sound.

With surprising speed it pulled itself along the deck of the Red Devil toward Aris. The claws left gouges in the deck as it gained speed.

The snapping of jaws became faster and more excited as it approached Aris who was now backed up against the lower wall of the cabin.

There was a whistling sound and a throwing knife hit the creature in the side of the body with a thud.

"Aris get up the ladder to the bridge now!" Malik yelled.

He drew another throwing knife from the small sheaths on the rear of his belt. The creature turned it's attention to Malik, as it did Aris quickly scrambled up the ladder that led to the relative safety of the Red Devil's upper platform.

The creature turned again to lunge at Aris as she tried to climb the ladder. Malik quickly threw the knife.

It whistled as it flew through the air as the first one had, the creature ducked and the knife embedded itself in the hull.

"Fast bugger aren't you!" Malik said.

"Malik catch!" The Captain threw down a pole with a hook on the end.

Malik caught the pole just as the creature leapt at him. He managed to wedge the pole into the creatures open mouth to stop it biting his head off but the force of the creature's impact forced him to fall over onto his back.

The creature fell on top and furiously slashed at Malik's chest with its two claws. Thankfully Malik was wearing the leather armour the Craftmaster had made and the claws just bounced off unable to penetrate.

"Aris when I say shock this bloody thing!" Malik shouted as he wrestled with the creature's head while avoiding a claw trying to slash at his face.

"But I'll hit you as well"

"Just get ready!"

Malik forced the creature's head up with the pole to create some space, he raised his knees into the space created then using both of his legs kicked the creature off of him. The creature landed in a heap against the stern rail of the Red Devil.

"Aris now!" He yelled and ducked his head under his arms.

Aris closed her eyes and held out her hand with her fingers bent slightly inwards. As she spoke the words of power, lightning crackled between her fingers. She opened her eyes and they shone momentarily with a brief bright red glow. A stream of lightning erupted from her hand and struck the creature forcing it up against the side of the Red Devil's hull.

The creature let out a scream and fell on the deck. Residual lightning arced over the surface of it's scaly body causing it to convulse and twitch. It gradually stopped twitching and finally lay still as Malik raised himself up and got back to his feet.

"Wait there!" He held up his hand at Aris before she could climb down the ladder.

She stopped and looked down over the upper railing. She watched Malik as he walked over to the throwing knife that was embedded in the hull of the Red Devil and pulled it free.

Carefully watching the creature's body he walked cautiously over to it in case it sprang back to life. When he reached the body he quickly knelt down on top of it pinning it down, using his throwing knife he slit the creature's throat.

He tapped the deck three times with the tip of the knife then wiped the blood from it and placed it back in the sheath behind his back.

Malik rolled the creature over and pulled the other knife out of the creature's side and was cleaning it when Aris approached the creature's body.

"What is that thing?" She asked while prodding the creature's corpse with her foot.

"Waterwraith" Said Captain Worthington climbing down the ladder to the deck.

"Nasty devil's these, eat bloody anything" The Captain lit another cigar and tossed the match over the side. "Now that I think about it five fishermen have gone missing from this stretch of water over the last couple of months, guess we know why now"

"Yes but why is one here? The water's far too warm for them here they like the cold waters further north" Malik said as he turned the Waterwraith's body over on to it's back.

"Perhaps it got washed down river during the spring flood season? Who knows" Captain Worthington said shrugging his shoulders. "We'll take it with us to the next town upstream. There is a bounty on Waterwraiths anyway and it'll bring some comfort to the townsfolk to see it's dead"

"Captain can I just ask, how do you know there was only one of those things?" Aris said looking around at the surrounding water nervously.

Malik and the Captain stared at one another for a few seconds.

"I think I'll just go and fetch my sword" Malik said slowly walking toward his cabin.

"I think I'll just go and start the engines" The Captain said and walked quickly back to the ladder leading to the bridge.

Aris stood alone on the deck of the Red Devil with the Waterwraith's corpse. She stared at the creature's still gently smoking body and thought for a moment.

"Hey don't leave me alone out here!" She shouted and chased after Malik.

Malik entered his cabin and was about to shut the door when Aris ran into it.

"Mind if I stay with you awhile?" She said.

"Sure, come on in"

Malik walked over to the storage chest bolted onto the wall.

"It's a bit cramped in here but you can sit on the bunk if you like"

"Thank you"

Aris walked behind Malik as he was unlocking the chest and sat down on the small bed.

"My Captain was right about you, you know" Malik said as he lifted the lid on the chest.

"Really? Right about what?"

"You are a powerful Elemental Mage"

"I suppose it helps when you are the daughter of the Arch Mage, and my mother is a member of the College Council" She replied.

"But you don't have any experience in combat"

"How do you mean?"

"You hesitated when that Waterwraith went to attack you"

"I…. I was frightened"

"I know, but if I hadn't been there it would have killed you!"

Malik pulled his bag out of the chest and then reached inside the chest again to retrieve his sword.

"Yes about that… thank you for saving me"

"Don't thank me just yet I may not be around next time" Malik said a little more harshly than he intended.

Malik slowly laid his sword down on the floor as if thinking of something. He turned and looked at Aris and rubbed his shoulder again she was staring at the floor.

"Do you want to be frightened the next time?"

"No"

"Good! I think I can help you" Malik smiled at her and stood up.

"Malik! You're bleeding!" Aris pointed at his leg.

A large red stain was growing in size on his left thigh.

"Damn thing must have caught me, I didn't even feel it" Malik ripped the material open and looked at the injury. He reached for his bag. "I've got a medical pack in here, I'll stitch it closed and put some healing herbs on it. It's not a problem"

"Wait a second let me try. Come here and stand in front of me" Aris said.

Malik slowly moved closer to Aris and turned so the wound on his thigh faced Aris.

Aris put her hands together and said something under her breath. A green glow surrounded her hands. She then placed her hands over the wound on Malik's thigh.

"That feels nice, it's warm" He said.

"There you go, all healed now" Aris said after several seconds.

The glow died away and Aris took her hands away from his leg. He looked down at his thigh, the bleeding had stopped and the wound was completely closed and healed.

"Thank you" He said rubbing his leg.

"Least I could do for you" She said and smiled at him.

"Well, let me return the favour by teaching you something new in the morning, where's your staff by the way?"

The following morning Malik knocked on Aris's cabin door. She opened the door a fraction and peered round the door.

"Oh Malik it's you, what's the matter?"

"Nothing its time for me to return the favour"

"Hang on a minute I'm not dressed yet"

"Perfect!" Malik said then noticed the look on Aris's face.

"Err what I mean is that it's good you are not dressed yet... Because I've got something for you that you will need today!"

He produced a wrapped package from behind his back and carefully passed it between the crack of the door and the doorframe.

"I had to guess at your size but I think they will fit. Get changed and I'll see you out on the deck, Oh and bring your staff with you"

Malik nodded at her and headed back toward the deck. Aris closed the door and walked over to her bed. She sat down on it and carefully opened the package Malik had given her.

Inside the package was a set of trousers, a shirt and an overcoat similar in design to Malik's.

She laid the clothes out on her bed and got dressed. She looked at herself critically in a small mirror on the wall. When she was satisfied she picked up her staff that was leaning against the bed and left her cabin.

Outside Malik was standing by a gangplank waiting for her with his hands behind his back.

"Thank you for the clothes. Where did you get them from out here?"

"Oh I made them for you from some of my spare new clothes" Malik said looking her up and down.

"Somehow I can tell these were your's, they are very much to your taste!"

"Sorry about that, I was rather limited with the materials. But they will last and you won't trip over them like you would in that white robe of yours"

"Oh I wasn't complaining!" Aris said quickly. "They are very comfortable thank you" She realized that the gangplank was down.

"Why aren't we moving?" She asked.

"The Captain say's there is some engine trouble so we are stuck here for the day while he repairs it"

He held out his hand.

"Which suits me fine for what I have got planned for today. Come on, we are going ashore for a little training session"

"Training? What kind of training?"

"I'm going to teach you how to look after yourself!" Malik said.

He helped her slowly cross the gangplank and onto the riverbank.

"I've found a nice spot that will do just nicely!"

Aris followed Malik up the riverbank and down a slope that lead to a grassy grove surrounded by trees and a gently running brook that lead away from the river.

"You've heard of the saying learning to walk before you can run yes?"

Aris nodded.

"Right well here you are going to learn how to fall before you can fight"

"I don't need to know how to fight I have my magic" She protested.

"Alright then"

Malik walked to a nearby tree and jumped up to brake a branch off of it. He drew his sword and used it to strip the bark and twigs off of the branch. Eventually he had a long pale stick, which he held like a short sword.

He walked back to the centre of the grove and stood facing Aris.

"Cast a spell and try to hit me"

"Why?"

"So you can learn something"

"I could kill you!"

"You wouldn't get the chance!"

"I would!"

"Prove it!"

"Fine!"

Aris held out her staff and pointed it at Malik. As she closed her eyes and began concentrating on casting the spell Malik started to run at her.

She opened her eyes to finish casting the spell only to see Malik in front of her. He span around so his body was out of the staff's line of fire and the wooden stick connected with Aris's staff sending it flying out of her hands.

He spun around again and ducked low sweeping Aris's legs out from under her with the stick. Aris landed on her back, Malik held the stick across her throat.

"That wasn't fair!" She shouted at him.

"Fights rarely are!" Malik said and withdrew the stick away from her throat.

"You have to take every advantage you can get" He held out his hand and helped her to her feet. "Let's see if I can teach you to give away as little advantage as possible!"

The two of them spent the rest of the morning in the grove Malik taught Aris how to fall and roll without injury on the thick grass. A few hours later the pair of them lay exhausted on the side of the grove.

"You know this is fun!" Aris panted as they lay back looking up at the sky.

"Really? I suppose so, I've never really though about it that much" Malik replied as he sat up. "I'm hungry how about you?" Malik said looking over at her.

"Starving"

"Right grab some of those dead dry branches from over there and meet me on top of the hill"

"Where are you going?"

"To catch some lunch"

Malik got up and headed up the hill and disappeared over the brow while Aris walked over to the tree and started to gather up the dry branches. She carried them up to the top of the hill and lay them down.

As she looked down she saw Malik standing at the side of the riverbank with his crossbow in his hands. Curious she walked down the hill to where he was standing.

"What are you doing?" She asked.

"Fishing" He whispered back. "Just wait, a big fish is going to jump any second"

"How can you tell?"

"Shhh"

A large fish leapt out of the water trying to catch a flying insect that was skimming the surface of the water. Almost without concentrating Malik fired his crossbow.

Aris noticed that the crossbow bolt had a length of string tied to the back of it. The fish was speared by the arrow and fell back into the water.

Malik put down the crossbow and pulled the string reeling the fish in. He lifted the fish out of the water and looked at it.

"This should do fine, what do you think?" He said.

When Aris said nothing he turned and looked, her mouth was hanging open.

"Let's eat" He said and set off up the hill again.

Aris still stunned finally closed her mouth and silently followed Malik up the side of the riverbank.

Malik reached the pile of dead braches and laid the fish on the grass. He arranged the branches into different sizes and broke some of the longer ones in half and made a small pile on the ground.

Aris came and sat down beside him and watched him. Malik reached into his shirt and brought out a leather pouch tied to some string around his neck. He opened the pouch and took out what looked like a ball of purple fluff and a cylindrical shaped piece of rock.

"What are those?" Aris asked.

"This is Fire Moss and it is your best friend when you are out in the wilderness!" Malik replied.

He pulled a small amount of the purple fluff from the ball and put the rest back in the pouch. He pulled the small ball of fluff apart separating some of the strands. Next he held up the cylinder and his sword.

"This is a flint also very handy to have"

"What are they for?"

"Well for those of us that cannot control the power of the elements, these two items will make a fire"

"Hey! I think I've heard of Fire Moss, it's only found in a few areas in Arlieana and is almost impossible to grow in the city"

"Almost but not quite impossible to do" Malik said smiling.

"It did take me a while to get it right"

He then gently put the small ball of Fire Moss into the middle of the bundle of twigs he had made. Next he took the flint and his sword and placed them close to the bundle.

"Watch yourself! This stuff is rather… energetic!" He said.

He ran his sword along the flint sending a shower of sparks on to the bundle of twigs. The Fire Moss erupted into a large plume of flame causing Malik to jump backwards away from the flame and almost roll down the hill.

Aris stifled a laugh as Malik lay on his back rubbing his face.

"I always manage to use too much of the bloody stuff!" He said getting back up.

Aris looked at Malik's face and started to laugh.

"What's up with you?" he asked as he piled more twigs and sticks onto the now successfully lit fire.

"You've singed your hair and eyebrows!" She said giggling.

Tears starting to roll down her face with the laughter. Malik's expression only served to make her laugh even more.

"Huh, well it's difficult to judge how much to use" He muttered.

Aris rolled onto her side, her shoulders were shaking and she had wrapped her arms around herself.

Twenty minutes and much stifled giggling later the fish was cooking on the fire. It had been skewered on to a stripped branch stuck into the ground so it was close enough to the heat to cook but not burn.

Malik lay on his back with his hands behind his head while Aris was sat next to the fire. Malik's sword lay on the grass between them.

Aris picked it up and looked at the red Spirit Stone set into the blade.

"Where did you find your Spirit Stone Malik?"

Malik looked up at her, his face was suddenly pained.

"It was in the ruins of my parent's house" He said slowly.

"Pardon?"

Aris moved closer to Malik and sat with the sword across her lap.

"I was about five or six years old at the time" Malik shut his eyes and continued.

"I don't remember everything that happened. What I do remember is that our town was attacked in the middle of the night, no one knows by who or why. I woke up under an overturned cart in the morning. The rain was pouring down"

Malik stared into the fire for a few seconds.

"The entire town was burned to the ground. I remember the smell of the smoke. It was thick in the air, as I went back to what was left of my home to see if I could find my parents"

"Did you find them?"

"No not there. As I was searching for them in the ruins of the house the floor gave way and I fell down into the cellar"

Malik sat up and checked the fish as it cooked on the spit.

"My father has always forbidden me from going down into the cellar, it was too dangerous he always said"

Malik leant over and gently picked up his sword off of Aris's lap and rubbed the stone with his thumb. The Spirit Stone glowed ever so faintly at his touch.

"Down there I found a small cave hidden behind a set of smashed shelves. My father must have originally built the shelves to hide the entrance. Inside I saw that different crystals had been grown there but they had all been recently smashed to pieces. I was going to leave when I noticed a faint glow in the dark."

Aris leaned closer.

"When I looked closer I found a dark coloured heavy cloth covering this strange crystal sticking out of a rock. When I touched it, it shone bright red then white and just let go of the rock. I took it with me, but it was years before I found out what it was"

"What happened to your parents, did you find them?" Aris asked.

"Eventually I did yes, among a pile of burnt bodies in the centre of the town"

"Oh Malik I'm so sorry"

"That's alright, it was a long time ago" Malik looked at the fish and gave it a prod with a stick. "Lunch is ready dig in!"

The afternoon passed by with Malik teaching Aris how to block attacks and counter attack with her staff. The wooden clunking sound of Malik's stripped tree branch connecting with Aris's staff could be heard well into the late afternoon.

"Very good you remembered to keep your balance, but what if I do this?"

Malik swung the stick at Aris with a right hand swing. She blocked as he then immediately sung to the left, which she also managed to block with her staff.

"You're a very quick learner! I'm impressed." Malik said lowering the branch.

Aris swung her staff at his head. Malik blocked with the branch and grabbed the staff under his arm locking it.

Aris put her hand on his chest and there was a flash of light. Malik was flung backward and landed against the hill.

Aris walked forward and picked up her staff. She brought the end of the staff down and pointed it in between Malik's legs.

"Thank you!" She said. "It's getting dark and I'm going back to the Red Devil are you coming or are you going to lie there all night!"

"I'll catch up when the world stops spinning!"

Aris ran up the hill and disappeared over the crest toward where the Red Devil was moored. Malik waited for a few seconds then jumped to his feet and ran to the top of the hill where he lay down and watched Aris run along the gangplank without any trace of fear or hesitation and into her cabin.

Malik smiled to himself and got up. He rubbed his ribs with his hand.

"Bloody hell she has got some power" He said to himself and made his way down the hill back to the Red Devil.

Captain Worthington was sat in the fishing chair smoking a cigar when Malik walked across the gangplank.

"Captain" Malik said nodding to him as he walked past.

"Evening Malik, the engine is repaired we can be underway first thing in the morning"

"That's good news Captain"

"Funny how it suddenly went wrong isn't it"

"I wouldn't know Captain, I'm not an engineer"

"Next time you can just ask alright"

"I'm sure I don't know what you mean Captain"

"Touch my engine again. And I don't care if you are a Crimson Guardian, I'll kick your arse right over the side of my boat"

"Goodnight Captain" Said Malik and walked to his cabin.

Malik sat down on his small bunk and took the bottle of pills out of the chest. He unscrewed the top and tipped out two pills into his hand.

A gentle knock sounded on his door. He quickly put the lid back on and threw the bottle into the chest.

"Come in" He said closing the lid on the chest.

The door opened and Aris entered she was wearing her white robe again but this time she had not put the hood up.

"I was just checking you were alright"

"My ribs ache a little but I'm fine. We are quite tough in the Crimson Guardians you know" Malik said as Aris smiled at him.

"Well as long as you are alright" She paused and looked down embarrassed.

"Would you mind teaching me some more?"

"Alright, I can do that"

"Thank you!" Aris beamed a large grin at him.

"Good night Aris"

"Good night" Aris replied and shut the door.

Malik opened his hand and swallowed the two pills. He then lay back and fell into another uneasy sleep.

"So tell me, just how do we shut down a Dark Gate?" Malik shouted.

He was sat in the fishing chair with his legs crossed. He cast out a fishing rod and started to fish again.

"Well I can either cast a special neutralize spell that I created or we could physically destroy the outer framework of the gate. They can only form the space-time fold if the whole of the frame is intact" Shouted Aris from far to the left of Malik.

"Are those the only two options we have?"

"Pretty much, are you sure that rope is secure?"

"Positive, see!"

Malik tugged on a rope tied around the bottom of the chair.

The rope led from the bottom of the chair up and over a bar and back down to an extended pontoon where it was tied around Aris's waist.

She was balancing on the pontoon as the Red Devil moved upstream.

"Is this good balance training?"

"Best I can think of while we are on the move!"

That afternoon they reached a small riverside town called Whitewater. Captain Worthington took the Waterwraith's corpse to the town hall to claim the bounty while Malik and Aris wandered around the Market.

"What are you looking for?" Aris asked Malik as they walked along a street.

"I'm looking for a pub"

"Why?"

"Well I could do with a drink, and they are also the best place to pick up any useful bits of information that might be floating around"

"Is that one over there?" Aris pointed at a sign across the street.

"The Seven Stars?" Malik read aloud. "Certainly sounds like one let's take a look"

They crossed the busy street and entered the Seven Stars pub.

The inside of the Seven Stars was quite dark. Around the outside of the pub there were alcoves with tables set into them. In the centre there was a number of tables and benches and at the back of the pub was the bar.

Numerous bar patrons of all different types were spread all over the pub. Malik walked through the crowd of seated people to the Bar with Aris behind him. He stopped at the Bar and nodded at the Barman.

"Yes sir what can I do for you?" The Barman asked.

Malik leaned to one side and looked at something mounted on the wall behind the Barman. He then leaned forward and talked quietly to the Barman.

At one point Malik showed the Barman the underside of his left wrist. The Barman looked at Malik's wrist then looked up at Malik and nodded.

"Go and take a seat at table 12 over there, I'll bring your drinks over"

"Thank you very much"

Malik led Aris over to the alcove and sat down at the table.

"What's going on?" She asked.

"We have a friend here"

"Why did you show him your wrist?" Aris asked.

Malik held his wrist out and showed her. Tattooed on the underside of his wrist was a red teardrop.

"What does that mean?"

"It's a Crimson Guardian tattoo. The Barman has a Crimson Guardian medal mounted on the wall behind the bar" Malik said as a large shadow fell across the table.

"This is our table" Said a voice.

A huge man was now standing in front of the table there was a number of other men behind him.

"Piss off and find another table" He said putting two huge hands onto the table.

Malik looked up at the brute of a man and cocked his head onto one side.

"No" He said calmly.

"Listen here shit for brains this is our pub and there is five of us. Now how do you want to do this?"

"I want you to turn around and find another table, there are plenty of others" Malik said leaning back and dropping a hand under the table.

The man hit the table with a huge fist causing the whole pub to go quiet.

"Since you are new in town I'll give you a chance to walk out of here mostly upright"

"Thank you, that is a generous offer indeed"

"All it will cost you is half an hour with your woman"

"I have a better offer for you" Malik's voice was still very calm and precise "Turn around now and you live"

"These are my guests" The Barman's voice came from behind the man.

"Goat, do I have to bar you again?"

The man called Goat slowly straightened up and turned around.

"No Mister Briggs"

"Good, now leave us be" Said the Barman.

Goat and his companions left the bar muttering as they went. The Barman placed 3 mugs onto the table and sat down next to Aris.

"My apologies about that, some of the lads here can get a bit rowdy when they have had a little drink"

"No need Mr Briggs" Said Malik his hand reappeared from under the table.

"You wouldn't have had chance to draw your sword up past the table" Mr Briggs said to Malik.

"I was planning on bringing it through the table and his thick skull"

"Ah"

"Mr Briggs may I introduce my partner, Elemental Mage Aris Calgar" He held out his hand to indicate Aris.

"A pleasure to meet you Aris" Mr Briggs said shaking her hand.

"I am Sergeant Briggs, retired now of course"

"Also a pleasure" She replied.

"So Mr Briggs what can you tell us about Torkle?" Malik said picking up one of the mugs and passing it over to Aris who took it. She looked at the contents before she carefully dipped a finger in and tasted it. Malik smiled.

"There has been a lot of people coming this way from the Northeast over the last few months." Mr Briggs picked up a mug and put it in front of Malik then pulled the last remaining one toward himself. "People are telling stories of small villages out in the wilderness that were once thriving but are now deserted of all life. Other villages have been burned to the ground"

Malik looked up at Mr Briggs from his mug.

"Were the bodies piled up in the centre of the village and burned?" He asked slowly.

Aris looked at Malik then turned slowly to Mr Briggs.

"How did you know that?"

"My town was attacked and burnt to the ground around fourteen years ago, the dead were piled in the centre of town and set alight"

"I see, I don't know if it was the same attackers but I spoke to a man two weeks ago who said he saw those that attacked his village. I didn't believe a word of what he told me"

"Why not?" Aris asked.

"Well he spoke of humanoid creatures larger than any man. He said they had dark green skin."

"With yellow eyes, wearing fur skin and skulls carrying a club the size of a small roof beam" Malik said staring into nothing.

Both Aris and Mr Briggs stared at him.

"Malik?" Aris asked.

"Hmm"

"How did you know that?"

"I'm… not sure" He said suddenly coming out of the trance.

"However you knew, you were spot on" Mr Briggs went on. "The man said that they took most of the village captive and killed those that resisted. As I said before I didn't believe him but now I'm not so sure"

"Is that man still around?" Malik asked.

"No, he left a few days after arriving. Why are you two heading to Torkle anyway?"

"There is reason to believe that someone is trying to reopen a Dark Gate there. We are to investigate the possibility, and if it is opened shut it again"

Mr Briggs looked from Malik to Aris and back again.

"Just the two of you"

"Oh yes don't worry we're specialists" Aris said and smiled at Mr Briggs.

Malik and Aris left the Severn Stars and headed back to the dock area.

The Sun was setting causing the light it gave off to become red in colour as the night started to draw in.

As they walked past an alley, a large hand reached out and grabbed Aris around the neck.

"Hello my pretty" A gruff voice said by her ear.

The man called Goat walked out of the alley holding Aris up so her feet were off of the ground.

"Boy's teach this worm how we do things around here while I take my apology out of her"

Five men appeared out of several alleyways and surrounded Malik. Goat dragged Aris backwards down the alley and into the shadows. The men were armed with various clubs and short swords.

"I don't suppose we could talk about this?" Malik asked.

One of the men swung a club at Malik. He ducked under the swing and punched the man square on the nose. The man screamed and dropped to the floor clutching at his nose as blood began covering his clothes.

Malik stepped over kicking him as he went and drew his own sword the blade brightly glowed red illuminating Malik's face.

He grinned. Some of the men took a step back.

"I guess not, such a shame"

Goat held Aris up against an alley wall with his hand around her neck. She tried to struggle but couldn't break free from his grip.

As Goat leaned forward Aris brought her knee up into his groin as hard as she could causing Goat let go of her giving her a chance to start running.

Goat gathered himself and ran after her easily catching up and barrelled into her knocking her to the ground. He started to rip Aris's clothes off.

Aris screamed at him and started to punch and kick to try and fight him off. Unfortunately her resistance only served to spur Goat on.

Aris closed her eyes bracing herself for the worst when suddenly there was a strange humming sound and Goat suddenly stopped and was very still.

Cautiously Aris opened her eyes. Goat was sat very still a sword blade was held under his throat. The blade was giving off a gentle red glow.

"Now then, gently let go of her and get up" A voice said to Goat.

Goat did so moving slowly and with great care. Aris backed away until she was against the alley wall.

"Aris, are you alright?" Malik's face appeared from behind Goat and into the dim dusk light of the alley.

Aris slowly nodded at him, she was shaking and never took her eyes off of Goat. Malik watched Aris then turned his attention to Goat the red glow from the sword blade suddenly doubled in intensity. The blade made a higher pitched humming sound.

"Shall I remove his face so you never see it again?" Malik said to Aris.

She didn't respond to him. Malik's sword made a sound as if the blade itself was screeching in rage.

"I am a fair man Mr Goat so I suggest you start running now" Malik growled into Goat's ear.

"You have five minutes before I come after you and start cutting pieces off. Do you understand?" Goat very carefully nodded.

The red glow faded from the blade as Malik lowered his sword. Goat turned and ran down the length of the alley and turned a corner. The only sound was that of his footsteps rapidly retreating into the distance.

Malik tapped his sword tip three times against the stone floor then walked over to Aris and knelt down beside her. She was staring at him as if thinking about something. Malik rubbed his shoulder again.

"Aris?" He said gently.

She didn't respond so he gently brushed her hair aside and saw her eyes were now closed. With great care he picked her up in his arms and headed back to the Red Devil.

Aris slowly opened her eyes and blinked, she jumped up quickly with a start until she realized she was back in her cabin. Looking around in the gloom she could see that moonlight was coming through the cabin porthole gently illuminating the room.

She moved her hand and felt something next to her. She picked up the object and in the moonlight she saw it was Malik's Sword. As she held it, the sword began to gently glow and made a low humming sound almost as if sword was purring.

Aris relaxed, the sound was strangely comforting to her.

She got out of the bed and removed the now torn clothes that Malik had made her and put her white robe back on. Carrying Malik's sword she went outside onto the deck of the Red Devil.

As she walked out onto the deck a voice sounded out from above.

"He must really care about you, you know"

Aris looked up.

Captain Worthington was sat on the upper bridge deck. His feet were resting on the railing. A red glow appeared in the darkness as he puffed on his cigar.

"What? He doesn't, he is ordered to protect me"

"Aris don't be daft, he left his sword with you! No Crimson Guardian would ever just leave their sword, especially one as rare as that one. I think it is more than just orders and you know that"

He got up and climbed down the ladder.

"He left it here to protect you"

"It's just a sword" She said.

"Really?"

Suddenly the Captain drew his sword and swung it at Aris. Malik's sword flashed red and made a high-pitched scream of rage.

There was a clattering sound as the swords collided. Aris watched in awe as Malik's sword moved without her will.

It parried the Captain's sword, then knocked it aside and held itself at his chest. The sword sounded like it was growling.

"See what I mean" The Captain said and lowered his sword. The glow and growling faded from Malik's sword.

"That sword has a bond with him because of that Spirit Stone. He must really want to keep you safe for the sword to react violently like that"

"Where is Malik?"

"Don't know, He brought you back here then ran back into town. He just told me to watch over you and he would be back by morning"

"Oh"

"You look a bit shocked. Do you want a cup of tea? I've got a pot on the stove in the bridge"

"I think… I think I could do with one, yes please" Aris said.

The sound of the engines starting awoke Aris. She was sat in one of the chairs in the Red Devil's bridge. Someone had put a blanket over her to keep her warm. Malik's sword was still lying protectively across her lap.

"Good morning" Said Captain Worthington from the helm seat. "Malik is out back if you want to give him his sword back"

Aris thanked the Captain and opened the bridge door. Malik was indeed sat at the end of the deck watching the water.

Aris climbed down the ladder and walked over to him. Before she could speak Malik spoke up.

"How are you feeling?"

"I'll be alright"

Aris handed him his sword back.

"Thank you for doing that"

"It's nothing" Malik replied putting his sword back into its sheath. "As long as you are alright that's all that matters"

"Why because you were ordered to look after me?"

"Well partly that yes" Malik looked down at the water again.

"Oh"

"And the fact that I've come to like you being around" Malik said a little faster than he intended.

Aris looked at something on the dockside that had caught her attention and then smiled at Malik's back.

"You know you really are an idiot sometimes"

Malik turned around and looked at her.

"But I really like you being around as well" She said and smiled.

"Now come and fix my clothes I want to start training again"

She took him by the hand and led him back inside.

As the Red Devil sailed away, up on the dock a crowd of men were looking and laughing at a man stripped naked and hanging upside down from a lamppost.

He swayed gently in the morning breeze. Mr Briggs walked along to see what was happening.

"Mr Briggs how are we going to get Goat down from up there" Said a man as Mr Briggs walked past.

"Someone go and fetch a knife or something and we'll cut the rope" He said to the crowd in general.

"Sorry Goat looks like you are going to have to land on your head, we won't be able to hold your weight" He shouted up to the man hanging upside down.

Goat groaned. Back on the Red Devil Aris grinned to herself.

The following two days passed without much incident although there was a noticeable increase in traffic moving downstream.

On the afternoon of the second day the Red Devil arrived at the town of Stonewall. As it turned out it was very well named indeed. A huge wall surrounded the outskirts of the town.

Only a handful of the tallest buildings were visible over the top of the wall.

The docks were separated from the town by a large stone gateway in the massive wall.

Malik and Aris stood on the deck of the Red Devil as the Captain manoeuvred it into a free docking bay. When the Red Devil was close enough to the dockside, an arm extended from the side of the boat and latched onto a mooring post securing the Red Devil to the dock.

The Captain climbed down from the bridge onto the deck.

"Well here we are" He said. "Welcome to Stonewall, you should check in at the Sheriff's office here. He will set you on the way to Torkle"

"And you Captain, what are you going to do?" Aris asked as she picked up a bag.

"I've got a few deliveries to make here but other than that I'm to wait here for your return so I can take you back to Founders Rock or wait for news of your death whichever happens first"

"Thanks for the vote of confidence!" Malik said.

"If I don't get word from you in a week I'm to report you as overdue to Founders Rock"

"Fine we'll send word back when we get to Torkle" Malik said and picked up his crossbow and slung it over his shoulder.

He threw some bags onto the dock and jumped up off of the Red Devil. He leant down and took Aris's hand and helped her up onto the dock.

"Thank you" She said and turned to the Captain. "Where can we find the Sheriff's office Captain?"

"West of the dock gate, it's next to the mail depot you can't miss it. Best of luck you two!"

The Captain waved at them as they walked toward the main dock gate that led into Stonewall.

The first thing that came to Malik's mind when they entered Stonewall was the drop in temperature. The high wall blocked a lot of sunlight from reaching the outer edges of the town.

The second thing that occurred to him was the lack of people. Normally a trading town such as Stonewall would be filled with the sound of traders and people going about their daily business.

Today there was nothing but a deathly silence.

"Where is everybody?" Aris said.

"I don't know" Malik replied as he looked around. "Look there's the mail depot over there"

Malik pointed to a set of large buildings next to the outer wall.

"The Sheriff's office must be next to it, so the Captain said"

The Mail depot was a large stone building with a set of large double doors that opened directly onto the street. The doors were currently closed as Malik and Aris walked past.

Attached onto the side of the Mail Depot was the Sheriff's Office, the sign hanging over the door slowly creaked backwards and forwards in the breeze that blew down the street.

Malik walked to the door and knocked. When there was no response he tried the door handle. The door swung open.

"Wait here a second" Malik said to Aris and went inside.

There was no one inside the Sheriff's office. Malik silently moved slowly around the office.

A stove was burning in the corner of the office. A pot of water on the top of the stove started to boil.

Malik stood still for a moment as he thought then walked over to the stove and moved the pot off of the heat. He opened the door and picked up a poker that was lying against the wall then used it to stir the stove fire.

"You can come out now I don't want any trouble" He said to the room in general.

"That is good to know, I would hate to have to shoot you in the back" a woman's voice said from an adjoining room.

A crossbow appeared around the doorframe, slowly followed by a woman dressed in brown leather and chain mail.

"And I would hate to turn you into a smoking pile of ash on the floor" Said Aris from the office doorway. She was holding a ball of flame in her hand, Malik smiled.

"Sheriff Killdare, I presume?"

"He used to be my husband but he was killed. Nobody else would take the job" The woman said and lowered the crossbow.

Malik nodded at Aris, the ball of flame disappeared.

"I am Crimson Guardian Owen and that is my partner Elemental Mage Calgar"

The woman looked from Malik to Aris.

"Sheriff Darcy Killdare" She said as she clicked the safety catch on the crossbow.

The Sheriff walked over to a desk and put the crossbow down and then sat back in the chair and put both her feet up onto the desktop.

"Now what can I do for you Crimson Guardian Owen and Elemental Mage Calgar"

"We have been told you can get us to Torkle" Aris said.

"Torkle! Why in the name of all that is scared would you want to go there for?"

"Our orders are to go and find out what is happening out there" Malik replied walking over and sitting on a chair.

"And you two are what Founders Rock sent? Do you know what has been going on round these parts!"

"Maybe you can enlighten us Sheriff" Aris asked.

"Three small settlements along the coach road between here and Torkle have all but been destroyed. Torkle itself is nearly totally deserted, as is Stonewall. The only people left here are those who cannot travel or have nowhere else to go. I'm one of the few people trying to keep things going out here"

"When did this all start?" Malik asked.

"About six months ago was when the first incident occurred. A family was found butchered at their home in the hills outside of Torkle. The strange thing was that only the older members of the family were killed. We know for a fact that there were two daughters and a son living there but there was no sign of them. My husband went out to investigate other missing people two months ago and has never been seen again"

"Any idea who could be behind all this?" Malik said looking at the Sheriff.

"None, I've heard mad ramblings of monsters carrying people off into the night. A beast the size of a house which smashes buildings to pieces and other such tales but nothing that made any sense to me"

"I see" Malik stood up and walked over to a map hanging on a wall he stared at it. "Well we are here to sort this out"

"I wish you luck" The Sheriff said. "I've already arranged for you to travel on the mail coach to Torkle tomorrow morning. You can sleep in the back room here tonight if you like"

"Thank you, that's very kind of you" Aris said.

"Not at all, it's nice to have some company for a change"

Later that evening in the back room Aris awoke shivering. Moonlight shone through a window illuminating the small room.

"Are you alright?" Malik asked.

"I'm so cold, sorry did I wake you" She said shivering.

"No, I hadn't gone to sleep yet"

Malik was lying on some bedding laid out on the floor. Aris was in the single small bed that occupied most of the back room. Malik looked over at her.

"You could come and sleep over here with me if you are cold."

"You don't mind?"

"As long as you don't snore" Malik said and smiled.

Aris got out of the small bed and pulled the blankets off with her.

Malik unfolded the bedding on the floor so Aris had some space.

She kicked him as she lay down beside him and Malik pulled his blanket over her and she cuddled up next to him.

"Mmm you're so warm... Malik can I ask you something"

"Go ahead"

"I don't snore do I?"

"Goodnight Aris" Malik said putting his arm around her.

With Aris breathing gently in his arms he gently fell into a deep sleep.

Malik opened his eyes warm sunshine shone on his face.

As he looked he realized that he was looking up at a blue sky and quickly jumped up.

"What the!?" He said to himself.

He was sitting on long yellowing grass. Not far away there was a large lake surrounded by trees. The sunlight reflected off of the ripples on the water.

Malik turned and looked all around, Aris was nowhere to be seen. Malik got to his feet and walked toward the lakeside. He couldn't remember why but the area seemed to be so familiar to him.

As he neared the lakeside he saw a small clearing with a fallen tree. Malik stopped and stared at it. As he did so a ghostly figure of a small boy slowly faded into view, he was sitting on top of the fallen tree.

The boy was holding a long stick with some fine string tied onto the tip. A twig was tied further down the string and at the very end of the string a piece of thin metal had been bent into a hook shape and tied onto the string.

The boy leaned over and pulled a beetle grub out of a hole in the tree and stuck it on to the hook. He then lowered the hook into the water until the twig floated on the surface.

"Err excuse me" Malik said to the boy.

The boy didn't respond but carried on fishing with his stick. Malik went to touch the boy on the shoulder, as he did so his hand went straight through the boy.

"That's... a little weird" Malik said to himself and tried again.

The same thing happened again when all of a sudden there was a scream in the distance. Malik and the boy both looked in the direction where the scream had come from then both started to run.

Malik was faster than the boy but somehow when he got to the area where the scream had come from the boy was already there. He saw that there was a waterfall and a small water pool in another little clearing.

A little girl was backed up against the rock face of the waterfall. A large Carnitoad was stalking her. It had two big round eyes, which swivelled as it watched her move. It opened its mouth and its long tongue with a horn attached to the tip shot out at the girl, it missed her and stuck against the rock face behind her.

"Don't move" Malik shouted at the girl but she didn't appear to hear him.

"Keep still" The little boy shouted and picked up a stone.

The Carnitoad pulled loose its tongue from the rock and it retracted back into the mouth with a gulping sound.

The boy threw the stone at the toad and hit it on the head. The Carnitoad slowly waddled around to look at the boy.

"Keep away from the water and run over here" The boy shouted as he threw another stone.

The little girl did so and ran behind him. The Carnitoad watched the girl run and as it opened its mouth to shoot out the tongue another stone hit it on the head causing it to let out a croak of annoyance.

The boy looked around and grabbed a fallen branch from the ground. He pulled some of the smaller branches off of it and held it up like a club. The Carnitoad licked its head with its tongue. Then with surprising speed it jumped at the boy and girl.

Malik dived and tried to tackle the Carnitoad in mid air unfortunately the Carnitoad just passed straight through him. Malik landed and rolled back onto his feet.

He saw the boy swing the branch and hit the Carnitoad aside with the branch. The Carnitoad landed on its back in a heap. It righted itself and lurched off back to the water where it jumped into the pool and dived under the water. The boy tapped the ground with the branch three times.

"Good morning you two" Malik and Aris were awoken by the Sheriff she was leaning against the doorway to the back room.

"Your ride is here, grab your gear and we'll get it loaded onto the mail coach"

"Thank you Sheriff we'll be ready in a few minutes" Malik yawned.

"Take your time" The Sheriff smiled at them and walked off.

Five minutes later Malik and Aris walked through the Sheriff's office and into the mail depot building via a side door.

Inside the mail depot a raised stone platform ran around the outside of the building allowed easy loading of items and people into any coach that was parked alongside. Malik and Aris stood on the platform looking around.

"We just have to refuel the coach's water tank before we can load it up" The Sheriff said walking up a set of steps that led to the raised platform.

Aris became aware of a chugging sound outside of the depot doors. The doors opened and what looked like a square box on four wheels rolled into the depot loading area.

It rolled to a stop and the top half of the coach swivelled around 180 degrees. Malik noticed that there was what looked like a chimney on the back of the coach.

The coach then appeared to reverse up alongside the raised platform.

"We are very pleased with the new mail coach" The Sheriff said watching the coach roll to a stop.

"We started using it just over a year ago and found it much faster than horses"

"I've never seen anything like it before" Malik said. "I mean I've heard of them but I've never actually seen one"

"They are not allowed on Founders Rock because of the risk of running over people" Aris said.

"The Master Healer would love that!" Malik laughed. "How fast does it go?"

"About thirty miles an hour in middle low gear as a rough guess we haven't really tried the other gears" The Sheriff replied.

Aris walked over to Malik and elbowed him in the ribs.

"Why are you grinning like that?" She asked.

"This is amazing, the water fuelling pipe up there drops down and water flows into the water tank on the coach"

"Where does the water come from?" Aris asked Malik.

"I imagine that there is a rain catcher up on the roof which collects water in a large tank." Malik pointed up near the ceiling

"Watch this"

A large flexible pipe came down from the ceiling. It was lowered slowly down by two cables connected to a gearing mechanism mounted on a wall.

The pipe was then attached to a nozzle on the coach by two depot workers.

One of the workers shouted something up to another worker on a gantry. A gurgling sound could be heard from the ceiling as water ran down the pipe and into the coach's water tank. One depot worker watched a gauge mounted onto the water tank. He was calling out gauge readings.

When he shouted and waved his hands at the gantry worker. The gurgling sound stopped and the pipe was detached from the coach and wound back up toward the ceiling.

"Right, now that's all sorted we can get the coach loaded now" The Sheriff said.

Malik had just finished loading their bags into the coach's storage compartment when the Sheriff wandered over to him.

"Malik, can I ask a favour of you?"

"Certainly Sheriff, what's on your mind?"

"Could you deliver a package to a friend of mine in Torkle"

"That should be easy enough to do. What's your friend's name?"

"Father Brian Spectre. He will be in the Torkle church near the centre of town. The church has become the unofficial hub of Torkle since all this trouble started. If anybody can help you when you are there it's him… He is uniquely qualified he helped my husband many times"

"Sounds like a handy man to know, thank you Sheriff"

"No, thank you Malik, I've already had the package loaded onto the coach"

Aris walked up to the coach and smiled at Malik as she climbed into the passenger compartment. Malik followed her and shut the door behind him. The Sheriff walked up to the window and leant inside.

"Look after each other when you get out there. If you need any help I'll try my best"

The coach started to move and pulled away from the raised platform. The Sheriff waived them goodbye as the coach rolled out of the depot doors and onto the street outside.

The coach rattled and chugged its way along the street and out through the large city gates toward the country plains.

The driver turned in his seat inside the coach.

"Is this your first time?" He asked Malik and Aris.

Malik was busy looking out of the window while Aris was hanging onto her seat.

"Yes" She replied, her eyes closed tightly.

"Don't fret, it smoothes out in a while when we hit the main coach road. Oh I'm Norman by the way" He said to Aris.

"Can we get up to top speed when we are on the road Norman?" Malik asked excitedly.

"Just for you I'll put in high gear!" Norman said smiling at Malik

"It's nice to meet someone else who likes these new coaches"

"They are just fantastic" Malik said grinning.

"I'm glad you think so" Aris muttered and pulled her hood over her eyes.

The coach drove off of the old dirt road that it had been driving on and mounted a newly built stone road where it accelerated away.

"How come the road doesn't go all the way into Stonewall?" Malik asked Norman.

"It would have been finished but when all this trouble started it got put on hold"

"I see, how are you doing Aris?"

"Better, now we are off that dirt track" She said.

"Good" Said Norman. "Hold on I'm going to put her into high gear!"

"Do you have to" Aris said but Norman was already pulling a lever into place beside him.

There was a clunk and the coach surged forward along the road. Malik and Aris felt the surge in acceleration press them back into their seat.

"Wow, this is great!" Malik said excitely leaning forward watching the countryside fly past.

"I think I'm going to be sick, The Red Devil was smoother than this" Aris moaned from under her hood.

"Look on the bright side you won't meet any Waterwraiths on the land" Malik said.

Aris groaned.

Later that afternoon they entered a wooded area. Trees surrounded each side of the road.

The trees cut out a lot of the late afternoon sunshine causing Norman to turn on a set of lights mounted on the outside of the coach to help him see the road in the gloom.

Aris was dozing quite happily now the coach had slowed down. She was resting her head on Malik's shoulder and seemed quite comfortable.

Malik was looking out of the window. The coach's speed slowed down further in the darker gloom as the sun set behind the trees.

"Malik, we are not far from Torkle now" Norman said

"That will please Aris…" Malik replied.

He started to turn his head from the window to look at Norman when he suddenly stopped.

"What's the matter?" Norman asked.

"I though I saw something large move in the trees"

"Don't worry as long as we are moving there is nothing to worry…about"

Norman stared through the window at something in the distance.

"Oh bugger!"

"What!?"

"A tree is blocking the road up ahead"

"Oh great. Aris wake up" Malik said shaking her.

"Mmm" She murmured.

"Wake up were about to be ambushed"

"Mmm… What!" She said and jumped up.

Malik was already climbing out of the back window.

"What are you doing?"

"Ambushing them back! Keep Norman safe"

He disappeared out of the window and vanished into the darkness.

"Does he do that often?" Norman asked.

"You get used to it"

The coach stopped in front of the fallen tree. The coach lights lit the area in front of the coach. Darkness surrounded the back of the coach and the areas on either side of the road.

"What are we going to do now?" Aris asked.

"Well I guess I could try and shift that tree with the coach" Norman said.

"I don't think we should get out of the coach so that's a good idea" Aris replied.

Norman slowly drove the coach up to the tree and gently started to push the thinner end of the tree trunk with the front of the coach. The fallen tree started to turn in the road as the coach pushed the lighter side.

"This might just work" Norman said.

"If we keep pushing this end of the tree a bit more we can back up and squeeze past"

Norman put the coach into reverse and backed it away from the tree

"Alright here we go!"

He put the coach into forward drive mode. The coach lurched forward and stopped. He tried again but the coach still wouldn't move.

"Maybe we are caught on something?" Aris said.

Suddenly the coach rocked violently side to side and a horrible howling echoed around the coach. The coach finally tipped over onto it's side throwing Norman and Aris about the inside of the coach.

Norman hit his head on one of the coach levers and lay unconscious. Aris scrambled upright. She ended up standing on a side door that was now the floor.

"Norman, are you alright?"

Aris rocked Norman with her hand but there was no response.

"Malik where are you when I need you" Aris said to herself.

She tried to open the other door but it was jammed shut. Instead she opened the back window and cautiously looked around before slowly climbing through. Once she had got out of the window she summoned a fireball that sat in her hand.

The light given off allowed her to see in the dark gloom. She carefully dropped to the ground and walked around the coach fireball at the ready, but there was nothing to be seen.

Aris suddenly felt very alone in her pool of light surrounded by the dark woods. A bush rustled behind her. She spun around, hand outstretched ready to release the fireball.

Another bush rustled on her left she turned again and caught a brief glimpse of two eyes which reflecting the light of her fireball.

Aris's breathing quickened she could feel her heart beating in her chest as panic started to set it.

She remembered one of her lessons with Malik. He had been teaching her how to tune into and sense her surroundings to find fish while on the Red Devil.

She hadn't managed to do it then. She hesitantly closed her eyes and concentrated.

As she calmed herself and brought her breathing under control she began to feel her surroundings with her mind. She began to feel the trees and branches moving in the breeze. She sensed the coach now on it's side and as she calmed herself she began to sense further away. As she stretched out with her mind she suddenly found an area that felt very, very wrong.

It was if the world was made up of smooth lines except for this one large area, it felt jagged.

As she probed it she felt it twitch. She turned and aimed her outstretched hand with her eyes still shut.

A fireball shot away into the darkness and exploded in the trees sending debris flying in all directions. She continued to turn loosing fireballs as she tracked the movement with her mind.

It was large and moving very quickly through the trees given its size.

The trees erupted into flames as Aris fired fireball after fireball into them. She sensed a change in direction. Whatever it was in the trees it was going to run across the road to the other trees.

She aimed ahead and loosed a single large fireball. The creature leapt out of the trees and caught the full force of Aris's fireball in the chest.

The fireball exploded.

Aris sensed that the creature was dead as the remains rolled along the road. It was as if an aura that surrounded the creature had been turned off.

She opened her eyes and took a deep breath. A length of woodland alongside the road was now gently burning where Aris's fireballs had impacted and ignited the trees and bushes illuminating the whole area.

She was about to walk back toward the coach when she froze. The same jagged feeling she had before was back. This time though it was right behind her.

She slowly turned. Standing over eight feet tall behind her was a huge ape like creature. It was standing upright on two legs and was covered from top to bottom in long matted hair. It raised both it's fists high in the air to crush Aris.

There was a red flash across the back of the creature's legs. The creature screamed and fell over backward. Malik appeared from behind the creature and as the creature fell he turned swinging the sword round.

There was a silken sound and another flash of red light. The creature slumped onto the ground, the head rolled to a stop not far from the body.

"That was a big sod!" Malik said tapped the ground three times then sheathed his sword.

He walked over to Aris.

"Are you alright?"

He gently put both of his hands on her cheeks and turned her head to look at a cut on her head. She knocked his hands away.

"Yes I'm fine, I just bumped my head inside the coach when it went over. Where were you anyway?" She said angrily.

"There were four of those things, I got the other two back there but these two chased after the coach before I could get to them"

Aris subsided as Malik looked up at the burning corpse on the side of the road.

"I see you handled yourself really well!"

"I missed the other one though"

She said looking down at the ground.

"Nobody's perfect!"

Malik gently lifted her chin so she looked at him. He smiled at her then a thought suddenly struck Malik.

"Where's Norman by the way?"

Malik pulled the unconscious Norman out of the coach and lay him down on the ground next to a fire Aris had made.

"He's not hurt badly, although he will have a headache when he comes round" Malik said putting his pack behind Norman's head.

"Now we just need to get the coach back on its wheels"

"Can you lift it up a little bit?" Aris said

"I can try, why?"

"I could create an air cushion under it to lift it up. I just need a small gap to start with"

"Alright hold on a minute"

Malik took his sword belt and armour off and laid them down by the fire. He walked to the coach and looked at it.

"Looks like the only place I can grip is this sharp thin lip under the roof, it will slice my hands to pieces if I'm not careful"

Malik looked thoughtful for a moment.

"Hold on, I've got an idea"

He tore the sleeves off his shirt exposing his bare arms. He wrapped a sleeve around each of his hands.

Malik turned so his back was against the roof of the coach and bent his knees. He grabbed the lip under the roof and grunted as he strained against the weight of the coach.

Aris stared at him, his muscles bulged on his arms as the coach creaked and lifted slightly off of the ground.

"Aris! Anytime now would be good!"

His voice stained as he concentrated all of his strength into lifting the coach.

"What! Oh sorry" She said shaking her head.

Aris held both of her arms out to either side of her. As she did so the wind began to gain strength. She brought her arms together.

A spinning column of air formed between her arms. It moved along the ground and flowed under the coach into the small gap Malik had created.

"You can let go now, I've got it" Aris shouted to Malik.

He let go and walked over to her swinging his arms round to get some life back into them.

"What happens now?"

"Well I give the coach a gentle boost and hopefully it will force it back up onto the wheels but…"

"But? What's the 'but'!"

"If I give it too much it will flip over in the air and then we are back to where we started, plus it might damage the coach more"

"Ah I see, well in that case I'll leave you to it then"

"Thank you"

Aris focused her attention on the coach. The wind began to build up around the overturned coach.

There was a slow creaking sound as the coach was slowly raised up higher. The coach was lifted three quarters of the way up when it stopped.

"What's wrong?" Malik asked.

"It's too heavy"

"I need to give it a push to get it back onto the wheels but I've used too much energy already"

"Can you hold it where it is?"

"For the moment yes but not for too long"

"Let me try something"

Malik ran at the coach and jumped at the side of the coach Aris was holding up with her magic. As he connected with the coach it rocked on the two wheels that were touching the ground.

He started to shove the coach in time with the rocking motion. He managed to almost get it to tip back onto its wheels when Aris shouted him.

"Malik! I can't keep this up much longer" Aris was beginning to shake from the strain of keeping the magic flowing.

"Just a little longer it's nearly there!"

He shoved the coach again. It stood on the edge of tipping then fell back. Malik shoved it back then ran around the coach and jumped up and grabbed the roof rack using his body weight to tip the coach.

The coach finally tipped back onto its wheels. The wind died away the only sound was the coaches suspension creaking from side to side as the rocking motion died away.

"That's got it, well done!" When she didn't reply Malik walked around the side of the coach. "Oh no"

Aris was lying unconscious on the floor.

Aris opened her eyes. It was still dark but a fire was burning brightly. She was lying under a thick blanket with Malik's arm around her.

She raised her head off of his chest. Malik looked like he was asleep. He was holding something in his other hand. She reached over and gently took a small bottle out of his hand. The bottle rattled as she shook it.

"Neurodoze" She read aloud.

She looked up at Malik's face. His face twitched every now and again as if he was in pain. Aris raised herself up to look at him properly when she stopped. Malik's sword was pulsating with its red glow while it was still sheathed.

Aris got up and sat still. There was something strange on the very edge of her magical senses. It was very faint and she wasn't sure at first if she hadn't just imagined it.

She stood up and walked over to the coach and pulled her staff from the baggage compartment.

She walked back to the sleeping Malik and held the staff close to him. A black crystal gently began to glow. The glow intensified as she moved the staff closer to Malik's head.

"Oh no!" She said and looked worriedly at him for a moment.

She bit her lip while she thought then with her mind made up Aris straddled Malik's chest and sat on him.

"Sorry Malik this will sting a bit" She said as blew on her hands.

She placed her hands on either side of his head and closed her eyes while concentrating.

Malik suddenly started to twitch and jerk violently, Aris had to struggle to keep her balance on top of him.

"Malik it's me, please don't fight me" She shouted.

Malik calmed and the twitching and jerking eased.

"That's it you know I wont hurt you" She whispered soothingly.

Malik settled back down and Aris rearranged her position on top of him before putting both hands back on his head again. She concentrated then slumped forward onto him as her mind entered his.

She opened her eyes again and found she was standing in a darkened room. There was a strange blue tint to all the colours.

It was always the same when she mind walked in another's mind. Malik was also here in the room. He looked as if he was suffering from really bad flu.

He was standing looking at a bed that was against a wall.

"I was so frightened I couldn't move" He whispered.

"Malik? What frightened you?"

Malik pointed at a doorway that suddenly appeared. There was a scream followed by a thud. Footsteps could be heard getting closer. A large figure appeared dragging a woman's body in one hand and a large club in the other.

The figure was larger than any man. It had dark green skin and wore battered black armour. Two yellow eyes scanned the room.

"That's a Black Orc!" Aris said running over to Malik.

"They are supposed to be extinct!"

The Orc walked past the bed then stopped. It sniffed the air then turned to the bed. Using the club it flipped the bed over with no visible effort. A small boy was cowering underneath the bed.

The Black Orc watched the small boy then swung the club round and hit the boy across the chest. The impact sent the boy flying into the air. He smashed through a glass window backwards.

The Black Orc faded from view leaving both Aris and Malik alone in the room.

"That was you?" Aris said.

Malik said nothing, the room faded and Aris found that she was now outside. It was raining heavily and the smell of smoke hung heavy in the air.

She saw the small boy crawling through the mud. He was holding his chest with one hand. There was a long gash across his chest, which he was bleeding from. He slowly crawled under an overturned cart and lay still.

Aris became aware of a black figure standing in the distance. There was something strange about it. It was something that shouldn't be here.

"You're not a memory. Who are you?" Aris demanded.

"I couldn't kill him then and now he resists my attempts even in sleep"

The figure walked forward toward Aris.

"It's you I can sense invading Malik's mind. He is under my protection leave him now" She ordered.

"You think you can make me little girl? I have more power than you can imagine"

The figure held out his hand Malik appeared in the air hanging like a rag doll on invisible strings. The dark figure clenched his fist and bolts of lightning stuck Malik causing him to scream in pain. Aris felt Malik's body jerk violently back in the real world.

"Leave him alone!" Aris screamed and cast a bolt lightning at the figure.

The bolt hit the figure in the chest and flung him backward where it disappeared. Malik was dropped out of the air and landed in the mud behind Aris. He lay still and didn't move.

The figure reappeared again in front of Aris.

"Not bad little girl. I actually felt that"

The figure slowly looked from Aris to Malik and grinned evilly.

"So you think you can protect him? Let's see how much you can take shall we"

The figure spread it's legs taking a wide stance. It fired another bolt of lightning at Aris as she cast her own spell. The two spells collided and exploded into a glowing ball of light.

"Is that all you can muster!" Aris shouted.

"Far from it" The figure sneered.

There was a sudden increase in power from the figure. His spell started to overpower Aris's own and the ball of light started to move toward her.

She countered by increasing her own power causing the ball of light to alternate back and forth between them as the battle of magic's raged.

"I'm impressed! But I'm afraid you are getting tired" The figure laughed.

Aris dropped down onto one knee under the strain of the magical conflict.

"Malik help me! Get up please!" She shouted.

Malik stirred on the ground.

"This is your mind. You have the power here not him!"

There was another bust of power from the dark figure, the ball of light started to creep closer to Aris again.

"Malik please!"

She sank down onto both knees and lowered her head.

A curved beam of red light shot across the ground past Aris and on toward the figure.

As it moved along the ground it entered Aris's spell and accelerated along the spells trajectory. The beam entered the ball of light causing the ball to flicker as red light danced across the surface.

The ball of light began moving rapidly toward the figure gaining speed as it did. The figure tried to increase the power yet again but the approaching ball of red light had far too much momentum. It struck the figure and exploded in a blinding flash of white light.

The figure screamed with rage and disappeared.

Malik sat bolt upright into Aris's arms. She held his head to her chest with both hands.

He wrapped both of his arms around her and held her tightly his breathing was deep.

"Malik, was that little boy you?" She asked gently.

Malik looked at her and opened his shirt. There was a large scar running across his chest where the rough edge of the club had cut into him. Aris ran her hand across the scar.

"It broke most of my ribs"

"How did you survive?"

"I don't know? I just did" Malik said shrugged his shoulders. "What just happened anyway?"

"You nearly died in your sleep that's what!" Aris said angrily shoving him with both hands. "Why are you taking Neurodoze!"

"The Master Healer in Founders Rock gave them to me. They are supposed to help me sleep, why what's wrong?"

"You idiot, didn't you know you had been cursed!"

"Cursed? What do you mean cursed?"

"Someone or something has been attacking your mind with black magic"

"I thought they were just nightmares! I kept waking up and couldn't sleep!"

"Your mind was defending itself by waking you up, Neurodoze stops you from waking"

"But I've taken them before?"

"When?"

"In Founders Rock, and on the Red Devil"

"Why didn't you tell me, I could have helped you sooner! Gods you haven't changed at all, even from when we were small"

Malik stared at her and blinked.

"Pardon"

"You really don't remember me do you?"

Tears started forming in her eyes as Malik looked blankly at her for a moment.

"I slept naturally for the first time in a long while when I was close to you. I also had a different dream in Stonewall" He said thoughtfully as memories slowly began to return.

"There was a small girl in trouble and a boy. I couldn't see his face…"

He looked closely at Aris and his eye's widened.

"You don't like toads do you?" He asked.

Aris smiled at him and wiped her eyes with her sleeve.

"No, I hate them"

"So it was you after all, was that a memory? Why can't I remember?"

"You have been under that curse for a long time. It's no wonder your memories are faded. Being close to me must have triggered something in your mind"

"Why didn't you tell me you knew me when we first met?"

"I didn't know it was you to begin with. I only realized after that man tried to rape me! You tapped your sword on the ground three times just like you did when we were small. I asked you why you did that, you said 'To tell my enemies in the underworld that I'm still here!'"

"My father told me that, he had been a soldier in the Royal Guard and that's what they all did"

"Do you remember anything else?" Aris asked hopefully.

"Not as such, little things are slowly coming back to me"

He looked up at her.

"Why were you at Halton anyway?"

"My mother and father went there to see someone I don't know why but it was something important. They were both excited about it whatever it was"

Aris looked at a symbol marked on Malik's right shoulder and traced the pattern with her finger.

"I went out to play by the lake and got ambushed by that bloody awful Carnitoad. Then you appeared and saved me, after that I spent almost all of my time in Halton town playing games with you"

Aris smiled at the memory.

"We had such adventures, exploring the woods and caves. I never felt afraid again because I was with you"

She stroked Malik's hair with her hand.

"Before we left you promised to always protect me when I was in trouble just like you did before with that Carnitoad"

Malik looked at his right shoulder and examined the symbol marked onto his skin. He felt like he was in a dream the world seemed to slow down. He gently took Aris's right arm and rolled the sleeve up. Then very slowly as if he was afraid he would hurt her or not find what he was looking for Malik turned Aris's arm over. On the underside of her arm was the same symbol marked onto her skin.

"I remember... We marked each other with that symbol we made up between us. We used burning apple juice and a reed stem from the lake. It stung like hell but you wouldn't let me stop until I had finished drawing it on your arm"

Malik held his hand up to his cheek as another memory resurfaced.

"When I had finished even though you must have been in such pain you still kissed me on the cheek and thanked me"

Malik lifted himself up and moved closer to her.

"This is in return for saving me this time" He said putting his arms around her and gently kissed her on the lips.

"Your welcome" She replied and kissed him again.

"Err sorry to interrupt"

A voice sounded out from the other side of the fire. Malik and Aris turned their heads. Norman had awoken and was sitting up by the fire.

At this point it struck them that Aris was sat on top of Malik who was only half dressed.

"Can I just ask? What in the Nine Hells has been going on!" He said.

Ten minutes later the sun had started to rise over the tree line and Malik along with Aris had finished explaining most of what had gone on.

Norman had walked over to the decapitated body of the ape creature and was prodding it with his foot when Malik joined him.

"It's a damn shame" Norman said.

"Big mountain apes are usually as gentle as falling snow"

"There was nothing gentle about the two I met back down the road" Malik said rubbing his side and wincing at a painful memory.

"Mind you, it is strange that they should be here" Norman went on ignoring him.

"It's much too warm for them at this altitude. They like the snow and cool temperatures up high in the mountains"

"You like them, don't you?" Aris said walking over to them and putting her hand on Malik's back.

He looked at her and put his arm around her shoulders.

"I do yes. When I was younger one of these mountain apes saved my life"

"What happened?" Aris asked.

"Oh I was young and stupid, I thought I could impress the girls by climbing eagle's peak on my own. While I was climbing a rock gave way and I fell. Luckily I only broke my leg when I landed. 'Oh good' I remember thinking, 'I'm going to freeze to death now'. Just when I thought I was done for, a big male found me and carried me down to a trail just below the mountain. A passing caravan found me and took me back to town"

"It's no wonder you like them" Malik said.

"I just don't understand why they would attack like that" Said Norman.

He knelt down and went to stroke the ape's fur when he stopped.

"Hey look at this, looks like something has burnt the fur and skin here!"

As they looked closer they could see that something had been branded onto the skin of the mountain ape.

"Looks like some kind of symbol? Aris do you recognize it?" Malik said kneeling down beside Norman.

Aris looked at the burnt area on the mountain ape and moved some of the fur away with her hand.

"It looks familiar, I think that it is some kind of control rune I'll have to check my books to confirm it though"

She traced the shape of the rune with her finger.

"I think it might be a good idea to get moving again. Norman, are you alright to drive?" Malik asked.

"I think so yes"

In the distance something howled, it was nothing that Malik had ever heard before. He turned and looked in the direction of the howl.

Aris walked beside him and tightly gripped his hand.

"Good, I'll feel more at ease when we get out of this wood. Aris I'll get your books out of the coach, you go and climb aboard. Norman can you go and get it started please"

"Yes Sir!"

Norman quickly ran to the coach and climbed inside. After a few seconds the lights came on and the engine started up.

"What was that?" Aris said.

"In all honesty I've got no idea and I don't really want to find out at this point. Come on lets get going!"

He led Aris back to the coach and climbed up the back of it while she climbed inside. He opened the cargo hatch and pulled out Aris's bag of books as the coach vented some steam. It started to make chugging sounds as Norman primed the coach.

Malik closed the cargo hatch and jumped inside as the coach lurched and started to move along the road again.

Malik slumped in the back seat and handed Aris her book bag.

"Well, all in all this has been an interesting night" Malik said making himself comfortable.

"It certainly has" She replied opening her bag and rooting through the books contained inside.

"I don't know why but I feel really tired now"

"Not surprising with all the strain your mind and body has been through I'm surprised you've lasted this long"

Aris found the book she was looking for and pulled it out of the bag.

"Ah this is the one, Malik?"

Aris turned to look at Malik when she got no response. He was sleeping peacefully with his head leaning against the side window. Aris smiled and dropped the bag onto the floor.

She then put her feet up on the seat and rested her head against Malik's chest using it as a makeshift pillow. She thumbed through some pages and started to read. A few minutes later, Malik still fast asleep put his arm around her. He mumbled something under his breath and carried on sleeping.

"I feel the same about you" She said quietly as she smiled and carried on reading.

The sun was just starting to rise over the mountains in the distance when the coach rolled into Torkle. Malik was still asleep when the coach stopped at the Torkle depot.

"Malik, Malik wake up!"

Aris shoved him several times to try and rouse him from his sleep.

"Alright you asked for it"

She held out her finger just in front of his nose. A tiny spark of electricity arced from her finger to Malik's nose.

Norman was on the back of the coach unloading the bags when he heard the scream from inside the coach.

"Poor guy, those apes must have really hurt him" He said to himself and carried on unloading the coach.

Malik climbed out of the coach rubbing his nose followed closely by Aris.

"Sorry but next time you should listen to me!"

"Just don't make a habit of it alright!"

Malik picked up his crossbow and slung it over his shoulder.

"You look much better now, not that you didn't look good before" She quickly added when she saw his expression.

"You just look more... full of life than you did before that's all"

Aris looked at the ground in embarrassment

Malik walked over and stooped down so he could look up at her face.

"Thanks to you I suspect"

He smiled at her and she lifted her head as he straightened up.

"Come on, let's see if we can find this Father Brian Spectre and give him his package"

Malik picked up his bag and slung it over his shoulder then picked up the largest of Aris's bags. Aris picked up the rest of her bags and pulled her staff out of the coach.

"The church is near the centre of town according to the Sheriff's directions" Malik said walking up behind her.

"I hope there is somewhere to eat around here I'm starving"

"I must admit I could do with something to eat myself, it was a bloody long night. Still let's see this Father Spectre then sort out something to eat"

"Alright, thank you for the ride Norman, Would you let Captain Worthington know we've arrived" She shouted as they walked toward the door.

A hand appeared over the top of the coach and waved them goodbye as they walked out of the depot.

"I'll let him know, Good luck you two" Norman shouted from behind the coach.

Malik and Aris walked out into the morning sunshine and looked around.

"Everything feels so cold" Aris said.

"It is unnerving that there is nobody about" Malik said looking around the deserted streets.

As they walked along the main street Malik noticed that all the doors and windows on either side of the street were boarded up and nailed shut.

"It looks like the town is dying" He said.

They walked past a Blacksmith's workshop. The door was banging open and shut in the morning breeze. Malik looked inside then put the door back onto the latch. Strangely the empty Blacksmith's shop unnerved Malik more than the lack of people. Malik found something deeply troubling about a cold unlit forge.

Eventually they reached the centre of Torkle, the church sat on the east side of the town centre. In front of the church there was a large stone structure that looked like a large warehouse with no walls. This served as the town's market square and would normally be full of people and traders.

On the west side of the town centre stood the town hall. It was also the residence of the Mayor and his family. Smoke was coming from one of the chimneys of the town hall indicating that some people were at least still around.

Malik wandered over to the church steps and looked up at the church. The doors were open. Malik walked to the top of the steps and peered inside.

Sunlight shone into the church through a large hole in the church's ceiling. Fallen debris covered the floor and had smashed some of the seating. Something large had crashed through the ceiling to get inside.

Malik looked up into the darkness above the hole when he heard a faint scratching sound. There was a faint rustling of feathers from somewhere near the roof beams high above him.

Slowly he took his bags and quietly put them on the ground. He pulled his crossbow around and up to his shoulder. He cocked it using the built in tension lever. There was a gentle click as the gears inside pulled the bowstring into place.

He held out his hand and pointed at the town hall he indicated to Aris to check it then keeping the crossbow to his shoulder carefully entered the church.

Aris carefully put her own bags down on the ground and held her staff with both hands. The gems on her staff glowed as she focused power into it.

She crossed the town centre and walked up the steps to the door. Carefully she pushed the town hall door open with the end of her staff then slowly she entered the building.

Inside the door was a main corridor with doors leading off to other rooms on each side.

At the end of the corridor there was a large staircase. It led up to the living quarters of the hall where the mayor and his family would normally live.

She saw light coming from a doorway under the staircase and headed over to investigate it. The doorway as it turned out led to a large kitchen area.

"Hello is there anybody here?" She called out.

"Hello?" A voice replied.

A face appeared from another doorway at the far end of the kitchen

"Just a second" The face said and then disappeared.

Aris entered the kitchen and looked around as an old man walked into the kitchen wiping his hands on a cloth.

"Boys" He said.

A hand was firmly placed on Aris's shoulder.

Thanks to Malik's training she instinctively brought her elbow back into the man's stomach knocking the wind out of him. As he bent forward she brought her staff around and it connected with his head sending him spinning onto the floor.

She pointed the end of the staff at the old man and a ball of spinning flame formed at the end. The old man stood with his arms in the air.

"Call them off" She said. The man nodded slowly.

"Alright boys come out slowly"

Three young boys came into the room from the back doorway.

"Who are you?" The old man asked.

"I'm Elemental Mage Aris Calgar. I've been sent from Founders Rock to help you"

"What, just you?"

"No my partner a Crimson Guardian is also here"

Aris lowered her staff and the fireball disappeared. Two of the boys ran over to the fallen man and helped him up.

"Sorry about that" She said as she helped the boys to pick up the man then they sat him in a chair.

He glared at her through his one open eye. The other one was already swelling itself closed.

The old man lowered his arms and gave a sigh of relief.

"I wonder if you could help me? I'm looking for Father Brian Spectre" Aris asked looking back at the old man.

"Really, well you are out of luck I'm afraid he is almost certainly dead" The younger man said.

"What happened?"

"We were all in the church about two nights ago when a large winged creature appeared out of nowhere and started killing people. Those that didn't run away were killed and eaten"

"The creature is nesting in the church now" The old man said.

"There may be some people still trapped in there but we have no way to save them"

"It's still in there? Oh no, Malik!"

She turned and ran out of the kitchen.

"Hey wait!" The old man shouted and ran after her.

Aris ran across the town centre toward the church when the old man caught up with her and pulled her to the ground.

"Are you completely mad you can't go in there!" He shouted.

"Malik's in there! Let go of me" She screamed.

"He's probably already dead!" The younger man shouted as he walked across the square holding his swollen eye. "Just the same as everybody else that went in there"

A horrible screech came from inside the church. There was a flash of red light through the church windows and something very large burst through the church doors backwards.

Most of the church's doorframe was blown out by the passage of the creature. It hit the stone market square structure in the centre of town causing part of it to collapse as it slid to the ground.

The creature was very big and had two arms and two legs with the head of a vicious looking bird. Two large wings were sticking out from its back. It was covered in bloodied black feathers.

There was a large cut running across the abdomen of the creature. It scrambled to its feet and raised its wings ready to take to the air. It began screeching defiance at the church.

Its two huge wings caused a massive gust of air that blew the dirt from the ground into the air and knocked Aris over. She covered her eyes with her arm to protect them from the rest of the flying debris as the creature took too the sky.

Malik walked out of the church in his right hand he held his sword and in the left was his crossbow. Aris jumped up and ran over to him throwing her arms around him.

"I thought you'd been eaten" She said kissing him and holding him tightly.

"Not by an overgrown buzzard like that"

"That was amazing!" The old man said as he came running over to them and stopped while he caught his breath.

"I've not seen power like that for a long time young man"

"Thank you, and who might you be Sir?"

"I am Mayor Falstaff of well... what remains of Torkle anyway"

The old man spread his arms wide indicating the whole of the town.

"This is my son and my grandchildren" He said turning and indicating to the group watching them from the doorway of the town hall.

"Pleased to meet you Mayor, could you do me one favour please?"

"What's that?"

"Duck"

Malik brought his crossbow up pointing at where the Mayor's head had been.

The large flying creature was diving straight at them from high above. It had its talons fully extended ready to slice Malik to shreds.

"Aris, could you enchant this arrow for me please?" He whispered in her ear keeping his eyes fixed on the creature.

"For you certainly, what would you like?" Aris replied also watching the creature's decent from above.

"Ice, I think that will do just fine"

Aris reached over and touched the arrow loaded in Malik's crossbow. The arrowhead took on a faint blue glow.

"Thank you"

There was a click as he fired the crossbow.

The arrow flew through the air leaving a faint blue trail behind it as it went.

The arrow hit the creature in the head causing it to veer off line from its original flight path. As it tumbled through the sky ice crystals began to form over the entire body of the creature as it fell toward the ground.

The creature was a solid block of ice when it crashed into a building on the far side of the town centre. The crash demolished most of the house. There was silence and no movement for several seconds. The building creaked then what remained of the roof fell in.

Malik gave Aris a quick kiss on the cheek and shouldered his crossbow.

They walked down the church steps and went to look at the large hole that now represented the front of a house. Malik and Aris both looked inside the building and saw that the large block of ice was still intact.

"Aris, would you care to do the honours?"

She looked side long at him as he held his hand out toward the ice block.

"You don't mind?"

"Be my guest"

Aris walked up to the ice block and tapped it a few times with the end of her staff then swung it as hard as she could at the ice block. There was a thud and the block of ice shattered into thousands of little ice shards along with shattering the frozen creature inside.

"That felt so good" She said walking back to Malik.

"Nicely done!" Malik sheathed his sword. "Now I think we had better go and get those people out of the church basement"

The Mayor led the way down to the church's large basement where they found a large wooden door that was bolted from the other side.

The Mayor banged on the door with his fist.

"Hello! It's Falstaff is anybody alive in there?"

A faint muffled voice could be heard from behind the door.

"Falstaff? Thank the Gods. Has the creature gone?"

"Better! It's dead we've got help from Founders Rock here"

"Ah good they have arrived, we have a lot of wounded down here that need help"

"Open the door and we'll get you out"

"We can't the doors hinges have buckled when that creature tried to get in here. Its jammed the door shut, can you force it from your side?"

"I don't know hold on a second"

The Mayor looked at Aris and Malik. Aris looked at Malik

"Your turn this time, if I blow the doors up it could hurt those inside" She said.

Malik looked at the door and drew his sword.

"Tell them to all get as far away from the door as they can"

Malik's sword began to glow as he built up his power.

"Get away from the door quick!" The Mayor shouted at the door then got out of the way himself.

Malik swung his sword twice at the door. It made a silken sound as it moved through the air then the door itself.

A large red cross appeared on the door where the sword blade had cut through the door, it glowed for a moment before it faded away.

Malik then sheathed his sword and walked up to the door.

He tapped on the door with his hand and it collapsed into four pieces.

"Bloody hell!" said the voice on the other side of the door through the cloud of dust.

"How many injured have you got?" The Mayor said walking through the doorway and into the room.

"We've got three seriously injured, Falstaff we need to get them help"

"Right, come on boys let's get them into the Town hall with the others"

The Mayor and the rest of his family ran into the other room and started to carry the worst injured out of the room and back to the outside.

"Is Father Brian Spectre here?" Malik asked one of the younger boys as he passed

"Oh yes granddad Brian, he was the one granddad was talking to, hold on I'll go fetch him"

The boy disappeared into the other room. He returned guiding a man dressed in long brown robes. The man's eyes were closed as he walked.

"This is granddad Brian Spectre" The boy said and nodded before heading back into the room to help the others.

"Pleased to meet you sir I am..."

"Crimson Guardian Malik Owen, yes? Where is your partner Elemental Mage Aris Calgar?"

"I'm here" Aris replied slightly stunned. "How do you know who we are?"

"I lost my sight many years ago but was given the gift of Far Sight in compensation"

The Mayor appeared again having got the injured out of the room and led the Father to an old wooden chair and sat him down.

"I've known of your coming for a while now but I didn't know the circumstances that we would meet, I must admit the appearance of that monster caught even me off guard"

"You can help us then?" Malik asked.

"Yes I can but first things first lets get everyone into the town hall I will feel much better for a large cup of tea"

"Sorry Brian, but we ran out of tea the other day" The Mayor said.

"Not to worry Malik has brought us some from Darcy in Stonewall" Father Brian said smiling.

He turned his head to look at Malik and regarded him critically with closed eyes.

"I think I need one as well now" Aris said and shivered.

Back in the large kitchen of the Town hall the recently freed people sat huddled around the large kitchen fire.

A large fresh kettle of water was hanging over the fire slowly coming to the boil. The Mayor's son was walking around with a large pot of tea filling up large mugs.

He saw Malik and Aris sat on a bench with Father Brian and walked over.

"How is Sarah doing William?" Father Brian asked him as he approached.

"She's fine my father says she will be up and about in no time now that we have got her out of the church basement"

"That is good news indeed. Oh did you want to say something to our friends here?"

"Yes... I just wanted to apologise for my behaviour before, I'm really sorry"

"Apology accepted, sorry for the black eye. If you will let me, I can fix that" Aris said.

She stood up she put her hand over William's swollen eye. There was a green glow from her hand again. When she took her hand away William's eye was healed.

"There that looks better" She said.

"Thank you" William said blinking his healed eye.

Aris nodded and sat down next to Malik again.

"That is a handy trick" Malik said as William returned to filling up tea mugs.

"I could teach you"

"Might be worth a try but I have to warn you I'm bloody rubbish at magic"

"Have you tried before?"

"I tried to learn how to create a flame by magic from some books in Founders Rock so I could start a fire in an emergency. I couldn't get it to work though"

"Ah but you didn't have me to teach you then" Said Aris taking his hand.

"I don't think I can, it's all a bit beyond me"

"What's the harm in giving it a try?" Father Brian said taking a sip from the mug of tea in his hands.

"Alright I'll give it another try" Malik said looking at Aris.

She beamed at him and moved closer to him.

"Right then give me your hand"

Father Brian took an unlit candle that was sat next to him and put it in front of Aris.

"Right, now we need something to light. Oh thank you Father"

Aris took the candle and sat it in front of Malik. She put Malik's hand on one side of the candle then got up and stood behind him.

She leaned over and took his other hand and held both of them in her own and positioned them on either side of the candle.

"Right now focus your concentration on the candle tip and I'll give you a prod in the right direction to get you going"

"It's hard to concentrate when you are leaning over like that" Malik said quietly so that just Aris would hear him.

Nobody noticed Malik suddenly jump as Aris stuck her knee sharply in the base of his spine.

"Concentrate" She repeated.

"Alright, Alright"

Malik stared at the candlewick he felt something odd happen inside him.

"It's me" Aris said inside his head. "If I demonstrate it in here you know how it feels when you do it"

Malik continued to concentrate on the candle as Aris gave him instructions on the inside of his head.

"Picture the candlewick burning. Then build up a small amount of power just like when you activate your sword"

Malik did so and felt heat build up behind his eyes.

"That's it keep focused on the candle… Right that should be enough now release the power at that point you are focusing on"

The candlewick smoked then lit itself. The flame gently bobbed about as Aris let go of his hands and sat down.

"See you can do it"

Malik looked at the candle in amazement and then blew it out.

"Wow do you feel tingly when you do it" He said then blushed when he realized what he had just said.

"Most of the time, I've got some really good ones to teach you!"

Father Brian cleared his throat.

"Remember that little trick it may well come in handy in the future"

Malik was still staring at Aris with his mouth open. He suddenly remembered where he was and shook his head.

"Err yes I will. Do you have any idea where we should start looking?"

"Falstaff would you be so kind as to fetch the map for me please" Father Brian called out.

The Mayor's face appeared from around the doorway at the back of the kitchen.

"Certainly Brian would you give me a few minutes to finish off treating these last few injuries"

"Of course, take your time"

The Mayor nodded and disappeared back around the corner again.

"I cannot give you an exact location but I can help to point you in the right direction.

The Mayor appeared at the table carrying a rolled up scroll.

"Thank you Falstaff, could you help me here"

Father Brian took the scroll from the Mayor and unrolled it on the bench. Malik and Aris came round to his side of the bench and looked down at the map.

"We are here in Torkle where the most recent incidents have been"

The Mayor said pointing to a point on the map.

"A month ago some settlements were attacked here and here on the way to Stonewall. Before that a Ranch was burned to the ground here not far from where we are. Around six months before that another Ranch owner here in the east had complained of missing livestock, then he and his family went missing shortly afterwards"

"Do you see a pattern Malik?" Father Brian said.

"Yes I do, it looks like the attacks started in the east and have worked their way here"

"Very good"

"What's this?" Aris tapped something on the far right hand side of the map.

"An old mining settlement up in the mountains but it has been abandoned for nearly twenty years"

Malik and Aris looked at one another then back down at the map.

"Sounds like a good place to start looking" Malik said.

"I agree, how long will it take to get there?"

"It is about one to two days travel on foot depending on how fast you move" The Mayor said. "There is a trail that runs along side the river about two miles to the north. It runs all the way to the old settlement"

"Can you tell us anything about the layout of the settlement?"

"Well from what I remember the settlement was built up around the mine entrance which is basically a large cavern leading into the mountain. The mines run for miles underground and there are airshafts cut all over the mountain. I think that there were some large chambers and buildings in the mine itself but I'm not sure"

"Why was the settlement abandoned?" Aris asked.

"As far as I know the mountain became unstable and parts of the mine collapsed in on its self. A lot of people died. It was decided that it was too much of a risk to reopen the mine so it was abandoned"

"I think that we should definitely take a look at the place" Malik said. "Mayor, can we get some supplies together?"

"Unfortunately we don't have a lot to offer at the moment. A supply cart is due to arrive here any day now but we should be able to put some basic stuff together for you"

"Thank you, is there much in the way of game in that area?"

"Oh yes there are plenty of rabbits and mountain deer at this time of year and the frost berries should be ripe by now"

"Great, we will be fine with whatever you can supply and if you happen to have a spare bottle of Frostbite I'll take that as well"

"I think we can sort that out. I've got some Frostbite in the wine cellar that I've been maturing for a few years you are welcome to a bottle. I even have a small pack tent you can use"

"Thank you that would be a really helpful added bonus"

The Mayor nodded at Malik and patted Father Brian on the shoulder and helped him to his feet.

"Come on Brian lets get you to your room for some rest"

"Oh thank you, it has been a trying couple of days a nice bed will be a welcome change"

"What's Frostbite?" Aris asked Malik as the Mayor headed off into the hallway next to the kitchen leading Father Brian.

"It's a type of alcohol fermented from the frost berries. It's strong stuff and has many uses other than getting really, really drunk"

"Like what?"

"Well it is great for stopping wounds going septic and can help keep you warm even in the bitterest cold"

"Sounds like good stuff"

"We used to have drinking games with the stuff back at the Brewers Maid Tavern in Founders Rock"

"I've never been in there" Aris said.

"When we get back I'll take you"

"Did you used to win? At the drinking games I mean"

"Me, no"

"Who did?"

"May did mostly" Malik smiled at a memory.

"Who's May" Aris said suspiciously.

"I suppose you could call her my adopted big sister. The Captain of the Crimson Guardians took me in after my parents were killed at Halton. May is his daughter"

"Why did he take you in?"

Malik gave her a sidelong stare.

"I mean I can't imagine the Captain of the Crimson Guardians taking just any boy into his care" She said quickly.

"When I asked him he said that he owed my mother and father and that it was the least he could do for them"

Aris put her arm around him.

"Sorry"

"Don't worry, I don't mind. He's a good man and May has always looked out for me along with Charleston"

The Mayor appeared again and walked over to Malik and Aris.

"We have a couple of guest rooms upstairs that you can use. They are the grand rooms used for visiting royal dignitaries but it seems only fair for you two to have the use of them while you are here"

"That is very nice of you thank you" Aris said.

"If you grab your bags I'll take you up so you can get settled"

Malik picked up his own bags and then Aris's larger bag containing her books.

The Mayor led them out of the kitchen and into the main hall. They climbed up the stairs to the first floor of the Town hall and walked along a corridor until they reached two sets of double doors.

The Mayor opened the closest set of doors and walked inside.

"These are our pride and joy!"

He flicked some switches on the wall beside the door. The room was illuminated by light emitted from crystals mounted all around the room.

"The two rooms are connected by a set of doors over there"

The Mayor walked over and opened the door leading to the identical room next door. He walked over to another door on the other side of the room and opened it.

"This is something really special!" He said and ushered them inside.

"Welcome to the Marble Bathroom. There is an identical bathroom next door as well. Each one has its own hot water supply and everything you could possibly need!"

Aris gasped in amazement and even Malik had to admit he was really impressed by what he saw.

White marble gleamed everywhere. In the centre of the room was a large bath. It looked large enough to bathe a horse in and still have plenty of room leftover for a small polo team.

Above it was a fountain that fed water into the bath like a small waterfall. On the far side of the bathroom was a large mirror with two basins all beautifully decorated with golden ornamental seashells.

"Make yourself at home my lad and I'll settle your partner in next door"

The Mayor ushered Aris out of the room to the room next door.

"Ah, errr well um" Malik started to try and object but gave up so instead he followed them out of the room and looked a little awkwardly at Aris.

"You will be fine" Aris said winking at Malik then followed the Mayor into the next room.

"I'll see what we can put together for a dinner. It may not be much but we are going to celebrate the return of our people and show you our gratitude!"

He nodded at Malik then closed the door leaving Malik alone in the large room.

"Guess I'll try and get the bath working then" He said to himself and wandered back into the Marble Bathroom.

After five minutes of fiddling with various knobs and taps Malik finally managed to get the bath to start to fill. While the enormous bath was filling up with hot water from the cascading waterfall Malik fetched a small pack out of his bag and laid it by the basin.

He went out of the bathroom and got undressed after looking in some drawers he found some large towels. He returned to the basin wearing one of the towels he had found.

He stared at himself in the mirror and rubbed the large scar that ran across his chest. He stood still, his eyes shut as the memories of his youth echoed in his head. He flinched as he felt the club hit his chest, the sound of the glass window breaking. Suddenly he caught sight of a black figure standing behind him in the mirror. He spun around but nothing was there only the water falling into the bath. He turned back to the mirror and the figure was still there.

"She won't be able to protect you forever, just like your mother couldn't protect you. And like her she will die trying"

The words echoed in Malik's head filling him with incredible rage. For a second Malik thought he saw a flash of blue light in the mirror. He blinked and the figure was gone. He blinked again and looked down at the marble surface. Cracks had formed around indentations his fingers had made into the solid marble.

"What the hell was that?" He said to himself.

He shook his head and hands and unpacked a shaving kit from the small pack and washed his face in hot water. He carefully shaved away the stubble that had accumulated over the last few days. When he had finished he threw the towel into a corner of the bathroom and climbed slowly into the bath.

He winced slightly as he sank into the hot water but soon relaxed as the stress and strain of the last few days and the encounter with the monster and strange figure in the mirror earlier melted from his muscles and mind.

He turned his head and saw Aris standing in the doorway. She was wearing a long white nightgown.

"Can I join you?" She asked.

"Of course, if you can find space that is"

Aris smiled and Malik watched her walk across the bathroom to the bath.

"Could you close your eyes please?"

"Hmm, oh right sorry"

Malik closed his eyes and heard Aris gently walk to the other side of the bath. He heard the rustling of her nightgown falling to the floor as she undressed.

Unable to help himself he opened one eye to see Aris. She had her back too him, he opened his other eye and watched her pick up her nightgown and hang it over an ornament. Malik suddenly felt a whole lot hotter despite the fact he was already in a hot bath.

He only just remembered to close his eyes in time as she turned. He heard the splash as she stepped into the bath.

"Alright you can open your eyes now"

Aris's head and shoulders were visible above the water, much to Malik's disappointment. He thought it was probably for the best though as he felt quite warm enough at the moment.

"Are you alright?" She asked.

"Err yes why?"

"You have gone all flushed in your face"

"I have oh… it's err…because of the hot water that's all"

"Oh" Aris looked as if she had something on her mind. "Malik"

"Hmm"

"Do you have a girlfriend in Founders Rock?"

"Nope, I mean I've got girls that are friends but I've not had a serious relationship"

"Why not?"

"I don't know I guess I've never felt really comfortable with anybody, why do you ask?"

"How do you feel about me?"

"You are something different altogether"

Malik turned his arm and tapped the symbol on the top of his right shoulder.

"Maybe it is because of our symbol but I feel at ease when I'm with you it's like nothing in the world matters anymore only you"

He looked across at her as she tilted her head to one side.

"I know it sounds bloody daft, I bet you have loads of men after you back at the Elemental College"

"One or two have tried, a really pushy one ended up with a broken jaw"

Malik smiled at a most satisfying memory as she lifted her arm out of the water and looked at her symbol marked on her arm.

"But I wasn't interested in them. I somehow always knew I'd find you again"

She swam across the bath and sat up on the same ledge next to Malik. He put his arm around her neck. The feel of her soft skin made him feel really flushed again.

"A while after I had left you and gone back to Founders Rock with my parents, my mother saw the symbol on my arm"

Aris turned her head on one side and rested it on Malik's shoulder.

"She got really angry with me. She said it was stupid of me to make a bonding spell like that when I was so young. I remember her yelling at me 'how do you know you made the right choice'"

Aris slapped the water with her hand making a large splash.

"We didn't speak for a week after that"

"What did your father think when he found out?" Malik nervously asked.

"Why? Are you worried?"

"I'm just curious that's all"

"He came and saw me when he got back after my fight with my mother. I though I was going to get shouted at again and he would break the spell, but he didn't get angry"

"No?"

"No, he just asked me about you"

"And?"

"He didn't look to impressed until I told him about the Carnitoad and how you tapped the ground with the stick"

She put her hand on his chest and gently traced the scar on his chest with her finger.

"He asked me what that meant and when I told him what you told me he burst out laughing"

"Laughing"

"Yes he was really happy about it. He told me that I couldn't have made a better choice and he would do all he could to make sure the bonding spell remains strong. He went and talked to mother and she suddenly changed her attitude when we next met"

"Sounds like I owe him a lot then"

"I think he must have known you to react the way he did"

"Don't know how, the only person I met that summer was you"

"What did your parents think?"

"They never knew and if they did they never said anything to me about it"

"I wonder if my father did know you, he was very insistent that I go on this mission. I'm very glad he was now"

Aris turned over and put her arms around Malik's neck. Malik put his arms around her waist and pulled her close to him.

"Me too, but let's not forget we do still have to sort this mess out"

She pulled herself close and kissed him.

"Tomorrow" He finished. "By the way just to let you know that I'm an honest person, I peeked when you were getting undressed"

"Really well I suppose that's alright I was watching you for a few minutes before you got in the bath"

"You cheeky sod"

Malik easily lifted her up out of the water. Aris wrapped her legs around his waist and pulled herself back down into the water where she sat on top of him.

"I suppose there is no point in being professional and not letting this get in the way of our assignment?" Malik said.

Aris cocked her head to one side and looked at him.

"At this point not a chance in any of the nine hells"

"Ah good I was just checking!"

He pulled her close and kissed her neck while running his hands up and down her back and around her legs.

Aris wrapped her arms around his neck again and pressed herself against him when someone knocked on the main door outside.

"Go away!" Malik shouted.

He ran his fingers through her hair and down her back again, the knocking continued.

"He's busy come back in an hour!" Aris shouted then giggled as Malik put his hand over her mouth.

The knocking started again with much more urgency.

"Oh for the Gods sake" He sighed.

"Don't..." He kissed Aris.

"Go..." He kissed her again.

"Anywhere" he kissed her one last time then stood up and got out of the bath.

"Don't forget one of these!" Aris said and threw him a towel.

Malik caught it and wrapped it around himself. Aris layback in the bath and waved at him with one of her legs as she watched him go.

"If this isn't life or death someone is really going to get hurt" He muttered to himself as he walked across the large bedroom to the door.

"Yes what is it?" He said hotly as he flung the door open.

The woman on the other side took a step back.

Malik stared at her, as she looked him up and down.

He looked down and at this point he remembered he was only wearing a towel.

"Sorry" He said quickly hiding behind the door. "I get really upset when people interrupt my baths"

The woman having got over the initial shock suddenly remembered what she had come for.

"Sorry sir but my father in law the Mayor needs to see you right now"

"Tell him I'll see him in the morning"

Malik went to shut the door but the woman shoved her hand against the door.

"Now, Sir" She said quite sternly.

Malik saw the look on her face and sighed.

"Alright, I'll be down in five minutes"

"Very good sir" She nodded at him then ran off down the corridor.

Malik shut the door and walked back to the bathroom where Aris was relaxing in the bath.

"What's the matter?" She asked him when she saw his face.

"Something's going on downstairs I'm going to take a look"

"Now!?"

"Sorry it sounds like something important. Don't look like that"

Aris pulled a face at him and stuck her tongue out.

"I don't like it any more than you do" He said as he picked up his clothes from the corner of the room and started to get dressed.

Aris stood up and climbed out of the bath. The water dripped off of her smooth skin and the curves of her trim body. She stood in front of Malik and put her hands on her hips.

Malik stopped and looked her up and down.

"I must be bloody mad" He said to himself.

"You promise to make it worth my while"

"I promise"

"Alright I'll let you off for now" She said and picked up a towel and wrapped it around her self.

She then picked up a smaller towel from the marble bathroom counter and wrapped it around her hair.

"But when you come back you are all mine" She said hugging Malik tightly before she walked out of the bathroom and into the bedroom.

As Malik followed her she threw the bedcovers back, flung the towel aside and climbed into the large bed.

"Don't keep me waiting" She said as Malik opened the door.

"Back in a flash"

He walked out then his head reappeared around the door.

"By the way I've one other thing I have to say"

"Yes?"

"Gods you have a beautiful body!"

The door closed and Malik was gone. Aris smiled and lay back on the bed putting her hands behind her head and sighed.

The Mayor was nervously waiting for Malik at the bottom of the stairs.

"Sorry were you in the middle of something?"

"No luckily I hadn't started yet" Malik replied. "What's the problem?"

"A man has just arrived and collapsed in the doorway"

"So?"

"So, he says he had escaped from the mining settlement and needs to talk to you urgently. He looks like he has been through hell to get here."

"How did he know I was here?"

"I don't know lad, but someone must"

"I really don't like this!" Malik sighed. "Alright Mayor I'd better go and see him before my night gets any worse"

"We've put him on a table in the kitchen and tried to make him comfortable but it doesn't look good"

"Right, get everybody to their rooms and tell them to lock their doors. I've got a bad feeling about this"

"Yes Sir"

The Mayor ran off down the hall and started gathering people together and ushering them to their rooms.

"Don't call me Sir it makes me nervous" Malik shouted after him.

Malik entered the kitchen with care. A small group of people were clustered around a table in the middle of the kitchen. They turned and looked at Malik with troubled faces as he walked over.

He beckoned them away from the table and recognized the Mayor's daughter in law who had knocked on the door. He gently took hold of her arm as she passed and pulled her closer so he could whisper in her ear.

"Please go and tell Aris I may need her" He spoke gently.

"I'll go to her room now and fetch her"

"Err no, she is in my room and don't worry if it takes her a while to open the door"

The woman gave Malik a strange look then realisation dawned and she smiled at him.

"Right you are Sir" She said then smirked at Malik as she went past.

Malik cursed his bad luck again, turned and walked over to the bench.

The man lying on the table was panting desperately. His clothes were torn and covered in blood while his hair was long and matted with mud and twigs. If he had lain still Malik would have been hard pressed to tell if he was alive or not. The wounded man saw Malik and sat bolt upright.

"Please Sir I don't have much time, please listen to me" He said panting desperately as he tried to get his breath. "There are more people enslaved in the mines. They are forcing us to dig something out of one of the caverns"

"Easy, easy" Malik whispered as he put his hand on the man's chest and gently pushed the man back down onto the table.

"How did you escape?"

The man suddenly gripped Malik's hand a look of total agony washed over his face.

"He tortured me with something he put on my back sir. He told me to run here and find you!"

"Who?"

The man arched his back in pain and gritted his teeth.

"I didn't know him" The man said through gritted teeth

"He has long white hair and his eyes are black"

The man gasped for breath again.

"Markings, he has markings on his n-neck"

The man let out a final gasp and slumped back dead on the bench.

"By the Gods" Malik gasped as he laid the man's hand across his body and looked at his face. It was frozen in sheer agony. Very gently Malik closed the man's lifeless eyes.

He turned and went to walk away to fetch the Mayor when the dead man's hand moved. Malik quickly turned and saw the dead man's hand was gripping his wrist very tightly. He tried to pull his arm free but the grip was like a vice.

The body opened its eyes they were completely covered black.

"Hello boy, it has been a long time since I last saw you" The corpse said.

The voice wasn't that of the man it sounded like several voices all speaking at the same time. The overall effect was quite disturbing.

"Who are you?" Malik said turning to face the corpse lying on the table.

The corpse laughed at him.

"You don't know me but I know you. Oh yes, you and your whole wretched family"

Malik's free hand gripped his sword handle. The blade glowed red as he pulled it from its sheath.

"It is a shame they wouldn't cooperate and just give me the crystals"

The corpse turned its head and grinned at Malik.

"It might have saved the town from being burned to the ground and while I couldn't have allowed his bitch of a wife to live I might have allowed some of the others to survive"

The corpse chuckled to itself making little bubbling sounds from the throat.

"When I find you I'll split you in half" Malik growled slowly.

"If, and only if you can survive long enough I've a message from my master"

"Oh really and what would that be?" Malik said raising his sword

"Die"

The corpse exploded sending body parts and gore flying in all directions as a large insect creature erupted from the inside of the body.

Two sickle shaped arms unfolded and sliced into Malik's chest cutting him deeply. Malik staggered back from the attack, ducked under the blades as they swung at his neck and recovered his stance.

He blocked the next strike at his head and his sword was locked against the two blades of the insect. It leaned its head on to one side then with lightning quick speed it kicked Malik with it's hind legs.

He let out a yell of pain as he was flung backwards by the force of the kick to the large wounds on his chest.

He landed awkwardly behind a bench and his sword was knocked from his hand as it hit a chair.

Malik got to his feet as the insect closed on him and swung a blade over arm at him. He dodged to the side and caught the arm on the down swing. Using the momentum he forced the creature to the ground and sat on its shoulder joint restraining the creature on the floor.

"Now I'm really angry" He said.

The creature started to let out a chattering sound.

Malik gripped the creature's trapped arm and using his leg as a lever started to pull. There was a cracking sound as the insect's exoskeleton began to break.

Malik increased the pressure and the arm broke off from the body. Purple ooze sprayed out from the arm socket covering the floor. The creature squealed but now because it was no longer restrained by its arm it shot from under Malik and spun over knocking Malik over onto his back. It brought the last remaining blade round and impaled Malik's right shoulder. The blade ran straight through the back of Malik's shoulder and speared the wooden floor underneath.

Malik screamed in agony but managed to grab the insect by the neck with his left hand and stop it from biting his neck with it's mandible's.

The creature chattered excitedly as it drew near to Malik's throat. It could sense Malik's blood flowing like a torrent through his veins and arteries. Desperately Malik felt for something he could use with his right hand. Even though his shoulder was pinned to the wooden floor he still had limited movement.

His hand brushed against a broken piece of chair. He grabbed it with his right hand. Using all the strength he could muster he lifted the insect up and jammed a knee in the space between him and the large insect.

"Let's see how you like it" He shouted at the insect.

With his left hand he gripped the blade arm that was impaling his shoulder and pulled. He screamed as the blade came free from the floor. With the new freedom and wincing with the pain from his shoulder he stabbed the creature in the large left eye with the chair fragment.

The insect screeched and reared up pulling the blade free of Malik's shoulder. The purple liquid oozed from the insects wounded eye.

Malik rolled over and got to his feet he saw his sword lying on the floor a short distance away and scrambled over to it knocking several chairs over as he fell forward. The insect was distracted trying to remove the stick from its eye by shaking its head and clawing at it with the remaining arm.

Malik finally managed to reach his sword, as he picked it up the blade flashed into life as he activated its power. He felt the energy from the sword flow through him enhancing his abilities.

The insect managed to pull the stick from it's eye and chattered loudly as it watched Malik with the remaining eye.

It wildly leaped at Malik with one last attempt to cut his head clean off. Malik ducked and spun around under the insects attack bringing his own blade up and around with him.

Malik's sword met little resistance as it sliced through the insect, which landed in two separate halves it's back legs wriggling of their own accord.

The floor was covered with the purple insect blood.

Malik limped over to the top half and trod on the insect's remaining arm blade as it was swung at him. Even now the insect was still trying to kill him.

Malik brought the sword down on the insect's head. There was a loud crack as the sword tip pierced the exoskeleton armour with ease. The sword was thrust with such force that the blade was buried far into the wooden floor.

The creature slumped and remained still.

Finally it was dead.

Malik pulled the blade free as Aris ran into the room.

"Malik! Oh Gods!"

She ran over and caught him as he fell to his knees. The red glow died from his sword and it clattered to the wooden floor as it fell from his grip. Blood dripped in an almost constant stream from his hand where the blood from the shoulder wound had run down the length of his arm. His shirt was coloured blood red from all the large wounds underneath.

Malik looked at her then looked down at his shirt.

"I don't think I'm going to be able to keep my promise tonight" He whispered just before the world went black and he slumped forward into her arms.

Malik opened his eyes and blinked. Sunshine shone onto his face through one of the large bedroom windows.

He was lying in the large bed of the guest room. There was a rattle from the doorknob and the door opened. The Mayor's daughter in law entered carrying a tray. Quietly walking over, she put the tray down on the bedside table.

"Nice to see you're still with us sir, how are you feeling?"

"All things considered not too bad, thank you. Where's Aris?"

"You are a very lucky young man to have someone like that at your side" She said smiling and pointed beside Malik.

He turned his head and pulled the covers gently back revealing Aris. Her arm was across Malik's chest while her head was resting on Malik's shoulder. He could see her gently breathing.

"She stopped the internal bleeding and healed most of the damage with her magic. It was really a drain on her and she passed out trying to completely heal you. My father in law stitched the rest and he put on a special balm to numb your body so you wouldn't feel any pain"

"I though I should be hurting more than I am" Malik said and gently stroked Aris's hair with his hand.

"How long have you two been together?" She asked pouring a cup of tea from the teapot on the tray. She handed the cup to Malik who gratefully took it and sipped a mouthful.

"Not long a few days"

"Is that all?"

"We knew each other as children but it has taken me fourteen years to find her again"

"Why so long?"

Malik took another sip and lay back again he winced slightly as his body made a formal complaint about the recent treatment it had received.

"Things happen, she had to leave and I got cursed"

Malik stroked Aris's hair again while the maid gave him a funny look. Malik looked up at her again.

"It is nice to be with someone who I feel completely at ease with. I don't have to prove anything to her she just takes me as I am"

"I know how you feel, I felt exactly the same way about somebody"

"What happened?"

"I married him!"

She smiled and gently took the cup from Malik.

"And thanks to you I am still here to be able to see my family"

"You're welcome… by the way I don't think I know your name?"

"It's Sarah Sir"

"Nice to meet you Sarah, I'm Malik"

"Nice to meet you also Sir"

Sarah nodded and walked out of the room closing the door behind her.

Malik looked down at Aris again and gently kissed her head then rested his head against hers and drifted off back to sleep. His hands gently caressed her hair as he slept.

It was late in the afternoon when Malik awoke again. He gently eased himself up and let out a little yelp of pain.

"Are you alright?" Aris said her voice full of concern as she sat up beside him.

"Yes I'm fine it's just a bit sore that's all, sorry did I wake you up?"

"No I was already awake, I was thinking"

"About what?"

"Well just how are we going to sort out the mess here?"

"I've been thinking about that myself. Before that poor man died downstairs he said that there were a lot of slaves being held in those mines. They are excavating something in one of the caverns and I bet it is the Dark Gate that we are after"

"So we free the captives, destroy the gate and go home"

"Yup, that's the same plan I came up with. There is just one thing though"

"Yes?"

"They are going to know we are coming. The man dressed in black that was putting the curse on me, I think he is the leader or something like that. He said he knew me and my parents"

"He did? How?"

"I don't know but he does seem familiar. Maybe it's something about his voice"

Malik shook his head.

"Anyway my plan is to travel only at night. Under the cover of darkness we could sneak into the mines undetected. When we're in we need to figure what to do first. As we do not know how many guards we have to deal with, it is safe to assume that we are outnumbered. That means we may only get chance to do one serious action before we are noticed"

"You mean it's either the gate or the captives"

Aris rolled onto her side and watched Malik.

"Precisely, I can't see a safe way to do both at the same time. There is too much uncertainty involved"

"We go for the captives. Now we know where the gate is I'll send a message to father and start getting us some support. Battlemage Airships can get here in a few days maybe less if there is one ready to depart. It would be easier to storm the mines by force without the captives being used as human shields"

Malik turned his head and looked over at her and took her hand holding it tight.

"I agree, we go to free the captives and get them to safety then attack the gate later with brute force"

"Agreed but we set out tomorrow night"

"Why?"

"You are in no state to rescue anyone yet, you surprised the Mayor that you were not dead when he saw your wounds. You even worried me silly when you blacked out and besides I'm starving. We haven't eaten properly for a while and your body needs some food to help it heal"

"Now that you mention it I am hungry"

"A full food delivery arrived today from Stonewall. The Mayor did say he was going to hold a grand banquet"

"Why?"

"I asked him that myself, he said it would do everybody good to celebrate a bit, but mostly I think his view is 'Why the hell not? There is more food than people at the moment and it will only spoil if it isn't cooked so why let it go to waste'"

Malik laughed and rubbed his sides.

"So my darling would you do me the honour of escorting me to the banquet"

Aris gave him a quick kiss on the cheek.

"With pleasure, I'd love to escort you too dinner"

Malik drew back the bed covers and looked down.

"Um... Aris why am I naked?"

"Well I had to perform a thorough examination to make sure nothing else was damaged"

"And?"

"Oh don't worry you'll live!"

She threw him some clothes winked at him and wandered into the bathroom.

"Tease" He shouted as he started to get dressed.

The downstairs of the Town Hall was filled with light. Every light crystal in the building must have been turned on. Aris gasped at the complete transformation from the cold dark imposing building that it had been the other morning when she first entered.

Noise was coming from an open set of large double doors across from the bottom of the stairs. As the pair reached the doorway they saw a huge table that filled most of the dining room.

A couple of girls aided by the Mayor's grandchildren were putting various plates of food onto the table. Another set of doors to one side of the dining room led to a smoking room. Voices and the occasional wisp of smoke filtered out of the open doors.

Malik and Aris walked over to the open doors. As they reached the doorway they heard the Mayor's voice rise above the others.

"Ahh here they are! Welcome"

The room was filled with people. Malik recognized a few of them from the church basement. There was a round of applause as Malik and Aris entered the room.

"Hello, what's all this?" Malik asked and smiled as the Mayor approached.

"This is a celebration my lad. The people that you see here have suffered greatly. Many of them thought they had lost loved ones but thanks to you some at least have been reunited. So I decided to show those that are here that not all light has gone out of this world just yet"

He slapped Malik on the back causing Malik to wince a little bit but only Aris seemed to notice.

"You are something my boy I still don't believe you are up and about after that bug opened up your insides the way it did!"

"My partner here has very talented healing hands"

Malik put his arm around Aris and gave her a hug.

"Well I've got used to you being around" She said nudging Malik gently with her elbow, the universal signal of 'shut up before you make a fool of yourself'.

"Do you like cigars at all?" The Mayor asked Malik.

"I am partial to one now and again yes"

"Ah, excellent!"

The Mayor nodded to a man who walked over and handed the Mayor a wooden box. The Mayor took the box and thanked the man.

"This is a small token of our appreciation"

He handed the box to Malik who took the box and opened the lid.

"King Royals! These are my favourite. Thank you so much everybody" Malik took a cigar out of the box and put it in his mouth.

"You are quite welcome" The Mayor replied and turned to Aris. He nodded at Sarah and she brought another box over. "This is for you my dear"

Sarah gave the box to Aris who opened it and gasped in amazement.

"Oh this is beautiful! Thank you"

She took a long pearl necklace out of the box and admired it. Set into the centre of the necklace was a large red ruby.

It sparkled brilliantly in the light. She held the necklace around her neck and turned to Malik.

"How do I look?" She asked.

"Stunning! It really suits you" Malik said his mouth hanging wide open.

"I didn't know you liked cigars?"

"I'm full of surprises"

His face suddenly became a mask of panic as a thought crossed his mind.

"Does it bother you?" He said quickly taking the cigar out of his mouth.

"Not at all my father smokes them from time to time, I like the smell it's comforting"

Malik gave a quick sigh of relief.

"At least I know what to take when I meet him for the first time"

He put the cigar back into his mouth and smiled. Aris put the necklace back in the box.

She walked over to Malik and took the cigar from his mouth. She put it in her mouth and cupped her hands around the tip. There was a flash of light and a gentle wisp of smoke trailed from between her fingers.

She lowered her hands and took a draw on the cigar causing the tip to glow red. She took the cigar out of her mouth and blew out a smoke ring and put the cigar back into Malik's mouth and kissed him on the cheek.

"All you will ever need is to just be yourself" She replied. "Now I'm going to get something to eat, I'm starving!"

She walked back into the dining room. Malik watched her go then blew out a stream of smoke. The Mayor nudged him and leaned over.

"That's a hell of woman you've got there! Are you two married?"

"No… but I'm giving it a lot of serious thought" Malik said taking the cigar out of his mouth and idly rolling it between his fingers as he thought.

He hadn't really thought that far ahead given how fast events had progressed but then again why not? One thing Malik was dead certain of is that no one was going to take her from him.

He put the cigar back into his mouth patted the Mayor on the shoulder and chased after Aris into the dining room with a large smile on his face.

When he entered the dining room Aris was moving rapidly around the table putting various pieces of food onto her plate. The plate was becoming increasingly full as she skilfully added more and more items onto the rapidly growing pile.

"Bloody hellfire! Where are you going to put that lot?" Malik asked

"Oh this is just starters" Aris replied as she finished chewing on a sausage.

She saw the look he gave her and shrugged her shoulders.

"Spell casting uses a massive amount of energy so we have to eat a lot of food to keep going. In fact elemental casting uses so much energy that female casters are forbidden to cast any type of spell while pregnant because of the risk to their unborn children"

"Good Gods, it's no wonder you are so trim!"

Malik stared in amazement as Aris demolished the plate of food. When she had finished off the last of the food on her plate she stood up again.

"You're not eating?"

"Oh yes I'm just giving you a head start!"

Malik looked sidelong at her and smiled seeing if Aris would take the bait.

She did.

"Really! You think you can out eat me Crimson Guardian!"

"Shall we find out then?" Malik said satisfied.

Three hours later and after everybody else had given up or gone to find something to sooth their full stomachs, Malik and Aris walked back along the corridor toward the guest rooms.

"I've never met anybody that can eat like that!" Malik was saying.

"Well I've never met anybody that could keep up with me before"

"Call it a draw"

"Alright" Aris said reluctantly.

"You are really competitive aren't you?"

"Not all the time"

"Alright how much then"

"About ninety percent of the time"

"Ah thought so!"

Malik opened the door and they walked into the room and held the door open for Aris. She walked in and he closed the door behind her.

"Alone at last" He said.

Aris stood in the middle of the room and turned to face him she held out her arms as he walked over. As he approached her she folded her arms around his neck and kissed him.

"I'm going to get ready for bed I won't be long"

She turned and walked into her room through the dividing door. Malik positively jogged over to the bed and flung back the blanket. He threw his clothes over the bottom of the bed and lay back with his right arm behind his head. His left hand touched the dressing that was across his chest where he had been deeply cut the day before.

"That's going to leave another nasty scar" He said to himself.

"I'm going to have to be more careful now"

The door opened and Aris entered wearing a long white flowing nightgown. Malik could see her figure through the thin material. The gown flowed around her as she walked across the bedroom.

Malik's mouth dropped.

She stopped before the bed and twirled around. The nightgown made the faintest of noise's as it moved through the air.

He tried his best to speak but found he had no voice anymore. Whoever the tailor was who had made the nightgown had made a masterpiece of seductive clothing it managed to convey all of the wearer's naked body without actually revealing anything at all.

"Do you like it?"

Malik tried to respond but the best he could muster past his lips was a sort of 'Muuuh' sound.

Aris satisfied that the nightgown had, had the desired effect upon Malik smiled and climbed into bed. She lay down beside Malik and rested her head on her arm.

"Malik before we go any further I just wanted to know something"

"What's that?" Malik said finally finding his voice and turning on his side.

"Have you ever… you know… with another woman?" She said looking down with embarrassment.

When she looked up she was surprised to see Malik also looked embarrassed.

"No, I mean I know how to do it! I've just never felt like it doing it before. I have pretty much gone from mission to mission without much time in between" Malik paused then asked. "How about you?"

"Me neither, it might be something to do with the bonding spell it keeps us only for each other"

"So you are saying I couldn't have had sex even if I wanted too"

"Well… yes and the same also applied to me as well. I didn't really know just how powerful the old magic's were

218

then. We both cast the spell of our own free will it all adds to the magic's power"

"Well you were my best friend I didn't want you to go. I remember thinking I'd do anything to keep you with me"

Malik moved a little closer and stroked his hand along her leg.

"That's why I suggested the bonding spell" Aris said.

"My older brother cast it with his wife in the Elemental College Hall when they were married. It was part of a grand ceremony. That's how I knew how to perform it"

"So is it like getting married?"

"Sort of yes, but without the involvement of any of the Gods. Like I said before it is ancient magic. It's mostly us Elemental Mages that cast it nowadays and we tend to make a big occasion of it. We give a little bit of our soul to each other and it pulls us back together no matter how far we apart we are"

She leaned over and gave him a kiss.

"And I'm so grateful it brought you back to me"

"I'm glad I found you again without you I'd be dead now, killed by an evil dream"

Malik rolled onto his back and Aris came over and cuddled up to him resting her head on his chest. He put his arm around her and held her close. Aris looked back at him.

"Do you really love me?" She asked.

Malik turned and looked into her eyes. Even in the gloom of the darkened room they still sparkled.

"I do love you and I am so sorry for not finding you before"

"I don't blame you but since you are with me again you can make it up to me"

"How?"

"Why do you think I'm wearing this nightgown? You are not getting away from me this time. I may not be experienced but I intend to have fun learning"

"Be gentle with me, I am injured you know" Malik said nervously as he pointed down at the bandaging across his chest.

Aris quickly sat on top of him pinning him to the bed with his arms trapped under her knees. She pulled the nightgown over the top of her head and leant forward until her mouth was beside Malik's ear. Malik felt her soft breasts press against his chest.

"I know you well enough to know that a little scratch like that wouldn't slow you down" She whispered in his ear.

Malik smiled and with ease flipped Aris over and swapped positions so Aris lay on her back with him on top.

"Well I guess you were right fancy that!"

Aris laughed and pulled the blankets up and over the both of them. The only sound that could be heard was a faint giggling sound coming from under the bed covers.

Malik awoke in the early hours of the following day it was still dark outside the windows.

He watched Aris as she lay in his arms breathing gently. He carefully ran his hand down her back. Her skin felt warm and soft as he touched her gently with his fingers.

"I can hear you thinking" Aris said and opened her eyes. "What's the matter?"

"I was thinking about how I could have possibly forgotten about you for all those years. I can't forgive myself for never looking for you in Founders Rock"

Malik's face dropped as he thought about it.

"Don't be so hard on yourself. You have been through a lot in those years, and besides I'm not upset. You are here with me now and that is all there is to it"

"I know but I can't help but feel a little afraid now"

"Why?"

"I'm taking you into almost certain danger and I don't want to loose you again"

Aris looked at him her face was suddenly stern.

"I'm here to do a job just the same as you are. I came here knowing full well the risks, even before I knew who you were. I've already seen you get hurt and it nearly brings me to tears thinking about it, but I've never once told you not to do your job so don't you dare tell me not to go because I could get hurt"

She pulled the blanket around herself and rolled over onto the other side of the bed. Malik was silent for a moment then spoke up.

"You know I really feel sorry for the poor buggers that are going to try and stand in your way in the Torkle mine!"

There was a movement from the other side of the bed as if a head had turned slightly.

"Aris, I want you to know something. I have never had a partner on any mission before now. I could never allow myself to fully trust another person with my life until now and that includes May and Charleston"

The covers on the other side of bed moved a little more suggesting someone craning closer to listen.

"What are you saying?" Aris's said from behind the blanket

"I'm saying that I need you with me on this assignment and if you will come, on all of the ones in the future as well. Gods know what could happen to us but I would rather face it with you beside me"

There was a pause then a movement under the blanket. Slowly the body under the blanket moved over to Malik's side of the bed.

Aris's head appeared out from under the blanket covering Malik's chest.

"Do you really mean that" She said.

"With all of my heart and soul" He said brushing her hair aside with his hand.

"Alright I forgive you" She said smiling "Now go back to sleep"

"No chance!" Malik said and pulled the blanket over them.

The sun gently began to rise over the landscape bringing the new dawn accompanied by the sound of faint muffled laughter.

Malik and Aris entered the kitchen in the early afternoon. Aris was dressed in the clothes that Malik had made for her previously.

"They look different from the last time you wore them, they look more feminine" Malik said admiring them.

"Sarah made some adjustments for me and made them fit me a little better"

"I though I did quite well considering I had to guess at your size by just looking at you"

"And now you have had a more thorough examination?"

"Ah well now I reckon I've got your size down to perfection!"

Malik patted her on her bum and gave her a kiss.

There was a lot more people bustling around now. The Mayor looked up from his bench where he was reading some papers and talking to Father Spectre.

"Hello you two, you're up late"

"We've been resting ready to set off tonight" Malik said as they approached.

"Very wise"

He gave Malik a wink and raising his eyebrows. Malik cleared his throat while Aris stared up at the ceiling and whistled quietly.

"I'll get one of the girls to make you both something to eat then"

He got up and wondered over to the kitchen door. Aris saw Sarah and nudged Malik.

"I'll be back in a second I want to have a chat with Sarah"

"I'll be here" He replied and kissed her.

Aris went over to the other side of the room where Sarah was talking with some of the other women while Malik sat down beside Father Spectre.

"Hello Father, how are you?"

"Oh I'm just fine thank you" He replied and leaned over. "There is something different about your young lady today"

"Really how do you mean?" Malik asked.

Malik looked over at Aris on the other side of the room.

"She seems more confident, perhaps more mature than she was"

Aris was laughing with the group of women then they all looked over at Malik then they started giggling again. Malik suddenly felt rather embarrassed.

"I'm not so sure about that"

He gave a little wave at the group. There was more laughter then they all waved back at him.

"Before you head out this evening would both of you come and see me, I want to give you both a blessing to wish you luck"

"Thank you. I never turn down any good luck when it is offered"

Aris waved at Sarah and walked back over to Malik smiling.

"What was that all about?" He curiously asked as she came and sat beside him.

"Oh nothing really, I just had to thank her for the advice she gave me the other day"

"What kind of advice?"

"Never you mind, lets just say you are talented in ways you never knew"

"So are you!"

Father Spectre gave a cough to remind them that he was still here and even though he could not see in the usual sense his ears still worked really well.

The Mayor and a girl appeared carrying a tray of food each.

"Here you go" He said putting a tray in front of Aris."Oh and by the way I found you a bottle of Frostbite. It is a good vintage so it should be rather... vigorous by now"

"Thank you very much. We'll be out of your hair at sundown" Malik replied.

The Mayor took the other tray from the girl and thanked her and passed the tray to Malik.

"It's been our pleasure having you here. Don't forget that a majority of people here now would have starved and most likely be dead in the church basement by now if you two hadn't arrived when you did"

The Mayor sat down again.

"We don't forget people who help us like that up here"

"We are just doing our job" Aris replied. "It'll take a few days but we will get those people out of that mining settlement and back here, will you be ready?"

"Yes I've got the coach coming back with more supplies. When you get them out we will be ready for them" The Mayor said nodding.

Later that afternoon Father Brian was sat alone in his room. He appeared to be staring at nothing but he moved and twitched as if he was watching some sort of vicious battle playing on the back of his closed eyes. There was a knock at the door and Father Spectre looked up at the door.

"Come in you two"

The door opened and Malik and Aris entered the room.

"We are just about to set off Father, you wanted to see us?" Aris said.

"I did indeed. I have something here for you both"

Father Spectre reached over to his side table and picked up a small box.

"Would you please both hold out your hands"

Malik and Aris did so. Father Spectre spoke a few words under his breath and opened the box. He took out two gold rings set in each ring was a small white gem and shut the box again. He spoke several more words under his breath as if whispering to the rings. They gently glowed for a second before they faded again.

"I can see that you both belong to each other, you produce an aura which is strongest when you are both together. I can see you are heading into great danger and so to help you I have these"

Father Spectre dropped a single ring into each hand.

"Malik put your ring on Aris's finger and Aris do the same with Malik's"

Malik took the ring in one hand and Aris's left hand with the other and slid the ring onto her finger. He was impressed at how easy the ring slid on. Aris put the ring she had onto Malik's finger. The ring felt so light on his finger but in a strange way it seemed to be fixed into place as if it belonged there.

"There now that wasn't hard was it?" Father Spectre said.

Malik and Aris stood admiring the rings.

"Nice workmanship on these rings" Malik thought.

"I think they are really pretty" Aris thought back.

They suddenly stopped and stared at one another.

"Good isn't it?" Father Spectre said.

"How did that happen?" Malik said to Aris.

"I don't know?"

They both turned and looked at Father Spectre in amazement.

"I can talk to Aris in my head"

"Congratulations young ones, you have both been blessed indeed"

Father Spectre smiled at them both.

"It is an old ceremony for husbands and wives. In the old days when a husband went to war he could still contact his wife through the rings they exchanged. These rings were made with a single sliver of a soul stone"

"But we aren't married?" Aris said.

"Only in the eyes of the law, but for those like me who see things... a little differently it is easy to see you are already bonded. Besides Aris you know that spell of yours wouldn't work unless you both truly loved each over"

Malik looked down at Aris and smiled he put his arm around her and pulled her close.

"Thank you very much Father they will prove very useful" He said.

"Go with my blessing children, and know you always have each other"

Malik and Aris thanked him and went to leave the room. Just before Malik left Father Spectre spoke out

"Remember Malik, shadows cannot exist in light"

Malik stopped and looked back at him. Father Brian nodded and Malik shut the door behind him. A few minutes later there was a knock at the door and Sarah entered.

"Here is your afternoon tea father" She said placing a cup beside him before she went and looked out of a window.

"Thank you dear" Father Spectre said picking up the cup without turning his head.

"Dad?"

"Hmm, what bothers you my daughter?"

"Can you tell me... will they be alright?"

"I don't know for sure. We have given them the best chance we possibly can"

"Do you think that nightgown you asked me to make worked? I didn't feel right using Far Sight on their private life"

"Oh yes it was very successful! I can see why the girls consult you in matters of love. The bond between them is much stronger than before.

He sighed and put the cup down again. Sarah walked over and sat by her father. He took her hand in his and held it.

"Let's just hope it is enough for all our sakes"

"And if it isn't?"

"Then there are very dark times ahead for all of us you should get ready"

"I'm not going to leave you here"

"If the worst happens you and William take the children and run away. Get to Founders Rock. Tell the King who you are, he will be in need of your gifts"

"Dad"

"This is my wish please Sarah"

"Alright, but I won't have to, he will not fail"

"How can you tell?"

"He nearly awakened yesterday"

"Are you sure? I didn't sense anything?"

"It was only for a moment, I was outside in the corridor. Anything that is standing in his path when he awakens is in for serious trouble his power is impressive even by Draconis standards"

"Hmm maybe there is hope for us" Father Brian gripped his daughter's hand tightly.

Malik walked down the steps of the town hall and wandered over to where Aris was waiting for him.

"It'll be dark before to long" She said as he came and stood alongside her.

"Good, the harder it is for eyes to see us the better"

He picked up one of the backpacks he had prepared with Aris earlier in the day. Malik grunted as he slung the pack onto his back and tried to put his other arm into the strap. Aris walked behind him and took the strap.

"Hold on a second… there! Try putting your arm through now"

"Thank you"

Aris walked in front of him and looked at his face.

"Are you sure you're up to this?"

"I'm fine it's just my shoulder is a little stiff that's all"

"Lair, I can tell by your face it still hurts"

Aris's thoughts entered his mind. He put a hand on her shoulder. She took it and held on with both her hands.

"Come on let's get going" Malik said avoiding looking into Aris's eyes.

He helped her put the smaller of the two backpacks on, then they both set off north out of Torkle toward the river and the trail that would lead them to the old settlement. There was a stone road heading north, it led toward the river and made travelling on easier.

It used to have been used by carts transporting goods to and from the river. At least it used to, nowadays there were no more settlements to the east or west so there was no need for any transport along this river. The Mayor had said this river wasn't connected to the Great Serpent River that they had travelled up to reach Stonewall. Instead this river ran from the east and emptied into a great freshwater lake in the west called Arlieana's Tear, so called because it was shaped like a teardrop.

Legend said that Arlieana's Tear was formed when the Dragonlord removed a mountain to make the island Founders Rock was built on. Malik was still unclear exactly how anything could physically move several hundred million tons of mountain range and dump it in the middle of an inland sea.

After half an hour they reached the trail and set off east following the river.

They hiked for several hours along the trail before they stopped for a rest. Malik sat on a rock and slowly took off his pack. Aris walked over and took the pack from him.

"Let me see your shoulder" She commanded.

"I'm fine honestly" Malik's thoughts replied.

"Please Malik" She spoke.

Malik gave in and undid his shirt. Aris put her hands on his shoulder and moved his shirt out of the way.

"Looks like the wound is infected the Reaper must have exuded venom or something from it's claw when it stabbed your shoulder" She said looking at the wound.

Around the outside of the wound black pus had started to weep from the wound when she removed the dressing.

"It feels like it's burning" Malik said and winced as Aris gently pressed her hand against the wound.

"Your body is fighting the infection but while it is it's also stopping it from healing"

The gentle green glow reappeared around Aris's hand as she concentrated on healing. She started swaying and Malik pulled her hand away. The wound was reduced and the black pus had stopped weeping from the wound.

"No more it's taking too much from you" Malik said steadying her.

"I'm fine!" She said stubbornly.

"Now who's lying?"

"But you're still hurt"

"It's much better I'll be fine I promise if we continue on another few hours it will be dawn and we'll stop to make camp and rest alright?"

"Alright" Aris agreed as Malik fastened his shirt again and put the pack back on.

Malik walked in front leading the way while holding one end of Aris's staff while she held the other. An hour before sunrise they stopped and Malik found a suitable concealed spot away from the trail where they could make camp while remaining out of sight.

He set-up the small tent the Mayor had given them while Aris rested on a fallen log.

"It's not very roomy but it is cosy" Malik said with his mind.

He walking over and sat down beside her. Aris looked at the tent then at Malik she smiled.

"It's perfect" she replied. *"I still find it strange talking to you like this"*

"I know, but it is handy. We can talk without making any sound"

Aris leaned her head against Malik's right shoulder and she felt him wince.

"Let me see your shoulder again"

"I'm alright it's a little sore that's all"

"Malik!"

"Alright, alright"

Malik took his shirt off and Aris looked at the dressing covering the wound on his right shoulder.

"You've opened the wound again, stay still"

Aris put her hands on either side of Malik's shoulder and the green glow that Malik associated with her healing spell gently illuminated the immediate area.

The green glow died away and Aris removed her hands and looked at his shoulder again.

"There you go, how is it?"

"Much better thank you" Malik said as he swung his arm around testing it.

Aris slumped back down on the log and yawned stretching her arms up as Malik put his shirt back on.

"Tired?" He asked.

"And hungry" She replied.

Malik stood up and picked Aris up in his arms he walked over to the tent and gently placed her inside.

"Rest for a while, it will be morning soon and I can start a small fire and cook some food"

He leaned over and kissed her then quietly left the tent, Aris was asleep in moments. He carefully pulled the blanket over her then closed the tent flap.

He walked over to his backpack and untied his crossbow and took some arrows from the pack.

Taking one last look around until he was satisfied the camp was sufficiently well hidden he set off into the woods, his footfalls making hardly any sound at all on the woodland ground.

Aris awoke with a start two hours later and looked around.

"Malik?" She called out then she heard his voice in her head.

"I'm here, I've got something for you to try, come on outside it's safe"

Aris pulled the blanket aside and crawled out of the tent. Malik was sat next to a small fire he had made. He leaned against the log while stirring a pot suspended over the fire by three metal rods.

"That's excellent timing its ready! You must have very special sense about food"

"Well I am an Elemental Mage you know, we have all kinds of senses"

Malik looked sidelong at her and raised his eyebrows.

"What?" She demanded.

She stood in front of him and put her hands on her hips. Malik smiled and patted the ground beside him.

"Well come over here and employ your taste buds. I think I've even managed to impress myself with this stew"

Aris walked over and sat down beside him, he ladled the stew into a bowel and passed it to Aris along with a metal spoon he had taken out of a leather roll beside him.

"You are well organized aren't you?"

"It's not my first time doing this"

Malik finished ladling another bowel full of stew he took another spoon out of the leather roll and laid back against the log.

"Good Gods!" Aris said.

"I didn't think it was that bad!" Malik said and looked down into his bowel.

"No I mean I've never tasted anything like this before it's delicious"

"Ah well the secret is in the fresh ingredients, I always think fresh rabbit tastes better"

"You know I don't think I've ever had rabbit like this before" Aris said eating the stew with considerable enthusiasm.

"I've often had to eat it when out in the field. You cannot carry much in the way of supplies when you have to move fast"

They finished the remaining stew in the pot and Malik took out the bottle of Frostbite. He carefully removed the cork and gently sniffed the contents.

"Bloody hell that's good stuff" He said and wrinkled his nose until his sense of smell returned.

He held the bottle away from his nose as his eyes started to run and turn red. Taking a small metal flask out of his pack and with great care he filled the metal flask and put it into the pouch that hung around his neck.

"Do you want to try some?"

"Alright why not, we're not setting off again until dusk are we?"

"That's the plan"

Malik took two cups out of the pack and poured a small amount of Frostbite into each cup.

"This stuff affects people differently. Me, it feels hot when it runs down my throat"

He passed a cup over to Aris. She carefully took a small sip and tasted the clear liquid.

"Mmm it's so sweet" She said and took a larger sip

"Hey careful that's strong stuff" Malik said but Aris had swallowed the whole lot.

"That is really nice can I have some more?"

Malik stared at his cup then took another sniff then a small sip.

"Bloody hell! How do you feel?"

"Fine! I'm tired but apart from that I'm alright. Are you coming to bed with me?"

"Yes in a minute I'll take care of the fire so it will not smoke and give us away"

Aris stood up and started to walk over to the tent.

Malik finished his drink and tipped the last few dregs onto the ground. He then collected the cups and bowels up.

While his back was turned, as he was busy putting them away he missed Aris's legs fall out from under her as she fell forward onto her hands and knees and crawled on all fours into the tent.

Malik turned around just as she crawled inside the tent.

"No effects at all! I think May has got some competition!" He said to himself. "Hmm, maybe the stuff must have gone off or something?"

The area of grass under where he had tipped the dregs of the cup started to turn brown and gently smouldered.

He covered the fire with earth using his hands to move the dirt. When he had put it out he then tried to stand. He gave up after the third attempt and crawled over to the tent and on the second attempt actually managed to crawl inside.

Aris lay on one side of the tent on her side. Malik entered and made himself comfortable. He lay on his back and stared at the ring on his finger. Idly he rotated it around his finger with his thumb.

Aris turned over and pulled the blanket with her covering them both. She moved close to Malik and rested her head on his shoulder. Malik gently lifted her head and put his arm around her so her head rested on his chest.

He sighed with contentment then sleep caught up with him and they slept the day light hours away in each other's arms.

As the daylight faded into night time Malik and Aris awoke. Aris started a small fire to boil some water for a hot drink while Malik took down the tent and packed it up.

When he had finished he walked over to Aris and put the packed tent down by the other equipment. She handed him a cup of tea as he sat down by the fire again.

"I'll make us a hot meal before we set off again" He said pulling some pans out of a pack.

"It will be the last one that I'll make for now. When we stop and make camp next time I won't make a fire or put the tent up, we'll be too close to the settlement to guarantee we won't be spotted"

"Alright but it had better be a large meal because I am famished"

"That's good I didn't want to carry too much stuff anyway in case we have to move fast"

Malik took four long flat metal packages and handed them over to Aris.

"Could you put these in the fire please"

"Flat bread?" She asked taking them from Malik and putting them in the fire.

"Best invention the Bakers Guild ever came up with! I'll be back in ten minutes or so, I set some snares this morning so I'll go and have a look what's for breakfast"

"I'll watch the bread and make sure it doesn't burn"

Aris stretched and leaned back against the log. Malik looked at her and then prodded her foot with his own.

"It's your turn to cook on the way back you know"

"I tell you what, you do the cooking on this trip and I'll look gorgeous for you" She said as she put her arm behind her head and posed for him.

"Is that so!"

"Oh yes, did I also mention you can do whatever you want to me when we get back to Founder's Rock"

She batted her eyelids at him while Malik stood and thought for a moment.

"Deal!"

He smiled and turned then a moment later he disappeared into the late afternoon light.

Aris watched the fire and prodded the metal tins occasionally with a stick.

After ten minutes the tins started to make popping sounds and began to expand, the sign that they were nearly ready. After a few more minutes the lids popped open slightly letting steam escape, indicating that they were cooked.

She fished the tins out of the fire with the stick and laid them out on the ground. She muttered a few words under her breath and the tops of each of the tins blew off up into the air with a loud pop.

The smell of fresh bread filled the air as the flat breads steamed and cooled. Malik returned carrying four large rabbits. He laid the rabbits on the ground by the fire.

"The bread is almost done it just needs to cool" Aris said as he sat down beside her.

"I love the smell of fresh bread" Malik said leaning over and giving her a kiss. "Could you pass me the large cooking pan please"

Aris rooted around in the pack and pulled out the cooking pan. She gave the pan a wipe with her hand and then handed it over to him.

"Thank you it's a bit gruesome this part" He said and pulled out one of his knives.

"It's not the first time I've seen you skin a rabbit"

"Oh yes! I remember now, it was when we went to look for the treasure of Water Drop cave"

"We never found the cave though"

"Well yes, but it was a lot of fun"

"Not when we got lost, that's why we ended up camping in the first place! If your father hadn't found us I don't know how long we would have been lost out there!"

"I wasn't lost! I knew roughly where we were!" Malik said while he ran his knife down the belly of one of the rabbits and started skinning it.

"Where were we then?"

Malik was silent while he finished skinning the rest of the rabbits and began cutting the rabbit meat into slices and dropped them into the pan.

"North of the river someplace"

Aris smiled and patted him on the shoulder then gave him a kiss. Malik finished cutting the meat and sprinkled some herbs into the pan from a small bag he had taken from his pack.

He then placed the pan into the fire and started to turn the meat with his knife as it began to sizzle.

"Do you enjoy it?" Aris asked.

"Hmm?"

"Cooking I mean, you seem to get pleasure out of it"

"A little, yes why do you ask?"

"It just doesn't seem like the thing a big tough Crimson Guardian would do"

"You might be surprised. We are taught to survive and eat pretty much anything. Some of us cook because we ate raw rabbit once, and decided we were not going to do that again unless it is a last resort! Besides when you don't sleep much you need to do something to keep your mind busy"

Malik tossed the meat about in the pan and returned it to the fire.

"I taught myself about medicine and spent a lot of time in the workshops making things"

"Like your sword you mean" Aris asked.

"It took me a few weeks to craft the sword but the real sod was fusing the Spirit Stone into the blade"

"I'm surprised you managed it. Fusing hasn't been widely done for a very long time and I only know of a very few senior people at the Elemental Collage who do it"

"There was a bit of trial and error involved I'll admit but I did find some text which helped as a guide"

"Really I've never seen any books in the college about it"

"It was in the Crimson Guardian Library in one of my father's journals"

"I thought you said your father had been in the Royal Guard"

"He was, how his journal ended up there I never found out"

Malik took the pan out of the fire and looking at the meat then turned it a bit more.

"Just right, could you pass me one of the flat breads please"

"Certainly"

Aris carefully removed a single loaf of flat bread out of a tin and handed it over.

Malik took two metal plates out of his pack and laid the bread on to one. He then tipped some of the meat onto the flat bread and folded it over making a hot rabbit sandwich.

"Not very delicate but you can eat it with your hands" Malik said as he handed the plate over to Aris.

"Thank you!"

She took the plate from him and handed across the other flat bread.

Malik put some meat onto his flat bread, folded it up and started to eat.

"Maybe when we get back home we could go on holiday and look for Water Drop cave again?" Malik said between mouthfuls.

"Maybe, you promise not to get us lost again?"

"I promise, I'll do my best!"

The moon slowly began to rise above the tree line as Malik and Aris sat around the small fire. It was high into the night sky when Malik and Aris began to travel along the riverside again. The night air was cold and very crisp, mist rose off of the river giving the impression that the water was steaming as it flowed past them. The effect was made more dramatic by the bright full moonlight, which bathed the world giving it a strange white glow.

Malik and Aris talked almost constantly as they travelled using their new found ability that Father Spectre had given them back in Torkle.

"You know when you enchanted that arrow for me?" Malik asked.

"Yes"

"How long does the enchantment last exactly?"

"Depends on what the spell trigger is. If they were enchanted to trigger on impact then the spell would wait until the arrow is fired and hit something"

"And you can enchant an arrow with any elemental effect"

"Pretty much, why?"

"Could you enchant me a few arrows when we next stop for a break"

"Of course, it's only a quick simple spell"

"Great! Thank you darling"

"That's alright just do something for me"

"What's that?"

"Make me a cup of tea please! I think my feet are going to drop off"

After a break and a very welcome cup of tea they continued along the track again. After an hours travel or so Aris noticed that the terrain had become much more harsh and rocky. She also noted that the temperature was dropping and the winds had increased quite significantly as they started to move higher up into the mountains.

They reached the outskirts of the mining settlement an hour before dawn. The outlines of the buildings could just barely be seen in the distance as Aris stared out in the early morning gloom.

She could see from where they were standing the settlement and the mountain behind it. The entrance into the mountain was hidden behind the buildings that made up the settlement, and would almost certainly be heavily guarded.

A massive waterfall fell into a large basin on the western side of the mountain and formed the source of the river they had followed from the west. Aris turned her head and watched the river flow toward the west, back to Torkle.

Malik tapped Aris on the shoulder and nodded toward a cluster of trees set away from the trail up a rocky incline.

"That looks like it might be promising" He spoke to her mind.

Malik took Aris's hand and climbed with her up and into the cover provided by the trees.

It turned out that the cluster of trees was in fact the very outskirts of a mountain forest. The tree bases were all at different heights as they had grown up out of the uneven terrain.

After looking around for a few minutes Malik selected a hollow in the rocks. A large tree root formed the floor of the hollow where it protruded through one rock face and entered another. The far end of the hollow had no wall as it led out to the cliff face. Aris dropped down into the hollow and immediately noticed a reduction in the wind that had been whipping around her and chilling her to the bone.

Malik dropped the pack into the hollow then jumped down after it to join Aris.

"We should be relatively safe here for the time being"

He took a blanket out of the pack and laid it over the tree's large root that formed the floor.

Aris sat down with her arms wrapped around her legs.

"I'm so cold, can we have a fire?" Aris said shivering.

"Sorry sweetheart, it would stand out like a distress beacon"

Malik sat down beside her and took another blanket out of the pack and wrapped it around both of them. He put his arm around Aris and she cuddled up beside him.

"How come you aren't cold?" She said through chattering teeth.

"I think I'm hot blooded"

"Well I knew that! Gods my hands are like ice, feel"

She slipped her hand under Malik's top and put her hand on his chest.

"Yaaah!!"

Malik jumped as if he had been bitten by something.

"You're nice and warm"

"And you're bloody freezing! Here drink some more of this"

Malik took the bottle of Frostbite out of the pack and opened it. He passed it to Aris who carefully took it and took a swig. She passed it back and Malik who also took a long swig from the bottle.

Aris lay back and rested her head on his arm. Malik put the bottle of Frostbite back into the pack and wrapped his arm around Aris again.

He looked down at Aris and looked thoughtful for a moment then he took some of his clothes out of his pack and folded them into a makeshift pillow. Then he gently lifted Aris's head and put the folded clothes under her head and just as gently lowered her head back down again.

He then made himself comfy and rested his head against hers. Malik gently stroked Aris's hair as he thought about the next night when they would finally enter the mountain. After half an hour of thought he finally drifted off to sleep as the wind howled over the top of the hollow.

He brought his legs up and curled into a ball, as their combined body heat and the blanket kept them warm. As far as Malik was concerned the wind could howl all it liked. Now, at this moment here, curled up under a blanket with Aris, he was happy and nothing the wind could do would stop that.

Malik awoke with a sudden jolt. Something had awoken him from his sleep. It was mid afternoon and the sun still had a few hours left before it set behind the mountain range.

He strained his hearing trying to find what it was that had woken him.

All was quiet even the wind had died down to a gentle breeze. Then suddenly he heard it. A rhythmic thump could be heard on the very edge of his strained hearing. There was also a sort of metallic clattering sound that followed after the thump.

He listened for a moment trying to identify the sound. As it got closer his eyes widened as he recognized another sound. There was a chant mixed in with the thumping sound. It sounded harsh and deep, there was the occasional snort and grunt that stood out from overall combination of sound.

Malik shook Aris and put his hand over her mouth as she was jerked into consciousness. He put his finger to his mouth then tapped his ring.

"What's the matter?" Aris said through her mind.

"We've got trouble!"

Malik started to quickly put the blanket away in the pack.

"What is that sound?" Aris thought as she heard the noise and listened.

Malik picked up Aris's staff and quickly handed it over to her.

"Orcs, lots of heavily armed Orcs and they are coming this way"

"Are they after us?"

"I don't think so. Here put these packs against the back there and keep as quiet as a mouse"

Malik picked up his crossbow and gently cocked it using the lever mechanism. He drew his sword and pressed himself the wall of the hollow and listened as the thumping got closer and louder.

Aris came and stood beside him keeping as close to the wall as she could.

"Sounds like a bloody battalion up there. I reckon at least fifty Orcs" Malik thought.

"Are they going to the settlement?"

"That would be my guess. I wonder if whoever it is that is in charge of commanding the mine has called for reinforcements"

"*What to stop us?*"

"*It's possible we have faced someone already on the journey here. That black figure we saw in my mind could well be the commander. He is too powerful to just be a grunt*"

"*If it was then he would know that we are coming*"

"*And that we are now a threat*"

A loud crashing sound indicated that the Orcs had made there way through the forest and were marching past the hollow. Both Malik and Aris tensed as the column of Orcs passed by the hollow. Aris shut her eyes and moved closer to Malik. After a few tense minutes the marching sound started to fade away as they moved on.

"*Aris keep very still and quiet*" Malik said into Aris's mind.

"*Why?*"

"*Look up very, very slowly*"

Malik slowly and very carefully eased his crossbow upwards.

Aris slowly looked upwards and saw standing up above them was a lone Orc looking out across the landscape.

It had dark skin and was wearing animal hides. It was looking at the settlement in the distance. It snorted and grunted to itself as it shuffled about on the ledge.

"Rear guard, it doesn't know we're here if it did we would know about it" Malik thought.

"Oh Gods"

"It's alright Aris listen to me I'll take care of him, but if this goes wrong run for the forest, forget the packs and just run, alright"

"What about you?"

"I'll be right behind you I promise"

The Orc turned it's head slowly scanned the horizon as if looking for something, it sniffed the air and grunted again.

There was a faint click.

It was the click of a safety catch being released.

The Orc looked down.

There was a thunk as the crossbow bolt was released. The crossbow bolt hit the Orc in the centre of the forehead. The Orc swayed and moaned for a second.

A hand reached up out of the hollow and quickly pulled it down into the hollow. The Orc's body jerked about as the muscles in the body convulsed.

The tip of the crossbow bolt protruded out of the back of the Orcs head. Malik quickly raised his sword and cut the Orc's head off at the neck.

"Why did you cut the head off?" Aris said shocked.

She was sitting against the back of the hollow with her head in her hands. Lifting her head she looked at the body again and put a hand across her mouth.

"I think I'm going to be sick"

Blood started to flow out of the Orc's neck and spread across the bottom of the hollow. The body finally stopped twitching and lay still.

"I'm sorry Aris, but it is better to be safe than sorry with these buggers, they can regenerate if given enough time"

"It smells horrible"

Aris watched the blood pool expand until it then started to drip down the sides of the tree root.

"Yes it does smell doesn't it" Malik said his voice sounded distant and almost like a growl.

"Malik are you alright?"

He looked up from the Orc to Aris and suddenly snapped out of whatever he was thinking about. His voice returned to normal.

"Sorry... just some bad memories that's all" He quickly shook his head to dislodge the memories from his head then continued. "I think we had better get going. When they realise that he is missing they will send out a search party to look for him"

Malik grabbed the body and took it to the end of the hollow where he then threw it out. The Orc's body bounced down the cliff face and disappeared from view. He kicked the head out after it and went back to Aris who was busy throwing the packs out of the hollow.

"I'll jump up and give you a hand to get out"

"Oh no need I'm fine thanks"

Aris bent her knees as a swirling mass of air formed around her feet. There was a gentle blast of wind and Aris jumped out of the hollow flipped in the air and landed on the ground up above.

"I was top of my class in Aerial Acrobatics"

"I'm impressed!"

Malik smiled then he jumped at one side of the hollow wall rebounded off of it and landed beside Aris where he gave her a quick kiss on the cheek.

"Come on let's get going, I've got a plan to get us inside the mountain"

He picked up his packs and slung them on to his back.

"What's that? Fight our way through at least fifty heavily armed Orc's with just the two of us?" Aris said it a bit more sarcastically than she had intended. The sight of Malik coldly chopping the Orc's head off and then the head rolling along the floor had upset her.

"A simple plan, but no all we need is an airshaft"

"Airshaft?"

"Airshaft" Malik said and smiled.

They quickly travelled away from the hollow and made their way up the west side of the mountain along a small trial they found. All the time they travelled they made sure they kept out of sight of the settlement. Eventually they reached the top of the mountain where Malik found what he was looking for.

"Perfect! That is what we are after" Malik said to Aris as they both peered over the top of a large boulder.

What they were looking at was basically a large hole in the top of the mountain. The hole was a large airshaft cut into the mountain. It supplied the mines below with fresh air. Many such shafts were cut all over the mountain range.

Standing over the hole on four large angled stone legs was a stone structure. A large windmill blade was mounted onto a tower next to the building. It spun quickly in the high winds that blew across the top of the mountain. A large rotating axle ran from the tower into the stone structure over the airshaft.

"Malik I've seen one of those before, that building over the hole should have a lift basket in it. It would have been used to take spoil out of the hole when the shaft was being built"

"Exactly and hopefully we can use it to sneak into the mountain. All we have to do is get rid of the guards nice and quietly"

"How do you know there are guards? The place looks deserted"

"See those chains running down the side of the shaft? I bet they are connected to a number of bells at the bottom of the shaft. A guard sees something up here, pulls a lever, alarm bells start ringing down below then the basket comes up the shaft with a large number of reinforcements"

"How could you possibly know that?"

"That's what I would do" Malik said and pointed.

"Look over there"

He pointed at the building suspended over the airshaft. A door had opened on a balcony that ran around the outside of the building. An Orc appeared and walked to a ladder and climbed down to another smaller gantry that ran around the building. It stopped and vaguely looked out across the landscape holding up a hand to shield it's eyes from the wind blowing and whipping around it.

"Come on let's take a closer look" Malik said and slid back down the boulder.

Malik and Aris moved quietly toward the airshaft building. They moved from cover to cover moving quickly and always keeping low to the ground. As they neared the building they lay behind a small out crop of rocks and shrubs.

Malik heard a faint bell ring from within the building. The Orc that had been walking around the gantry of the building stopped and climbed down onto a third smaller metal gantry that ran under the building. It leaned over the side of the gantry and looked down into the shaft.

A loud clicking sound could be heard from the building and four sets of large metal chains began to rise up into the building. A loud clanking sound could be heard from within the airshaft.

"I wonder what's going on?" Malik said to Aris as they peered out from behind the rocks.

"Looks like something is coming up"

A large metal cage slowly appeared out of the shaft and stopped level with the top of the shaft. A metal gate was opened in the cage and the Orc started to shout at something in the cage.

"Oh no!" Aris said shocked.

Three pairs of men and women came out of the cage carrying large containers full of earth and rubble. They wore torn and tatty clothes and were shackled together in pairs by a long chain.

The Orc on the gantry climbed back up to the building and disappeared back inside. A minute later it reappeared walking down some stairs that ran down one of the support legs of the building. It was closely followed by two other Orcs each one carried a long whip.

They headed purposely over to the group of slaves that were unloading the containers of earth and rubble out of the cage.

"Aris, I think I can guess what they are planning!" Malik growled as the Orcs had now surrounded the slaves. "We take the Orc's quick and quiet in case there are any more up in the building"

Malik took off his pack and drew his sword. Aris nodded at him and her staff began to glow. They both heard the crack of a whip followed by a scream.

Malik nodded and they both quickly disappeared into the shadows.

A container had fallen over spilling the rubble it contained over the floor. The Orc's were taking a lot of pleasure in whipping the pair of slaves who had been carrying the container.

One Orc flicked its whip around the male slave's neck and pulled him forward onto the ground dragging the female slave with him.

The slave grabbed the whip in an effort to try and stop the coil from strangling him. Another Orc kicked him in the ribs causing him to curl up. The two Orcs started to laugh.

There was a silken sound and a grunt from behind them. They turned and saw the third Orc with a red glowing blade protruding out of the front of it's chest.

The blade disappeared from the front of the chest as it was pulled out from behind and the Orc fell to one side revealing Malik standing where the Orc had been.

His sword flared red.

"Boo"

The chest of the Orc holding the whip coiled around the slave's neck exploded in a flash of blue light.

Aris appeared into the light. The end of her staff gently gave off a stream of blue smoke.

The last remaining Orc turned and started to run back toward the stairs that led to the building.

"Darling" Malik said and nodded in the direction of the retreating Orc.

Aris nodded then pointed her staff at the Orc. A blue ball of light formed on the tip of the staff and shot off after the running Orc. The blue orb accelerated and struck the Orc in the back and the orb exploded in a ball of blue light blowing a large hole in the Orc's chest.

The body slumped and tumbled over and over as the momentum of the body rolled it across the ground until it finally stopped.

"Remind me not to aggravate you too much!" Malik said to Aris as they walked over to the slaves.

The female slave was kneeling by the male slave. She had his head in her lap and was uncoiling the whip from around his neck as Malik and Aris approached them.

She looked up and Malik held up his hands in a calming gesture.

"Don't be afraid we're here to help you" He said softly as he kneeled down beside them.

Behind the containers the other slaves watched then when they realised they were not in danger they slowly came out one at a time.

"I'm a Crimson Guardian, are there any more Orcs?"

The woman shook her head.

"No there were only ever three of them that we saw"

She looked at the slave on the floor.

"Please, can you help my husband, he can't breath properly"

Malik carefully took the man's head and gently turned it from side to side. A bruise was forming where the whip had been coiled tightly around the neck. The man was having serious trouble breathing as his throat had begun to swell up and was already turning black in colour.

"Aris I need your help with this!"

She came and knelt down beside Malik and the man.

"I'll need some room, cut the chains so we can move him easier"

She put a hand over part of the man's throat and a gentle green glow appeared. The man took a gasp of breath.

"Right" Malik said and stood up.

He drew his sword and gently took the woman's arm with the chain attached and laid it on the ground.

"He won't be able to cut it" The woman said to Aris.

"We have already been trying back in the compound it is hardened steel"

Aris looked at the woman and then up at Malik.

"You don't know Malik" Aris replied then turned to the injured man again.

"Cover your eyes with your other hand!"

Malik's sword flared bright red as he placed the tip of the sword an inch above one of the links. He brought the sword straight down on the chain and there was a blinding flash of red light.

The light faded away, when the woman opened her eyes the chain link was in pieces and Malik's sword was embedded into the rock floor.

Malik pulled the sword free and put it back in its sheath.

"Thank you darling, could you lift him on onto one of those containers for me" Aris asked.

Malik easily picked the man up and laid him out onto the top of an overturned container. The other slaves had now all come out from behind the containers they had been hiding behind and were all watching Aris.

Malik pulled a lock pick tool out from the sleeve of his outfit and walked over to the other slaves.

"Don't worry I'll have them off in a moment" He said as Aris put both of her hands on the man's neck.

The glow grew in intensity as Aris increased the power of her spell.

Malik started to pick the locks on the shackles of the other slaves until one by one they clicked open and fell to the ground. When he turned around to check on Aris the green glow died away from her hands.

"There we go, He should be back to normal in a few moments" Aris said taking her hands away from the man's neck.

The man opened his eyes and then blinked then he sat up and looked around as his wife put her arms around him.

"What the hell just happened?" The man said to Aris.

"You had a crushed wind pipe. Luckily I could heal it before you choked to death"

"Oh, thank you!"

"It's my pleasure"

Malik walked over and took the man's wrist and started to fiddle with the lock.

"Just give me a few seconds to get this off" Malik said as he worked the lock.

There was a small click and the shackle came free from the man's wrist. Malik turned to the man's wife.

"Alright your turn now"

After a few seconds he undid the shackle from the woman's wrist as well. The man rubbed his wrist where the shackle had been rubbing him.

"It feels so good to get that thing off at last. By the way my name is Charles and this is my wife Clara"

The man called Charles put his arm around Clara.

"Nice to meet you both" Clara said.

"Over here is Fred and Glenis and also Martin and Ruth"

The other slaves nodded or waved as they were introduced.

"Who might you two be then?"

Malik sat down on a container next to Aris.

"We're from Founders Rock sent here to help I'm Malik and this lovely lady here is Aris"

Aris waved at the assembled group. Charles looked from Malik to Aris

"Only the two of you! They have a bloody army of Orcs down there!"

"Unfortunately they have a few more now" Aris said.

"I just don't believe it! Why didn't the King send the army to help?"

"We are uniquely qualified" Malik said calmly.

"How's that?"

"Aris is an Elemental Mage and I'm a Crimson Guardian"

"Oh yes a girl weather witch is going to be a great help here!" Charles said bitterly.

Clara suddenly caught sight of Malik's expression as he suddenly flinched. Clara put a hand firmly on Charles's shoulder and whispered something in his ear. He looked at her and then from Malik to Aris and back again.

"Are you sure?"

She nodded at him and Charles's face went pale as he turned to face Aris.

"Err sorry about the weather witch comment, it has been a bad couple of months for us all" He muttered a little sheepishly.

"Not a problem I wasn't really listening anyway besides I have a very tough skin it takes a lot to upset me" Aris said shrugging her shoulders.

Charles smiled and looked up at the building.

"Let's see what we can find in the way of food up there"

"Charles, won't the guards below get suspicious about you being missing?" Aris asked.

"Not really, we were not going back down again. We wouldn't have survived this job as they were going to kill us after we had finished"

"Why?"

"It keeps the other slaves in line, we were randomly selected"

He stood up and put his arm around Clara.

"Come on let's get out of this cold air and get warm"

They headed up the stairs to the building up above the shaft. Aris slowly removed her hand out from the back of Malik's armour.

Malik sighed with relief and relaxed.

Her fingers crackled with electricity.

"That wasn't very fair you know" He said.

"I didn't want you to belt him one, they have been through an awful time here"

"I wouldn't have hurt him"

"Oh really!" Aris tilted her head to one side and looked at him.

"Well maybe only a little!" He said on reflection.

Aris slapped him on the bum and smiled.

"How did you come up with this idea of an airshaft anyway?"

"Remind me to tell you about Deepwell mine sometime"

"Why?"

"I'll tell you later, come on let's see what they can tell us about what goes on down below"

The Guard building had indeed been an old mining tool. It had been used to lower miners down to bore out the airshaft. Malik could see shelves of dusty old metal hats and old looking pick axes hanging from a wall.

The engineers that had built it had just abandoned the building after the airshaft had been completed. The Orc's had simply adapted it to there own uses.

The old fireplaces had been reopened and a bright fire was burning within. The room was surprisingly warm given the relatively small size of the fire.

Inside the building a massive axle ran through the wall from the windmill tower outside. The axel was connected to two large cogs angled the shaft down through the floor. There it connected with a system of cogs and gears that would lift or lower the huge cage in the airshaft.

"What did they have you doing down there Charles?" Malik asked as they sat around the fireplace.

"We were removing the spoil from a large cavern that they are excavating. Seems there is something large down there in the bowels of the mountain that they want to uncover"

"What about the rest of the slaves? Where are they held?"

"They are held in a cavern not far from the bottom of this airshaft. We call it the compound. It's a large cavern next to the old accommodation for the miners which the Orcs are using as a barracks"

"Is the barracks between here and the compound?" Malik asked.

"No but there is no need as the compound is well guarded"

"How is it guarded?"

"There is a large wall that runs around the outside of the compound and a large gate which is guarded on either side by two towers with guards posted on each one. A patrol runs around the inside of the wall making sure no one tries to climb out and keep everyone inside under control"

"What about the barracks any guards there?"

"Only a couple of sentries on the main door to the barracks they don't really have much call to guard their own barracks here"

"That's good news for us then. Where is the closest storage bay to the airshaft?"

"There is one which is by the compound cavern so the workers can get tools and equipment on the way to the main cavern"

"Is there any blasting powder in there?"

"Oh yes about thirty kegs at least"

"Malik, what are you planning? I don't like it when you get that look on your face!" Aris asked.

"Just a little surprise for our Orc friends" Malik said smiling as he turned to the rest of the group.

"We can get the rest of the people trapped down there out. But I will need some help to do it"

The group looked at each other then Charles spoke up.

"You rescued us, so I guess we are all in"

"Thank you, everyone." Malik smiled. "Right this is what we are going to do. First we need to get our hands on some blasting powder. Who knows the storage area?"

"That would be me" Martin said raising his hand.

"I've spent a few weeks in there handling the materials"

"Good, Martin and me will secure the storage bay and find the powder"

"Aris you remove the sentries from the main door to the barracks quick and quiet and wait for us"

"Alright" Aris said nodding.

"Everybody else wait until we get the powder then come and give us a hand to move the powder kegs"

At the bottom of the airshaft two Orc guards listened to the cage rattle as it was lowered down the airshaft.

The cage clanked to a halt at the bottom of the shaft and one Orc guard looked over at it and saw a couple of containers still in the middle of the cage.

It opened the cage and after looking around the cage from the doorway it shrugged and started to close the cage again when it heard a faint scratching sound coming from a container.

It carefully walked over to the container and looked inside. A sword blade thrust out of the container and pierced the Orc's chest. The Orc slumped forward and it's body was lifted and tossed over the container and out of view.

Malik silently lifted himself out of the container. He drew a knife from behind his back, took aim and threw the knife at the other Orc guard. The knife cut through the air and struck the Orc in the back of the head killing it instantly.

"Do you really have to throw Orc corpses at me!" Aris hissed.

She appeared from behind one of the containers and put her hands on her hips.

"Sorry sweetheart I couldn't see you back there"

Malik lightly landed on the floor of the cage and quickly looked around. When he was satisfied that they hadn't been detected he and Aris quickly opened the rest of the containers letting the others out who had been hiding in them.

The dead Orc guards were stuffed inside one of the containers they had stacked up outside of the cage to conceal their bodies from view.

The inside of the mountain was surprisingly well lit considering it was far underground where no light could penetrate. Large crystal lights gave off a gentle glow illuminating the area in an almost pleasant light.

In some areas there were large torches burning brightly from the walls, shadows danced across the tunnel walls and floors in the flickering light.

Malik looked at Martin who first pointed down a tunnel before he turned and pointed at another larger tunnel. Malik nodded at Aris and she ran quietly over to the larger tunnel and pressed herself against a wall. She then listened for a moment and then disappeared down the tunnel toward the barracks.

"Malik, will she be alright on her own?" Martin asked.

"She can look after herself" Malik replied.

"Alright everybody else wait here while Martin and I secure the storage area. If there is any trouble, get back up the shaft and head for Torkle as fast as you can"

The group nodded at him and took up positions around the chamber keeping alert and on the look out for any more Orcs that may be around.

Malik set off with Martin down the tunnel toward the storage area. Along the passage Martin tapped Malik on the shoulder and they stopped in some shadows and pressed themselves close to the tunnel walls.

He looked down the tunnel toward the entrance of the storage bay. At the end of the tunnel was a lone Orc guard. It was lazily leaning against the wall and yawned occasionally. Malik watched it for any signs that it might dose off to sleep. Carefully looking around he realised that there was no way he could possibly sneak up on the Orc without it seeing him.

Looking around he picked up a small stone, which he threw down a side passageway.

The Orc jumped to attention at the sound of the rock bouncing down the passageway and drew a large axe from behind it's back.

Carefully the Orc crept toward the dark passageway. Malik watched it from his hiding place in the shadows as it flattened it's back to the wall beside the passageway and listened.

It quickly rounded the corner and stood with it's axe raised ready to attack.

Malik took the opportunity and made his move, moving quickly and with barely any sound he closed the distance on the Orc. He put one hand around it's mouth and pulled the head back while he drove his blade through the Orc's back slicing it's heart in two and killing it instantly.

He lowered the body to the ground and dragged it into the dark passageway where he hid it in the shadows before taking another look around.

When he was satisfied that there were no more guards present he beckoned Martin to follow him and they moved on to the store entrance.

The entrance to the storage area was a large set of double doors with a wooden beam holding them shut.

Malik and Martin carefully lifted the beam off of the door and lay it down before they pushed the doors open and entered.

Martin hit a control on the wall inside the storage area and some crystals began to glow providing some light inside the storeroom.

It was larger than Malik had been expecting. Tall shelves filled each of the two sidewalls. Ladders attached to runners on each side provided access to the higher shelving units. Toward the back of the storage area was a raised platform and a cart.

The platform allowed easy loading of goods onto the cart ready for transportation.

"Where is the powder kept?" Malik asked.

"Over here at the back of the room"

"Excellent go and get the others quick" Malik patted him on the shoulder.

Martin nodded and ran out of the storeroom while Malik took hold of the cart stood up against a wall and pulled it to the raised platform. He carefully started to load the kegs onto the cart one at a time.

"Sweetheart, how are you getting on?" Malik thought using his ring to communicate with Aris.

"I'm here at the gate to the barracks there is two guards here but they are half asleep!"

"They won't be a problem for you then?"

"Of course not, but Malik, something is worrying me a little"

"What's that?"

"Does this all seem a bit too easy"

"I know, keep out of sight and remove those guards when I give you a signal"

"Alright, I'll be here waiting"

"Aris, please be careful!"

"You too"

Martin and the others arrived back at the storage area as Malik jumped down from the cart.

"All right here's the plan I'm going to set a booby trap by the barracks to blow the doors and hopefully trap a majority of the Orcs in the barracks area. I need you all to line the tunnel to the shaft with a single keg of blasting powder every twenty yards or so along the tunnel. Charles can you get word to the rest of the captives in the compound?"

"Clara could. She has snuck in and out of the compound before now without any one noticing"

Charles put his arm around Clara and smirking with pride at his wife's achievement.

"Great, Clara can you get in and tell everyone to be ready. We are going to blow the gate to pieces. When the gate is down everybody will run for the airshaft and be sent up in the cage in as big a group as possible. Once out they should head west and follow the river to Torkle as fast as possible. A Battlemage Airship is en-route here so if possible meet up with them. Aris and I will provide cover at the airshaft for those going up in the cage. Does anyone know roughly how many trips we will have to make up and down the shaft?"

"At a guess I'd say we will need to make two maybe three trips to get everybody out" Fred said as he pulled a small hand trolley from a rack.

"Good I think we can just manage that. Let's get moving the faster we get this done the better"

Malik nodded at Clara who gave Charles a kiss and ran down the tunnel toward the compound. Everybody else started to load the kegs of blasting powder onto hand trolleys and wheeled them out of the storage area.

"Martin can you give me a hand to pull this cart down to the barracks door please"

Martin nodded and stood by Malik, they both gripped a handle of the cart and it creaked as they pulled the cart slowly out of the storage area and down the tunnel toward the barracks.

"Aris we are on our way. Remove those guards for us please"

"Consider them removed!" Aris voice replied in his head.

Outside of the barracks the two guards were standing to attention. Aris watched as a party of Orcs marched from a larger main corridor and entered through the double doors, which closed shut behind them.

As the doors banged shut the two Orcs relaxed and sat down on some old chairs and started to grunt and growl in the Orc language.

Aris crept forward staying close to the shadows until she could clearly see both of the Orcs.

She aimed her staff at the closest Orc and the end of her staff gently glowed blue.

She fired a single ice dagger from her staff then quickly aimed the staff and fired a second. The first ice dagger hit the closest Orc in the back of the head piercing it with such force the tip of the icicle protruded out through the front of it's head. The Orc's blood splattered onto the wall in front of where the Orc had been sitting.

The second Orc had seen the glow from Aris's staff out of the corner of it's eye and had already been rising from the chair. The second ice dagger hit it in the chest throwing it backwards against a wall where it pinned the Orc.

The Orc made bubbling noises and blood poured from it's mouth as it tried to call for help. Aris walked forward holding her staff out in front of her. She suddenly saw that it was desperately trying to reach out and grasp a chain that was a just out of reach of it's left hand.

It looked down at the dagger sticking out of its chest and grasped it with both hands and started to pull on the dagger trying to loosen it from the wall behind.

"You things just don't give up do you?" Aris said as she approached the Orc.

The Orc gave one last pull on the ice dagger finally freeing itself from the wall behind. The Orc pulled the ice dagger from its chest and launched itself at Aris with the ice dagger held like a knife.

Another ice dagger sank into it's chest throwing it back against the wall again but not with enough force to pin it this time. The Orc gasped for breath coughing blood from it's mouth

"This is for what you bastards did to him" She growled.

The Orc started to move again but another four ice daggers slammed into the chest one after the other.

The Orc's body slumped down to the floor as Aris walked over and aimed her staff at it's head and fired another final ice dagger through the Orc's skull making a sickening cracking sound as the dagger met no resistance.

"Just to be sure" She said to herself.

She wiped her brow and gave a sigh she then heard a noise behind her and she span around with her staff ready.

"Hold on it's me!" Malik's voice rang out in her head. She lowered her staff and ran over to the cart.

"Any trouble sweetheart?" Malik said as he looked at the Orc slumped on the floor with the six ice daggers sticking out of it.

Aris looked back at the Orc then turned to look back at Malik's face.

"Nothing I couldn't deal with"

"Good give us a hand would you, we need to close the doors and stick that beam back in place first of all"

The barrack doors had originally opened outwards, probably when it had been used for something else before it had been converted into living quarters.

At some point the doors had been altered to open inwards so the other side could be barricaded to protect those inside in case of a siege. Malik planned to use that fact to full advantage. The original old braces could still be seen on the outside of the doors, meaning a beam could be dropped in place and stop the doors from opening inwards.

Aris pulled the double doors closed while Malik and Martin lifted a beam from the cart and gently slotted it into the old braces on the doors.

Malik then returned to the cart and picked up a keg of powder and put it on top of the beam. He picked up one of the old chairs and stood on it so he could open the keg. He turned to Aris.

"Aris can you pass me one of those mugs and enchant it with fire on an impact trigger please"

Aris smiled at him as she realised what he was planning. She took one of the Orc's mugs from the table. The mug flared red for a moment before it returned back to normal.

"There you go be careful with it!"

She handed the mug up to Malik.

"Thank you kindly" Malik said and gave her a kiss on the lips.

He saw Martin was stood watching them. Aris turned her head to Martin.

"It's alright we're together" She said to him.

"I did wonder" He replied.

Malik put the mug into the keg of blasting powder with extreme care then put the lid securely back on.

Martin smiled and put another two kegs by the doors for good luck. They all stood back from the doors for a moment and admired their handy work.

"Alright here is the plan, Orcs hear explosion in compound. They try to open doors and find them locked. They break down doors to get out, the powder keg falls, enchanted mug explodes igniting blasting powder and there is the mother of all booms!"

"Sounds like a good plan, you know Malik you really have a cunning mind"

"Why thank you sweetheart, come on let's get back, Clara should have got into the compound by now"

The three of them ran back down the tunnel to the rest of the group who had just finished putting the last of the powder kegs in the tunnel.

As they arrived Charles walked over to them wiping his brow.

"Clara is in the compound"

"Any problems?" Malik asked.

"No, she got in easy"

"Right, let's get the rest out. I need you to get the cage ready for the first group of people to go up out of here. When the last group is out disable the mechanism to stop them using the cage to follow"

"Not a problem, we'll be ready"

"Good, come on Aris let's go and make a really big hole!"

Smiling at Aris he put his arm around her waist and led her down a tunnel. As he passed he picked up a keg of powder and put in on his shoulder.

They walked past the booby trapped barrack doors and carried on down the corridor that ran further into the mountain. As they quietly walked down the corridor a door suddenly opened in front of them. Aris flung Malik into a dark alcove and pressed herself tightly against him. She whispered words under her breath and the crystal lights in the corridor became dimmer causing the shadows to become darker and hide them from view.

Two Orcs appeared out of the open door and walked down the corridor toward them. Aris pressed herself even closer to Malik as the footsteps got closer. She could smell nothing but his scent. It filled her senses as she tried to concentrate.

"Gods does he know what he does to me without even trying" She thought to herself as she closed her eyes.

The Orcs stopped in front of Aris and Malik. She felt Malik's body tense as he prepared himself to move.

"Don't move, I can keep us hidden" Aris thought's filled Malik's mind

"Alright I trust you" He replied.

Aris felt his body relax slightly. Silently his hand moved up to her back and pressed against her. The lights flickered as she momentarily lost concentration.

The Orcs looked at the lights that had flickered then grunted at one another in Orcish. In the alcove Malik could feel Aris's heart beating against his chest. Her head rested against his. He could feel her body gently shaking. Unable to stop himself he ran his fingers up her back. Her body responded to his touch and the lights flickered again. He could feel her warm breath on his neck it. It felt as if every nerve was tingling with excitement. She moved her hand down to his thigh and ran her hand around it.

"How can she do this to me?" He thought as his heart usually calm and under complete control began to beat wildly out of control.

Suddenly he had to breathe in. He took a deep intake of air and smelt her sweet hair. The effect nearly made his leg fall out from under him. Aris reacted to his body. She put her other hand around his other thigh and ran her hands around the back of his legs and up around his bottom pulling his waist closer to hers.

"Oh Gods I can't take this much longer" He heard her voice in his head.

A third Orc appeared out of the door and shouted something to the other two Orcs. They turned and walked back to the door and went back inside closing the door again. Malik and Aris were left alone again in the alcove.

Aris gently moved away from him and looked at Malik's face, even in the gloom of the dim light his eyes shone.

"They've gone" Aris whispered as she tried to get her breath back.

"Yes" Malik gently panted.

They stood still, doing nothing but look at one another as they both breathed in each other. Moving as one they suddenly came together. Their lips locked to one another as they both lost control. They parted as they managed to regain some self control.

"We can't do this now" Malik panted

"It's wrong" Aris agreed.

Malik picked her up and spun her around pressing her against the wall of the alcove. She wrapped her legs around his waist and pulled him close. He kissed her down her neck her body quivered with the sensation.

She pulled his head to hers and kissed him tasting his lips.

Suddenly she pushed his head back.

"We have to stop" She gasped.

"I know, we can't do this, its wrong, very wrong"

Malik put both his hands against the wall and braced them. He looked as if he was fighting a titanic inner battle against himself as he tried to prise himself away from Aris. Their self control only just won the battle and they both slid to the ground their backs leaning against the wall as they both tried to catch their breath.

They turned their heads and looked at one another as they panted.

"Nobody has done that to me before" Aris whispered as she patted Malik on the leg.

Malik looked at her then nodded. There was a joint thud as they both banged the back of their heads against the alcove wall behind.

The corridor finally got larger and opened out into a huge cavern. They crept around the outside of the large cavern keeping out of sight they climbed on top of some large rock formations. They climbed higher until they had a good view of the compound.

The entrance to the compound was pretty much as it had been described to them. The main gateway had a tower in front of it and Malik could see the second tower on the other side of the wall.

There was also a makeshift bridge that spanned the gap above and between the two towers.

"Let me see if I can spot the guards anywhere" Aris said.

She closed her eyes and spoke some words under her breath. When she opened her eyes again they briefly glowed red.

The world looked different when viewed with magic. The cavern was lit up as if it were the middle of the day. When using this spell, Aris was also able to see the aura given off by living creatures.

She looked at Malik and was surprised to see his aura was dim but as she watched him there were brilliant sparks which flared when he moved hinting that his power was hidden away somewhere deep inside.

Malik looked at her and smiled, Aris smiled back. She knew full well the potential he had. Her father had told her stories of his friends Tiber and Darcy Owen. Malik was heir to their combined strengths, but they hadn't revealed themselves yet.

Aris turned back to the compound and saw two strangely coloured auras on the far tower that was inside the compound. She also noticed two more auras glowing through the wall closest to her and Malik. From what she could see it looked like the four auras were talking with one another.

Aris tapped him on the shoulder and pointed at a tower.

"Two Orcs are talking on the top section of the inner tower"

Malik took his crossbow and picked a handful of arrows from his quiver and then selected two with green arrowheads. He slotted one into the top of the crossbow. Next the other green arrow was inserted into the quick loader mechanism on the underside of the crossbow the crossbow string clicked into place as he cocked it.

Aris put a hand on his shoulder.

"There are two more on the ground. They should be coming through the gate now" She said used her ring to speak directly into Malik's mind.

"We'll have to wait and see what they do" Malik replied while lowering the crossbow.

The gates opened and two Orcs appeared. They shut the gates behind them and put a large bar across the gates to securely hold them shut.

One of the Orcs took a strange looking crystal out of a pouch and touched the wooden bar with it. The bar flashed black for a moment then went back to normal.

They then walked off out of the cavern down a side passageway that led deeper inside the mountain.

"That looked like a holding spell to me. We won't be able to remove the bar without that crystal"

"No need, we have a keg of blasting powder, if we cannot remove the bar we just remove the doors!" Malik replied as he patted the keg of blasting powder carefully.

"You know you are a real 'know it all' at times"

Malik looked sidelong at her.

"But I love you in spite of that"

Malik smiled and took her hand.

Silently they moved closer to the compound. When they were in a new position Malik raised his crossbow taking careful aim. Aris could hear his breathing slow down as he concentrated.

"Aris let me know when the closest Orc on the tower inside the compound turns his back."

"Alright"

Aris focused her attention on the far tower and carefully watched the Orc.

"I think it's going to move in a few seconds"

Malik seemed to have stopped breathing altogether.

On the far tower the Orc turned and looked out across the compound.

"Now!"

There was a twang from of Malik's crossbow then a click as he re-cocked his crossbow then another twang as he fired again.

The two arrows flew straight and seemed to accelerate as they flew through the air. Instead of dipping and falling back to the earth they continued to travel on a straight path.

The first arrow struck its target in the chest and pierced the Orc's heart. The second Orc heard the impact of the first arrow and turned to see what had happened. The second arrow arrived and hit the Orc in the shoulder spinning it around and over the tower railing. There was a distant thud as the Orc hit the ground.

"Wind enchanted arrows, I love it! Come on!"

He jumped up pulling Aris up with him, he picked up the powder keg and they both ran toward the compound gate.

"Aris deal with the patrol and get every one away from the gate"

"Right!"

They both approached the compound gate at a run. Aris jumped into the air there was a blast from a column of twisting wind as she launched herself high into the air and flipped over the wall and disappeared from view. Malik heard her land on the other side of the wall.

Malik set the keg of blasting powder down against the gate and knelt down. He pulled out an arrow with a red arrowhead from his quiver. A roar made him turn his head, he saw an Orc charging at him with a large battle axe held high above it's head.

Malik's hands blurred as he pulled a knife out from behind his back and threw it at the Orc. The knife whistled through the air and struck the Orc in the throat. It dropped the axe as it pulled the blade from it's throat and fell to the ground. Blood spurted from it's neck.

He loaded the new red arrow into his crossbow and rolled forward suddenly as he heard a noise behind him.

An axe head buried itself into the ground where Malik had been kneeling, in a fluid motion Malik was on his feet again and turning.

He kicked the Orc that had been sneaking up on him from behind causing it to stagger backward pulling the axe out of the ground as it went.

Malik raised his crossbow holding it underarm as the Orc dived for cover behind one of the towers support legs and vanished from view.

Malik quickly followed it around the corner but it had disappeared from view.

Keeping the crossbow in front of him at all times Malik quietly walked forward and looked around the immediate area while slowly moving forward checking every hiding place.

He turned around another tower leg support but still nothing could be seen. He slowly walked under the tower. Still nothing.

Malik sniffed the air when suddenly an arm reached down from above and snatched his crossbow from his grip.

Malik ducked as an axe head was swung at neck level from above.

He felt the breeze off of the axe head on the back of his neck as it passed over the top of him.

There was a thud behind him as the Orc landed on the ground. It had let go of the beam it had been holding onto with the claws on its feet.

It tossed Malik's crossbow aside and grinned while it raised the axe above it's head and stepped forward bringing the axe down on Malik.

As the Orc attacked Malik stepped forward catching the axe handle with two hands before it got too much momentum and power from the Orc's swing.

Unfortunately this brought Malik face to face with the Orc. The smell almost made him gag.

Without his sword drawn Malik couldn't use his spirit stone to give him his extra powers and all of his strength was focused on the immediate struggle with the Orc.

Malik resorted to his combat training and quickly sidestepped and released tension on the axe handle. The Orc fell forward with the axe unable to compensate for the sudden lack of resistance.

It buried the axe head into the wooden support leg of the tower. As the Orc tried to recover Malik quickly grabbed the Orc's head from behind with both hands rammed it into the blunt end of the axe head buried into wood. While the Orc was stunned he twisted as hard as he could.

There was a loud crack as the Orc's neck broke and the body fell to the ground.

"I hate bloody Orcs"

Malik wiped his brow and picked up the crossbow again. He checked it wasn't damaged and then cocked it again.

"Aris, how are you doing?"

"Malik there's something wrong here. There are no guards or anything"

"I agree this is becoming too easy! Are the gates clear?"

"Yes I've moved everybody back you can fire when ready"

"Cover your ears then"

He raised the crossbow and fired the red arrow at the powder keg.

As it travelled through the air the arrow began to glow a bright red. It pierced the side of the powder keg and exploded. The blasting powder ignited and after the initial explosion of the arrow there was a much larger second explosion.

Malik covered his eyes with his arms as a huge wall of dust blew past him.

When the dust had finally settled he could see that the gate had been blown apart by the force of the explosion.

The large beam that had secured the gates shut lay on the floor beside the wreckage of the gates.

Aris appeared over the top of the wreckage of the gates waving her arms in an effort to blow the dust away from her face. Behind her the other captives cautiously followed Aris out of the compound.

"Bloody hell Malik, it's a wonder the whole mountain didn't hear that"

Malik shrugged his shoulders then a loud roar from behind him made him turn slowly around.

"Oh hell it's Borug!" A woman's voice screamed out.

"Who the hell is Borug?" Aris thought.

"I think we are about to find out" Malik replied.

He became aware of a slow thudding sound and could feel vibrations coming through the ground in time with the thuds.

Coming out of a side tunnel was the largest Orc Malik had ever seen. It must have been five or six times the size of an ordinary Orc and had chain wrapped around each of it's hands forming a set of makeshift gauntlets.

It pounded the ground with a huge fist causing the ground to crack. Malik felt the ground vibrate from the impact. He turned to fully face Borug.

"Aris get them to the lift. If the Orcs start to follow you ignite the powder kegs and blow them to hell"

"You're not taking that thing on by yourself, I'm staying!"

"Go the others need you to keep them safe, I'll be fine"

Malik dropped his crossbow to the ground and drew his sword. The blade flashed into life as he activated its power. The patterns on the blade glowed brilliantly in the gloom of the cavern.

"I'll meet you at the lift that's a promise now go!"

"Alright but you had better not be long" She said as she ran over and gave him a kiss before leading the group of captives toward the lift.

He watched her go and saw her glance back at him before they rounded the corner and disappeared from view.

Borug roared and hit the ground again and started to run after the captives. Malik turned and started to charge toward Borug. His sword left a trail of red light behind him in the gloom of the cavern as he accelerated toward the charging giant Orc.

Aris ran ahead leading the group out of the cavern and down the long corridor toward the lift shaft. Up ahead the same door opened and the three Orcs from earlier appeared and stood in the corridor.

"Oh bugger off" Aris shouted still running.

She held out a hand and bolt of lightning erupted from her palm. The lightning bolt struck the centre Orc and arced off of it into the other two Orcs standing on either side. The three stood twitching as the electricity flashed and continued to arc between them.

As Aris and the group got closer to them she waved her hand and the lightning discharged itself into the nearest crystal light. The crystal light became blindingly bright with the massive surge of energy. It tripled in size as it took advantage of the excess energy to grow in size.

The group ran past the barracks doors, as Aris passed by there was loud Orcish shouting coming from the other side of the doors followed by a thump. The group stopped and turned to look back at the doors.

There was another loud thump and the doors shuddered. The powder keg on top of the bar started to wobble.

"Run, fast!" Aris yelled.

They all ran as fast as they could away from the barracks double doors.

There was another louder thump from behind the doors.

Aris turned and looked over her shoulder. She heard another loud thump followed by a loud cracking sound as the bar finally broke.

"Everyone get down!"

There was a pause for a moment then the explosion came. They felt the force of the explosion's shock wave through the ground. Aris could see the flames roaring along the tunnel behind them.

She stood and braced herself and held out both hands in front of her. Blue light surrounded her hands and she pointed both hands at the floor.

Ice quickly started to form at the point she was aiming at. The ice quickly grew, as it spread up the walls it also moved outwards away from the walls and began to fill the tunnel.

In a matter of moments the tunnel was blocked by a thick ice wall. The explosion hit the wall and caused a large crack to appear along the ice.

Sweat appeared on Aris's brow as she put more energy into holding the ice wall together. Chunks of rock and debris continued to thud into the ice wall causing more cracks to appear and spread away from the already growing large crack along the surface of the ice barrier.

After a few seconds the explosion died away as quickly as it appeared. Aris lowered her arms and gave them a shake to get the blood flowing again. The ice barrier shattered and collapsed to the ground where it started to melt.

Aris took a deep breath then turned around.

"Let's keep moving we're nearly there"

The group ran on while she turned and looked back down the tunnel for a few seconds then followed the group.

Borug had stopped and was watching Malik approach at a fast sprint. He crossed his huge arms and braced himself.

Malik launched himself into the air and kicked Borug with such force that the impact forced the Orc back into a wall which cracked and threw up a large cloud of rock dust.

Malik flipped backwards and landed back on the ground. He stood ready with his sword out in front of him. The red glow from his sword shone through the dust cloud.

The dust began to settle and Malik saw the outline of the huge Orc appear. Other than the change in position the Orc hadn't moved a muscle at all.

Borug lowered his arms and grinned at Malik with huge yellowing teeth.

"Alright you are stronger than you look" Malik said and drew back his sword and attacked again.

Borug surged forward and knocked Malik's blade aside and punched him with enough force to lift Malik clean off his feet and sent him flying through the air.

Malik hit the top of the tower outside the compound and crashed through it down to the ground where he unsteadily got to his feet and leaned against a tower support trying to catch his breath.

Borug charged toward him and smashed the tower in half with a swing of a fist. Malik rolled to one side as the debris of the tower fell around him.

Malik feeling a little dizzy put a hand to his head. When he took it away his hand had blood on it.

"Oh great" He said to himself.

He quickly dived to one side again as a huge fist struck the ground where he had been.

Malik rolled wildly and his hand knocked against a small keg of blasting powder. Looking at Borug then the remaining tower behind him Malik thought fast.

He grabbed the keg and ran toward Borug again and dived in between Borug's legs as the huge Orc brought both fists down in an attempt to smash Malik.

He rolled to his feet and ran to the other tower just inside the compound wall and climbed up to the tower platform as Borug smashed what remained of the wall and gateway aside.

Malik looked frantically around the tower. He found what he was looking for and cut some loose rope free with his sword. He took out one of his knives and tied one end of the rope around a handle on the powder keg.

He held the knife and loose end of the rope in his left hand with the keg under his arm while he held his sword in his free right hand and summoned his power again.

Borug approached and gripped the tower with both hands. Timbers began to creak and snap sending splinters of wood everywhere as Borug started to exert massive forces on it.

Malik ran across the tower platform as the wooden beams and planks began to shatter and jumped from the tower and drove his sword into Borug's body just below his left collarbone.

Borug reared back in pain and the force of Malik's attack and stumbled backwards, as he did so he tripped over the wreckage of the gateway and fell onto his back sending a huge cloud of dust into the air.

The cavern vibrated with the impact of the giant Orc's body causing parts of the cavern roof to come loose and smash into the cavern floor.

Malik quickly drew back his arm and stabbed his knife into Borug's chest and tied the loose end of rope to the knife hilt.

He pulled his sword from Borug's body and a huge fist punched Malik again, the force of the punch flung him against the cavern wall.

Malik slid to the floor and as the world started to spin again he tried to get to his feet and stumbled falling to the ground again. A grunt followed by the sound of wreckage moving told him that Borug was getting up again and if he couldn't move himself then he would be in serious trouble.

Malik managed to get up and gather him self, he picked up his sword which lay beside him and reactivated its power again as Borug also got back to his feet.

The keg of blasting powder hung from the knife buried into his flesh.

When Malik used his sword to increase his power, the world around him seemed to slow down as his reflexes and reaction time were further enhanced by his Spirit Stone.

He stood and watched as Borug slowly reached down and with one hand and little visible effort picked up a huge rock that had fallen from the cavern roof.

Borug threw the man sized rock at Malik with tremendous force. With a flick of his wrist Malik brought his sword up, there was a flash of red light as the rock was sliced apart. The two halves thudded into the ground on either side of Malik and there was a clicking sound as the cut edges of the rock cooled.

Malik quickly scanned the cavern looking for his crossbow as Borug roared in rage and beat on his chest.

He spotted the handle of the crossbow protruding out from under some broken planks where the first tower had originally stood.

As Malik turned his head back he saw that Borug had picked up another large stone and had his arm back ready to throw.

Malik started to run toward the wrecked first tower and dived over a pile of rubble and rolled onto his feet again and continued running.

Behind him he heard the impact of the rock into the pile of rubble and wreckage. Splinters of wood and broken planks flew past him as he ran.

He felt something sting his left leg and right arm but ignored it and continued running.

Malik drew a handful of arrows from his quiver as he ran and sorted them throwing wrong ones aside one by one until he found one with a red coloured arrowhead. He tossed the remaining ones aside, pulled the crossbow from the wreckage as he passed and jumped behind the remains of the first tower.

Malik quickly loaded the arrow into the crossbow and cocked it. He heard a loud roar from Borg and he peered over the top of the tower remains.

Borug had actually picked up the second tower and held it over his head with both arms.

"Oh, I've had enough of this" Malik said and aimed the crossbow.

Borug took a step forward to balance himself under the weight of the tower and drew back his arms ready the throw it.

Malik fired the crossbow and ducked behind the remains of the first tower as the arrow flew through the air and struck the keg of blasting powder hanging from Borg's body.

The arrow exploded and ignited the powder keg causing another second much larger explosion just as it had with the compound gate.

Malik felt the shockwave of the blast rush past him with a deep rumble that shook the cavern. Dust and debris fell onto Malik as he lay panting on the ground. He checked the wounds on his leg and arm to see how serious they were then picked him self up off of the floor.

He turned and was about to walk away when he stopped and slowly turned.

The remains of the second tower sailed out of the cloud of smoke and dust turning end over end. Malik threw his crossbow aside and just managed to dive out of the way before the whole structure came crashing down.

The dust cloud gradually settled revealing Borug who was holding his right hand on the large open wound on his chest. Blood poured from between his fingers and he dropped onto one knee drawing in huge gasps of breath. He managed to stand up again and they both stood watching each other.

"You're a lot stronger than I first thought, I'll give you that"

To Malik's surprise Borug bowed his head at him in a nod of acknowledgement.

Borug suddenly grabbed his head and threw it back roaring in pain.

Malik took a step back and raised his sword again in preparation for the next attack but Borug had dropped to his knees howling in agony. He arched backwards with his head bent back further. He was still clasping his head with his hands.

Just as suddenly as he started Borug was suddenly silent. He slowly lowered his hands then he lowered his head and opened his eyes.

Both of his eyes were completely black.

Borug opened his mouth and took a breath then the same voice Malik heard back in Torkle echoed from Borug's mouth.

"You try to cause me no end of problems boy!"

"Try me face to face and I'll severely inconvenience you" Malik growled.

"Do you think you have accomplished anything? The only thing you have done is save me the time of having to kill those maggots"

Borug gave a chuckle then picked up a fallen support beam and threw it like a spear at Malik.

Malik easily dodged the beam as it flew past him and embedded itself into the wall behind him. The exposed end of the beam vibrated gently.

"So you've finished uncovered the Dark Gate then?"

"Did you figure that out yourself or did you need your little weather witch to help you?"

"You haven't managed to activate it then, oh dear is it beyond your abilities? What a shame!"

Borug laughed at him and stood up.

"The gate will be open in a matter of hours not that you will live long enough to see it!"

Borug charged again at Malik and swung his right arm down to crush Malik. There was a flash of red light from Malik's sword as his powers were activated and he leapt into the air over the top of the fist as it impacted into the ground creating a large crater.

Malik landed on top of the fist and ran along Borug's arm.

He jumped again as Borug tried to swat him away with his left arm.

Malik twisted in the air and landed behind Borug's head bringing his sword down into Borug's neck just below the skull.

Using all his strength Malik forced the blade down into Borug's body severing the spinal cord.

Borug gave a grunt and toppled forward into the ground.

Malik removed his sword and jumped down. As he walked around the body he could see Borug's face.

The huge Orc's eyes had returned to normal, they watched Malik as he approached.

Slowly they closed and the body gave a final sigh. Malik put his hand on Borug's head and bowed his head.

"Malik please tell me you are alright?" Aris's voice sounded out in his mind.

"I'm fine sweetheart" Malik opened his eyes and raised his head. *"We have a problem though"*

"What's that?"

"The gate is fully uncovered but isn't active yet, How long until the Battlemages get here?"

"A few hours at least"

"Alright how many people have you got out?"

"There is one group left to go up. The lift is on its way back down now"

"I'm coming back to you, let's get out of here and wait for the reinforcements"

"Hurry up then the lift is here now!"

"I'm on my way now"

Malik tapped the ground with his sword then sheathed it and gave one final look at Borug's body then turned and sprinted toward the entrance to the cavern.

As he ran down the corridor he came to the barracks. In his battle with Borug he had never heard or felt the explosion from the barracks.

Wreckage littered the tunnel and the entrance to the barracks. The two large doors had been blown inwards showering those on the other side with deadly splinters of wood. A large number of dismembered Orc bodies were scattered around the inside of the barracks.

Malik stopped and looked around he felt that something was watching him but he couldn't seem to sense where it was coming from.

Something large and heavy landed on Malik from above forcing him into the ground. Two large Orc hands gripped Malik's throat from behind and started to squeeze.

Malik managed to lift his body from the ground giving him self some room to move. He flipped onto his side bringing his elbow back as he did.

The Orc loosed one hand to protect itself from the ground and as it did Malik's elbow connected with the Orc's skull knocking the Orc off of him. It recovered and drove an elbow into Malik's chest before returning both hands around Malik's throat.

Malik tried to pull the hands off of his throat but he didn't have the strength left to remove them without his sword. The Orc leaned closer and sneered at Malik, this was the moment Malik had been praying for.

He quickly brought his right arm inside the Orc's arms and struck the Orc on the nose with the palm of his hand.

There was a crack and the Orc slumped forward as the broken nose bone shot up and into it's brain killing it.

Malik removed the hands and took a deep breath, coughing he pushed the Orc's body off and slowly sat up.

"That'll teach you to drop in uninvited" He muttered.

Malik stood up and was dusted him self off when he suddenly stopped and slowly looked up. Standing in what had until recently been the barracks gateway was a squad of ten Orcs.

Malik stood and stared while the Orcs stared back.

"Oh bugger!" He said and sprinted off down the tunnel

The Orcs stood still for a moment and looked at one another, then as one they gave chase down the tunnel.

"Aris! We have company!" Malik thought as he sprinted down the tunnel toward the lift shaft.

He jumped over a large pool of water that had not long ago once been Aris's ice barrier and skidded to a halt.

He reached up and took some arrows from his quiver. He selected one with a white arrowhead and hid behind a large fallen rock that had been dislodged from the ceiling. He heard footsteps approaching from further up the tunnel.

He readied himself and when he heard the splash of a foot entering the pool of water he stabbed the arrow into the water.

Lightning burst out from the arrow and danced upon the surface of the water. For the Orcs that had entered the pool they stood there unable to move as the electricity passed through their bodies electrocuting them. The lucky ones who hadn't entered the pool of water stood on the far side growling and snorting.

Malik sprinted off again back to the lift shaft when he came across the first of the blasting powder kegs that Charles and the others had set up earlier.

"Aris, I'm nearly with you start the lift" Malik thought as he approached the lift shaft.

Up ahead he heard the chains of the lift start to rattle as the cage began to lift. He rounded the corner and entered the lift area. Up ahead he saw the cage with Aris waiting in the doorway with the cage door open.

The lift had just begun to rise up into the airshaft.

Aris saw Malik running toward her when he suddenly drew his sword and changed direction as she turned her head she saw several Orc archers one of them was taking aim at her.

Malik flicked his wrist and a moment later the Orc was knocked off it's feet with another of Malik's knives sticking out of its chest.

"Shut the door I'll grab on to the underneath" Malik shouted to her as he cut down another Orc.

The lift had stated to enter the Airshaft and if the door was still open it would jam the lift and stop it from moving. Another problem is that it is impossible to open the cage door while the lift is in the shaft because of the tight fit of the cage in the shaft.

The last Orc archer drew back it's bow to shoot Malik but before it could release the arrow Malik swung his sword and cut the Orc's bow and arrow in half, for a few seconds the Orc stood motionless then fell in half.

"Get over her now!" Aris screamed as the cage rose higher into the shaft.

Malik ran over and jumped up and caught the bottom of the cage where he hung. As he rose up into the shaft one of the Orc's that had chased him earlier jumped and barrelled into Malik knocking him from the bottom of the cage.

Malik hit the ground on his back knocking the air out of him. Another Orc pinned him to the ground and stopped him from reaching his sword.

Malik saw Aris up above. She was on her hands and knees on the bottom of the cage. She was shouting something but he couldn't hear what she said.

A large Orc filled his view grinned at him, pulled back it's fist and swung it at him.

"I love you" He thought to her.

The world went black.

Malik slowly opened his eyes and looked around, he was being held up by two Orcs. The Orcs had a strong grip on each of his arms stopping him from moving.

Strangely Malik noticed that they hadn't taken his sword from him. It remained in its sheath hanging by his side.

He looked up and noticed a figure was standing in front of him. The figure was draped in long black robes. Malik couldn't see the face as it was hidden by a large black hood.

"Hello boy, after so long we finally meet again"

"Who are you?"

"Don't you recognize me? Well it has been a long time. The last time you saw me your parents were still alive, well briefly anyway"

The figure drew the hood back revealing a human head with long white hair and dark black tattoos around his neck.

"Bloody hell, I know you, you're Tethis!"

"Mayor Tethis if you don't mind boy" The figure said grinning evilly.

"No, it can't be! Why would you destroy your own town?"

"Oh he didn't want to at first. But he didn't have a choice after I took his body from him"

"Took his body?"

Malik thought for a moment then realisation dawned.

"You're a Shade aren't you! A bloody parasitic shadow!"

Tethis smiled and clapped his hands together then came closer to Malik. The two Orcs lifted him up.

"Well done, I can see you do have some intelligence after all, much like your mother. It's a shame I had to have her skull crushed she had such a nice body"

The two Orcs were suddenly dragged across the ground as Malik suddenly surged forward toward Tethis. He was stopped when one of the Orcs kicked him in the chest and stamped on him a few times.

"I see you also have your father's strength" Tethis said as Malik was lifted back up to his feet. The two Orcs doubled their grip on Malik's arms just in case.

"He was very strong, it is a shame I had to have him killed but he just didn't see my way of thinking"

Malik coughed and spat some blood from his mouth as he raised his head.

"I must say they were both very clever" Tethis casually continued. "Do you know they managed to find a way to actually grow magic crystals? That alone made them both dangerous enough to warrant killing them"

"And the town, why destroy that?"

"Just for the fun of it really. My Orcs were getting board and needed some exercise. Besides it would be silly to leave any survivors to tell what they had seen"

Tethis stood up and walked over to Malik and grabbed him under the chin then knelt down to look him in the face.

"Which brings me right back to you, you were the only survivor of the raid on Halton"

"There were others"

"Not for long there wasn't" Tethis sneered.

"My curse killed them off one after the other but yet you survived for all these years. I could feel your life force constantly taunting me. But now that you are here, I really want to enjoy wiping every last trace of it from the face of this pathetic planet"

Tethis released Malik and raised his arm and the Orcs lifted Malik up onto his feet. Another much larger Orc entered Malik's view.

"Do you recognize him?" Tethis asked. "He is the one who killed your mother and gave you that scar on your chest"

The Orc swung a large club around and smashed it into the ground. Tethis walked over to the Orc and placed a hand on the Orc's chest.

A black mist surrounded the Orc. The Orc took several deep breaths of the mist and roared. The Orc's already large muscles bulged and grew even bigger. The two Orcs holding onto Malik let him go and ran out of the way.

"Finish the job" Tethis said to the Orc and stepped away.

"I've let you keep your sword boy as I want you to think that you have a chance"

Malik said nothing but kept his eyes fixed on Tethis. He drew his sword from its sheath. Malik's blood ran down his hand and dripped onto his sword.

The Orc roared again and charged at Malik who remained still. As the Orc bore down on him he spoke to Tethis.

"My father's crystals, did you destroy them all?"

"Not that it matters to you but yes they were all smashed!" Tethis replied smiling.

The Orc continued to close on Malik, it held the club overhead and was about to start swinging it downwards. Malik lowered his sword.

"You missed one"

The blade flashed into life and a bright flash of red light as he swung his sword around and sidestepped the Orc.

The Orc staggered forward to slow itself down as it had missed Malik.

It turned around raised its club again then stopped and fell into two halves as Malik turned and attacked the two Orcs cutting them down as they tried to restrain him again.

He turned and charged at Tethis his sword shined vibrantly and growled in rage.

Tethis looked surprised and just managed to raise his hand before Malik reached him.

Malik dropped to his knees and buried his sword in the ground as he fell. The red glow died away from his sword as his concentration failed.

"Not so easy when your heart is being crushed is it?" Tethis said he walked over to Malik and knelt down beside him and whispered in his ear. "Do you want to know the tragedy in all this?"

Malik gasped for breath.

"Your mother failed in her mission. All she was ordered to do was protect your father while he worked on his crystals but over the years they fell in love and you were a result" Tethis licked his lips enjoying every minute of Malik's pain. "You know she might have even been able to save your father if she hadn't been pregnant with your sister"

Malik's spirit stone roared in rage. Tethis grinned as Malik's head dropped.

"My father wouldn't have been killed by your stinking Orcs" Malik gasped.

"That is true, take comfort boy he killed a great many of my Orcs as he tried to protect the people he was with. Unfortunately he couldn't stop me crushing his heart like this"

Tethis held out his hand and slowly clenched his fist. Malik screamed in pain.

At the top of the airshaft the lift finally emerged from the mountain and clanked to a halt. The cage door opened and the last group of the captives exited and joined with the others.

Aris was the last to leave the cage, as she slowly exited Charles ran over to her.

"Where's Malik?"

"He is still down at the bottom of the shaft. Can you send me back down I've got to go and fetch him"

"You must be mad if you want to go back down in there!"

"He would come back and get you or me" She said anger building in her voice.

"I know, I know but we disabled the controls for the lift we can't move it again"

Aris suddenly dropped to her knees and cried out in pain, she put her hands around her head and bent forward.

"What's the matter?" Charles asked kneeling down in front of her.

Clara ran over to them and helped Charles to lift Aris up off of the ground and sit her on an upturned container.

"They're killing him!" She cried and tried to run for the cage.

Charles held onto her arm holding her back.

"Don't be stupid!" Charles said pulling her back.

"Charles let her go" Clara said.

Charles looked at her then at Aris and slowly let her go. Clara nodded to Aris as she looked back.

Aris ran back to the cage and held out her hand. There was a flash of light and the cage was blown backwards away from the shaft. The chains and fixing's made a horrible noise as they bent and snapped under the intense force placed on them.

The cage broke the last of its fixings and tumbled end over end down the side of the mountain.

Aris stood at the side of the shaft and looked down then turned to face the group of captives behind her.

"Head west just like Malik said. A Battlemage Airship is en route here meet up with them and you will be fine"

"Good luck!" Clara shouted to her.

Aris nodded and jumped backwards into the Airshaft and disappeared into the darkness.

Malik gasped for breath and held a hand to his chest. It felt like his heart was being torn from his chest.

"It's a very stubborn muscle the heart it just doesn't want to stop beating!" Tethis said increasing his power.

Malik screamed in pain and fell forward.

"Oh how long have I waited to hear such a wonderful sound"

Tethis closed his eyes and listening intently to the sound of Malik's scream echo around the cavern.

Tethis suddenly opened his eyes and looked at the airshaft.

"Looks like someone is coming to try and save you" He said and nodded at a group of Orcs.

The Orcs grouped around the bottom of the bottom of the shaft with their weapons drawn.

"Looks like she is just in time to see you die"

A massive swirling vortex of air hit the bottom of the airshaft blowing the assembled Orcs into the air and flinging them into the walls of the cavern.

Aris landed on the ground with the lightest touch and launched a ball of flame from her hand at Tethis.

Tethis didn't move instead he just stood still as the fireball approached. Two feet before the fireball reached Tethis it was deflected by an unseen force and struck a wall where it exploded, the blast of super intense heat melted the solid rock turning it bright red.

Tethis turned his attention from Malik to Aris.

"Not a bad attempt witch" He said and raised his other hand.

Aris was flung into the air and pinned to the cavern wall.

"But not good enough" He grinned and turned his attention back to Malik.

"I'll give you a choice, who dies first boy? You or your love"

He clenched his fist squeezing Aris's heart causing her to scream.

The scream triggered something within Malik. Rage suddenly filled him as the scream echoed in his mind. The image of his dead mother filled his mind, another image entered his mind. Lying next to his mother was Aris, blood covered her face as her eyes stared at Malik.

Malik blinked, his vision began to change. The world was somehow becoming more defined and detailed as he looked up he could see Tethis was surrounded by a large black swirling aura.

The pain in his chest began to subside as the rage within him grew. His sword began to glow brighter as his concentration returned.

Tethis suddenly became aware of Malik's resistance and dropped Aris to the ground where she lay. He concentrated his now free hand on Malik using all of his power. Malik felt an increase in the pressure on his chest but as the rage continued to grow even fiercer the pain died away.

"What? That's not possible!" Tethis gasped as Malik got up onto one knee and grasped his sword.

The blade glowed red with an incredible intensity as the rage continued to grow within Malik. The glow started to change from red to bright orange and then to a pure white light.

The cavern began to vibrate as Malik raised himself up onto his feet.

Malik stood still grasping his sword and swung it while it was still buried into the cavern floor. The sword moved without encountering any resistance from the ground Malik swung the blade again and stuck it back into the ground where white light erupted from the gash in the ground.

White light moved like a wave across the ground tearing and splitting it apart. Tethis crossed his arms and braced himself as the wave of light hit the same force that had deflected Aris's fireball. Rather than be deflected, the wave of light held fast against the force and flowed around it.

It looked like there was a bubble around Tethis that was protecting him from Malik's attack. The white light flickered and danced over the surface of the shield constantly compressing the bubble making it smaller.

Malik let out a roar of rage that was more animal than human and the wave doubled in size and the vibrations grew in intensity. Parts of the cavern roof were shook free and fell to the ground Tethis screamed and tried to dive to one side as the light overpowered him.

Back in his study in Founders Rock, Captain Heald was sitting at his desk writing on some papers when there was a knock on the door.

"Enter"

May entered the study carrying a pile of papers closely followed by Charleston carrying another pile.

"I've got the next lot of reports for you father"

"Oh thank you May, what are you doing here Charleston?"

"Err well I was just err"

Charleston tried to speak but just ended up standing to attention holding the pile of papers and looking very sheepish.

"Charleston is being a perfect gentleman and helping me to carry in the papers"

"A perfect gentleman? Charleston!?"

The Captain looked from May to Charleston then realization dawned. He took in a deep breath to start shouting then suddenly stopped. He turned quickly and faced toward northeast. Even though it was a brick wall he seemed to be looking at something.

"Father what was that?"

"It feels like Malik's energy" Charleston said.

The Captain turned around and saw both May and Charleston staring in the same direction he had been.

"What did you say Charleston?"

"It feels like… no it is, its Malik!"

"He's right I'd know that energy signature blindfolded" May agreed.

"But what does it mean, has he awoken?" Charleston said looking at May.

"You two know about awakening? You both can sense… can you…"

The Captain suddenly stood up and walked over to the study door.

"We need to talk, now!" He said and closed the door.

The light faded and Malik dropped to the ground unconscious, everything was very still the vibrations stopped and the dust settled.

Several Orcs arrived from the tunnel that led to barracks. They ran over to help Tethis who was struggling to stand up. When they got to him they saw Tethis was missing his right arm as well as some of his shoulder and upper torso.

Tethis looked at Malik and Aris then he turned to one of the Orcs

"Lock the boy up in the cells, make sure he cannot reach that sword"

The Orc grunted and picked up Malik and slung him over its shoulder then picked up Malik's sword and headed off down another tunnel.

"You, help me to my quarters and you bring the girl with you" Tethis ordered the two remaining Orcs.

"I'll make you pay boy" Tethis growled as the Orc helped him to walk down the tunnel.

Malik slowly opened his eyes and blinked, his head was spinning and his body felt drained. He was lying on a stone floor in a dark room. He sat bolt upright and reached for his sword only to find it was gone.

"Easy boy don't try to move too much just yet" A voice said.

Malik turned around and saw that sitting against a wall on the other side of the stone cell was a man. Now he was awake Malik was feeling his strength return.

"Who are you?" He asked.

"Mathias Killdare" The man said.

"Killdare? As in Sheriff Killdare?"

"You know me?"

"I met your wife in Stonewall. She said you were dead"

"Darcy! Is she safe?" Mathias asked anxiously.

"Yes, she has taken over your job as Sheriff"

Mathias smiled.

"I guess she would think I was dead, It feels like I've been here for years"

"What happened?" Malik groaned and sat up against the wall.

"I was investigating these mines after all the people went missing and got captured by those bloody Orcs. Who are you?"

"Malik Owen, I'm a Crimson Guardian. My partner and I were sent to try and sort out this mess. Did they bring anyone else here?"

"No only you"

"Gods I hope she is alright"

Malik got to his feet and stretched, he was feeling much better now. In fact he felt stronger than before.

"Aris can you hear me?" Malik thought but there was nothing but silence.

He walked over to the cell door and examined it. It was a large heavy wooden door with iron bars forming a small window.

Looking out of the small window Malik saw a large table in the middle of the room beyond the cell door.

A group of Orcs were sitting around the table looking at Malik's equipment. Malik put a hand to his head as it throbbed. He closed his eyes and remembered the encounter with Tethis.

"What happened to me?" He thought to himself. *"I felt powerful much more than before, I could sense the magic coming from Tethis and shield myself from it"*

He opened his eyes and looked over at the table again. He felt the connection with his sword. He concentrated on the table again as he got the same feeling he had earlier.

His eyesight sharpened on the area he was concentrating on. He saw his sword lying on the table. He closed his eyes again and sensed that an Orc was reaching for the handle.

"What are you doing? Mathias asked.

Malik held up his hand and turned back to the window. At the table one of the Orcs reached over and picked up Malik's sword and looked at it.

"Got you" Malik said.

Malik's sword glowed white and the Orc's arm blurred as it moved on its own accord. In a few seconds it had cut down the other Orcs sitting around the table then turned on the Orc holding the sword itself. The sword drove itself through the Orc's chest. The Orc fell over backwards and let go of the sword grip.

"That takes care of the guards. Now let's do something about the door"

"You won't be able to move that door" Mathias said. "The door bolts are set well into the wall"

Malik stood at the door he concentrated and felt his power increase again. It was different from his sword's power. When he summoned power from his Spirit Stone it flowed into him from the sword. This power was different, it came from within him and it felt good.

He kicked the door.

The part of the wall that the door lock was set into exploded and crumbled. The doorframe fell away and the door slammed into the outside of the cell wall.

"Bloody hellfire!" Mathias said coughing and waving the dust away.

"What happened to me?" Malik said staring at the remains of the doorframe.

"Well whatever it was just keep in front of me please!"

Malik walked over to the table and retrieved his sword from the Orc's body.

"How did you do that?" Mathias asked as he took a sword and shield from a rack hanging on the wall.

"Not a clue I just sort of did it!" Malik said as he cleaned the blood from his sword.

"Any kind of plan about what we do now"

"Yes find Aris, kill the Shade followed by anything else that gets in the way"

"Simple, I like it! By the way this door leading out of here is locked would you mind?" Mathias said while he rattled the door latch.

A white blade appeared through the door and moved easily up and down through the wood and metal that made up the door. The sword then disappeared back through the door and what was left of the door fell into two pieces.

Malik and Mathias stepped over the remains of the door and climbed up the stairs that led out of the cells.

"How do we find this Aris of yours? These tunnels run for miles under the mountain"

"She's this way" Malik said pointing down a tunnel that led deeper into the mountain.

"How do you know?"

"I can smell her scent. She was carried down that tunnel by an Orc"

Malik turned and pointed in the other direction and put a hand on Mathias's shoulder.

"Head up this tunnel you will find a small vent shaft that leads straight up and out of the mountain. There are no Orcs that way, the air is much too clean"

Malik turned his head and looked down the tunnel in the other direction and sniffed.

"They are all in that direction"

"What are you going to do?"

"What else I'm going to find Aris. When you get out head west to Torkle you should find the rest of the captives along the way. A Battlemage Airship should also be on the way here to help"

"Alright Malik, you be careful down there"

"Say hello to Darcy for me"

Mathias smiled and nodded. He stopped and stared at Malik for a moment and shook his head then turned and ran up the tunnel to the vent shaft.

Malik watched him go until he rounded a bend and disappeared from view. He then turned and headed along the tunnel deeper into the bowels of the mountain.

As he moved along the tunnel Malik was finding it easier to control his new found abilities. He discovered that he could see very well in the dark when he wanted to and that he could concentrate his sight and zoom in on things he wanted to look closer at.

A rat ran quietly down a side tunnel, to Malik it sounded as if the rat was wearing steel boots. He watched it run up the side tunnel following every move from where he was standing.

He reached the end of a tunnel where it formed another junction in the massive maze of tunnels that ran under the mountain.

He stood in the middle of the tunnel and sniffed again. He could smell both Aris's scent and also the scent of the Orc that had carried her down the tunnel. He followed the scent until he reached another door where he stopped and sniffed the air again.

He identified three scents going into the room. Tethis, Aris and the Orc went into the room beyond the door.

Carefully he opened the door and entered the room. Inside was a central large room with several other doors situated around the outside. Some of the doors were open revealing smaller rooms. The central room was covered in strange markings and on one side was a shrine of some sort with a folded blanket set on the ground in front of it.

Moving silently he searched the rooms one at a time. The last room he looked in was clearly Tethis's bedroom. In the middle of the room was a large bed draped in black silk.

He could smell both Aris's and Tethis's scent coming from the bed this was enough to start making him nervous. As he moved closer to the bed he detected that Aris's scent moved off away from the bed and through another door on the far side of the bedroom.

Malik moved closer and when he pulled back the bed sheet he found Tethis's body lying on the bed among the blood soaked bed covers. Malik was no stranger to seeing dead bodies but even he had never seen so much blood.

It looked as though Tethis's body had retained all the blood inside the body then at a given point it had all just flowed out from the wounds Malik had caused earlier.

Malik slowly backed away from the bed keeping his eyes fixed on the body in case it suddenly sprang back to life.

Casually he reached out with his right hand and grasped something in the shadows. There was a choking sound and when Malik brought his hand back he held an Orc by the throat. With ease Malik held the Orc and arms length and lifted it off of the ground. It's feet dangled in the air.

The Orc struggled to try and break Malik's grip but the grip was too powerful.

"What happened here?" Malik said calmly and quietly.

The Orc grunted and struggled trying to break free.

"I know you were here and I know you carried the girl"

The Orc continued to struggle but Malik pulled it close to his face. The room began to vibrate again and a low rumbling could be heard. The Orc's face became a mask of terror as it looked at Malik's eyes. There was a faint blue glow emanating into the room from somewhere.

"Don't make me ask again" Malik growled.

"Room go black Tethis, die. Girl walks away"

The Orc grunted and pointed to the door. Malik slowly turned his head toward the door and dropped the Orc to the floor.

"Run and hope I never find you again"

Malik walking to the door as the Orc rubbed it's throat, turned and ran out of room back toward the tunnels as fast as it could.

Malik carefully opened the door and peered around it. A long tunnel slowly descended downwards. By the looks of it this tunnel was newly constructed. There were new wooden support beams put in place to support the roof of the tunnel. Malik followed the tunnel downwards until it stopped being dirt and became stone.

Malik looked around at the sides and ceiling of the new tunnel. They were made from caved stone and at the far end of the tunnel was a large set of stone doors. One of the doors was already slightly open.

As Malik looked back he realized that whoever had made the tunnel from Tethis's Room had dug down and through the ceiling of an existing tunnel made long ago which had caved in.

Crystals hung in special ornamental holders from the walls casting a dim light that filled the tunnel. Malik carefully walked along the stone tunnel keeping to the shadows. He saw another larger passage way joined the tunnel further along. There were signs of a lot of recent activity had been through the larger passageway.

As he neared the stone doors he suddenly became aware of a strong power coming from behind the doors. Malik approached the half open door and with one arm put his hand on and gripped the door.

He pulled and the door moved a little then jammed against some stones lodged in the joints.

Malik concentrated and felt the change come over him again. He gripped the door and pulled again with the one hand. This time the stones lodged in the joints crumbled and shattered and the stone door swung open. Malik let go of the door and flexed his hand.

He looked at his arms and legs but they looked perfectly normal to him but they felt stronger and more powerful. It was as if there was a switch inside him that he could use to turn this new found power on and off.

Carefully he looked through the open stone doors. Behind them was a large round cavern all covered in the same cut black stone that the tunnel behind Malik had also been made of.

In the very centre of the stone cavern on a round raised platform the Dark Gate stood. It was made up of two large triangular frame works made of a strange grey material. Standing at the base of the Dark Gate was a figure dressed in a long black robe. Malik could tell from the scent that it was Aris.

"Aris?" He called out softly

She didn't answer him instead she just stood still looking up at the Dark Gate.

Malik looked around the cavern then carefully stepped out from the doorway and walked toward Aris. He called her name again as he approached, but she still didn't answer him. Against every shred of his common sense Malik approached and carefully put a hand on her shoulder.

"Aris are you alright?"

Her hand moved from under the black robe and a ball of lightning erupted into Malik's chest throwing him backwards.

Malik landed on his back and skidded to a halt. His armour smoked gently around the large round black burnt area where the lightning had touched him.

"Never better half-breed!" Tethis's multi vocal voice said.

Malik looked up and Aris turned around and took back the hood. It was definitely Aris but her eyes were covered entirely black just like Tethis's had been before. Her body twitched every now and again as if some battle was going on inside her.

"Oh Gods what have you done too her Tethis?"

"I've simply taken her body" Tethis said and slid the robe off of Aris's shoulders.

Underneath the black robe Aris was wearing the uniform Malik had made her aboard the Red Devil. Aris's hands moved up and down her body feeling every curve of her body.

"It is such a nice body don't you agree?" Tethis's voice said.

"My scouts found your camp and these clothes are very special to Aris!"

Malik gritted his teeth together as he could feel the rage building in him again as he got back to his feet.

"You may have overpowered me before but I bet you cannot bring yourself to hurt this body"

Malik drew his sword and activated it. The sword glowed with a brilliant white light. Aris waved a hand and her staff appeared in her hand. She then aimed the staff at Malik and fired several large fireballs at him.

Malik moved his sword and with barely any effort deflected the fireballs away from himself into the surrounding walls of the cavern where they exploded turning the black stones bright red with the heat.

Malik stepped forward and suddenly stopped when Aris twitched and fell to her knees.

"Malik!" Aris's voice echoed around the cavern instead of Tethis's

"Aris!"

"Kill me now! Quickly I cannot hold him back much longer"

"No! I'll find a way to free you! Please trust me!"

Aris screamed and Tethis voice returned.

"She is very stubborn and just won't go quietly" Tethis said.

Aris stood up and fired another fireball from the staff. Malik jumped high into the air avoiding the fireball and came back down with his sword outstretched.

Aris gripped the staff in both hands and held it up to block the strike.

The staff and sword connected and a massive shockwave spread out from the epicentre where sword and staff met. Malik forced Aris's body down onto one knee. The glow from his sword increased until there was a blinding flash of light and Aris's staff shattered in her hands.

There was a scream from Tethis and Aris fell backwards onto the floor. Malik raised his sword to strike and stopped.

"You disappoint her, boy"

Aris brought both hands up and fired a massive blast of lighting that struck Malik in the chest. The blast forced him backwards his sword fell from his grip and as it clattered on the floor the light faded from it.

Malik hit the wall behind and before he could move Aris appeared in front of him and gripped him by the throat and pinned him up to the wall with one hand. She brought a knee up and drove it into Malik's chest knocking the air out him.

Aris held out her free hand and Malik's sword was lifted into the air by an unseen force and flew through the air. She caught the sword by the handle and impaled Malik through the stomach pinning him to the wall behind.

Malik screamed in pain as Aris let him go so he hung from the wall by the sword.

"How does it feel to be killed by the one you love?" Tethis whispered in Malik's ear then backed away.

Malik gripped his sword by the blade to ease the pressure of his body on the sword's blade. The pain caused him to gasp for breath and he spat out some blood from his mouth.

"How strange fate is!" Tethis said spreading Aris's arms wide and turning to face the Dark Gate.

"Do you realise that you have delivered the very knowledge I need to reopen the gates again"

Tethis's voice laughed as Aris turned around to face Malik again.

"The knowledge held in this woman's mind is fantastic. And I have you to thank for bringing it right too me!"

"Drop dead and we'll call it even" Malik spat some more blood from his mouth.

"Don't be so bitter boy, you will live long enough to see the beginning of the next chapter in this planet's history"

"You mean the sapping of life from the planet itself"

"I mean when this world becomes full of beautiful shadows"

"Shadows?" Malik said quietly to himself.

The words of Father Spectre rose in his mind.

"Shadows cannot exist in light" Malik said and looked up at Aris.

She walked over to the Dark Gate and placed a hand on its base. The two diamond shaped frames started to slowly rotate. As they started to move faster a small black hole slowly began to form in the centre of the gate.

Malik's sword began to glow red as he gripped it by the blade. Blood dripped from his hands as his grip tightened around the sword. He gritted his teeth and pushed forward on the blade. As he pushed the sword forward he felt him self move slowly away from the wall. He pushed harder and felt the unpleasant sensation of the blade begin to move through his body.

With one final effort he freed the sword from the wall and let out a yell of pain as he dropped to the ground gasping for breath. He pulled his sword free from his own body and gripped it by the handle. Rising onto one knee he used his blade to help himself stand up.

"Tethis!" Malik roared in anger. "I won't let you have her!"

His sword changed colour again and glowed white as he changed. Aris turned and looked back at Malik as the room began to vibrate with Malik's gathering power.

Malik took a step forward and plunged his sword into the stone floor. The cavern was filled with an intensely bright white light as Malik's power was released into his sword in one massive energy burst.

Aris crossed her arms over her eyes to try and shut out the light but there was nowhere to hide from the blinding light that reflected off of every surface in the round cavern.

Behind Aris tendrils of darkness broke away from her body as Tethis's presence was burnt from her body and soul by the light. The tendrils grouped together and disappeared into the small black hole in the centre of the Dark Gate.

Aris fell to the ground and lay still as the light faded from the cavern. Malik fell back to his knees gasping for breath and clutching at his stomach. He fell forward and lay on his side.

His sword remained buried in the stone floor of the cavern. Behind Aris the Dark Gate revolutions slowed to a stop and the black hole disappeared.

Aris's body twitched and she lifted her head up then slowly raised herself onto her elbows and looked around. When she saw Malik lying on the ground she struggled to get to her feet. She managed to get up and run a few more steps toward him before she fell again.

Aris got back up and ran to him. She fell again just before she reached him and crawled over to him.

"You're back!" Malik quietly said and smiled at her.

"Malik I'm so sorry!" She cried as she picked his head up and rested it in her lap.

Tears formed as she looked at his wound and the blood pool that he was lying in. Blood continued to flow from the wound in his stomach. Aris gently lay Malik's head down and moved to his side. She placed both hands on the wound and the gentle green glow appeared as she tried to heal him.

Sweat started to form on her brow as she tried to concentrate. She yelped and the green glow flickered and died.

"Malik I can't stop the bleeding! I don't have any magic left"

"Around my neck in the pouch is the vial of Frostbite. Pour it into the wound"

Aris reached around his neck and took the leather pouch and opened it. She removed the small metal vial of Frostbite and twisted the lid off.

After gently moving Malik's hand she poured the contents into Malik's wound.

"Now what?"

"Could you hand me my sword and the flint out of the pouch please"

Aris got up and pulled on Malik's sword, it glowed red at her touch then came free out of the stone floor. Aris laid it down on the floor next to her as she tipped the contents of the pouch into her lap and sifted through the items until she picked up the small cylindrical flint.

"What are you going to do?" Aris asked handing him the flint and sword.

"Hopefully stop the bleeding really quickly"

He tried to sit up, winced at the pain and gritted his teeth as he lay back down again.

"Let me do it"

She took the sword from his hand and held it on the flint like Malik had done before when he lit the Fire Moss.

"Aris, are you sure you want to do this?" He asked her.

"No are you?"

"Not really no! But do it anyway" Malik said through gritted teeth.

Aris ran the sword across the flint causing sparks to fly from the flint and ignite the liquid Frostbite.

There was a loud whooshing sound and tall flames jumped from Malik's stomach. He screamed in agony then was silent as he fell into unconsciousness.

Aris gently stroked his hair and kissed him on his fore head. She cradled his head in her lap again and gently rocked back and forth quietly crying for a few minutes until Malik coughed.

He opened his eyes and blinked, then looked up at Aris.

"That was a bloody stupid idea wasn't it!" She said and smiled.

Malik laughed and grimaced in pain.

"Don't make me laugh, it hurts too much! I'm glad to see your eyes again. Black didn't suit you at all"

Aris smiled back and looked down at his wound. The burst of flame had stopped the bleeding from Malik's stomach.

"The bleeding has stopped, how do you feel?"

"I've been better" Malik said quite honestly and groaned.

"Can you move?"

"I think so, give me a hand up sweetheart"

Aris stood up and reached down with her hands. Malik took them and she gently helped him up to his feet.

"I wonder where those blasted Battlemages are?"

"They can't be far away now" Aris said.

"Well they can bloody well destroy this damn gate when they get here then"

They turned around and started to walk away when Malik stopped.

"What is it?"

"Something is wrong? I can feel it"

"Feel what?"

"The gate it's pulsating!" He said and slowly turned around.

The Dark Gate started to spin again and this time it was spinning much faster than before. The black hole in the middle grew much larger and filled the gates framework. Malik pushed Aris behind him and raised his sword.

"Don't be stupid, you are in no condition to fight"

"If I change I can hold them back"

Malik's blade came to life again and glowed white instead of red.

A huge dragon's head appeared through the Dark Gate. It was black in colour and had huge black eyes. It extended it's head out through the Dark Gate on a long neck which ran back thorough the gate as it's body was too big to fit through the gateway.

"Bloody hell it's Tethis!" Malik yelled.

The dragon took a deep breath and breathed out a massive stream of fire from it's mouth. Malik threw Aris to one side and dived to the other. They both rolled up onto their feet and ran as fast as they could to either side of the dragon.

"Aris!" He yelled and threw his sword through the air to her.

"What am I supposed to do with this?" She shouted as she caught the sword and ducked under another stream of fire.

"When I distract him you go and destroy the gate. No matter what happens just destroy the gate!"

He stood up straight and Aris saw the change come over him. Before she had only detected the traces of something powerful hidden deep inside Malik but now the power radiated off of him in huge amounts. The room rumbled and vibrated with his growing power.

"How did you do that?"

"Get to the gate!" Malik shouted and began walking toward the dragon.

The dragon watched Malik carefully it's huge head swung to follow him as he moved. Aris carefully started to move slowly around the back of the dragon's head to get to the gate.

The dragon suddenly rounded on Aris and opened it's mouth to incinerate her.

Malik struck.

He moved much faster than he had before and appeared by the dragon and kicked the underside of the jaw throwing it's head upwards. The stream of fire burned the roof of the cavern turning it bright red.

Aris ran on and when she looked again she saw the dragon look down and thrust it's head down at Malik.

The huge jaws were open wide ready to bite into him but somehow he managed to catch them with his hands before they could close on him. He stood holding the dragon and it's open jaws back. The dragon tried to pull and shake it's head free of Malik's grip. Strangely the massively powerful dragon seemed unable to move or lift the comparatively small man that was hanging on to it's jaw. Instead it changed tactics and started to force itself down onto Malik.

Aris saw Malik's legs start to dip under the force of the dragon. She ran to the spinning Dark Gate and held up Malik's sword.

The sword began to glow red as she willed it to activate and suddenly felt a surge of power fill her as she held the sword.

Malik dropped down onto one knee as the large jaws began to close in on him. Aris swung the sword at the spinning outer frames of the Dark Gate.

There was a clattering sound as the sword connected and sliced through the frames as they span past leaving a glowing red trail through the air.

The spinning mechanism suddenly became unbalanced as it lost structural strength. Then under the massive rotational force parts began to snap off and fly from it as it began to break apart under the strain.

The black hole flickered and started to shrink. The dragon screeched and tried to pull away to get back through the black hole.

"Oh no you are staying here you bastard!" Malik shouted and took a firm grip on the dragon's lower jaw and pulled it back.

The black hole flickered and disappeared with a final flash of black light.

Since the dragon's neck was now no longer connected to the rest of it's body it fell to the ground and twitched as the muscles went into spasm.

Malik threw the head to the ground and gave it a kick with his foot sending the huge head and neck skidding across the floor where it slammed into a wall causing cracks to appear in the walls surface.

Aris ran over to him and threw her arms around him. She looked at his face and took a step back when she saw that his eyes were glowing blue. In the gloom of the cave they shone brilliantly. As she felt his power return to normal the blue glow died away until they were back to normal.

"How did you do that?"

Malik took a step forward toward her and she took another step back.

"I don't know, it just happened when Tethis hurt you. Now I can turn it on and off when I need to" He looked down.

"Aris do you think I'm a monster?"

Aris stepped forward and put both hands on his face and kissed him.

"No more than me, I've always known there was something buried deep down in you"

Malik smiled and put his arms around her and hugged her tightly. When he let her go he looked down at her clothes and noticed she had blood on her clothes.

"Have you been hurt!" He asked quickly.

"No"

He looked down at his own shirt he was bleeding from the wound in his stomach again.

"Oh damn it" He said and fell forward into Aris's arms.

Malik slowly opened his eyes and blinked in the sunlight that shone through the open window. He eased himself up onto his elbows and looked around.

"Aris?"

"She's resting next door" Father Spectre said from a corner of the room. "She stayed with you since your were brought here. Sarah came in earlier and found her asleep. So we moved her next door where she can rest more comfortably"

"Thank you"

Father Spectre smiled and got up and walked over and sat down again in a chair closer to the bed.

"Father, how did I end up here?"

"The Battlemages arrived and stormed the mine. They found you cradled in Aris's arms. They were able to stabilise your condition and brought you both back here to Torkle"

"What about the captives?"

"Safe, the Battlemages saw them coming down the mountain led by Mathias Killdare and sent a small party to escort them here safely"

"Good" Malik said and lay back.

Father Spectre looked down and then raised his head when Malik spoke.

"Father something happened to me in the mountain"

"Yes I know"

"You do?"

"For those of us who are gifted with… special senses shall we say, your awakening was similar to a very large volcano suddenly erupting"

"Awakening?"

"Hmm yes that is the best way of describing it. You have questions no doubt but it is not for me to answer you. Those answers await you back in Founders Rock"

Malik opened his mouth to argue but Father Spectre held up a hand.

"I can tell you that you are no monster you are Draconis just like your mother, father and even Aris. You are still you in every little detail only that your true potential has revealed itself. As for Aris she truly loves you with all her heart and always will so don't worry"

Malik shut his mouth and went to get up out of the bed throwing back the bed covers.

"Draconis?" He said to himself.

"I've organised for some tools to be left in the Blacksmith's Smithy for you" Father Spectre said standing up distracting Malik from his inevitable question.

"You won't try and stop me from moving?" Malik said surprised.

"Why bother it wouldn't do any good! Besides look at your wound"

Malik slowly lifted his shirt and peeled off the dressing that was bandaged to his stomach. The wound had closed and scabbed over. The surrounding skin that had been burnt by the Frostbite flame was slightly red in colour. As he rubbed it with his fingers parts of the scab fell away revealing newly healed skin underneath.

"By the Gods!"

"No not them, just simple biology" Father Spectre said. "Oh by the way the Mayor wanted to present you with something to show his appreciation for all your help in saving the captives"

Father Spectre pointed his cane at a box that was lying next to the bed.

"I thought this is what you would want. Aris will be asleep until tomorrow morning. Fighting Tethis's will took a lot out of her, poor girl"

Malik knelt down and opened the box.

"This is perfect thank you! Although I would quite happily have paid for it" He said smiling.

"You will make up for it in other ways I have no doubt. You have removed the dark shadow on these lands and it is you who will bring life back here whether you know it or not" Father Spectre replied.

He smiled at Malik and then left the room.

Malik picked up the box and ran out of the room excitedly. He then ran back in and put his clothes and shoes on then ran out again.

He ran down the street to the Blacksmith's Smithy and dashed inside. The Smithy was in very good condition and it didn't take Malik long to get the forge alight.

People were busy removing boards and repairing some of the houses and as they walked past the Smithy they stopped when they heard the hammering coming from the inside. Some of them stopped to watch Malik work as he laded some molten metal into a sand moulding he had made.

The daylight faded until the light from the Smithy spilled out onto the street casting silhouettes on the ground. Some of the crystal streetlights flickered into life as Mayor Falstaff walked down to the Smithy and knocked on the open door.

"How are you doing lad?"

"Nearly finished, could you do me a favour please?"

"Certainly what is it?"

"I could do with a beer! It's a bit hot in here!"

"Not a problem lad I'll be back in a minute" Mayor Falstaff said and disappeared back up the street to the town hall.

He returned a few minutes later carrying two bottles of beer. He entered the Smithy as Malik was working at the forge. By this time he had taken his shirt off and was shaping a piece of sliver metal with a small file. The Mayor noticed that the wound on his stomach was now completely healed.

"Here you go" Mayor Falstaff said putting a bottle down by Malik.

Malik put the file and piece of metal down and picked up the bottle by the neck and flicked the bottle cap off with his thumb. The Mayor tried to remove the top off of his and gave up. Wordlessly he handed it to Malik who gave the Mayor his opened one and flicked the cap off of the new bottle with his thumb again.

"Thank you" Malik said holding the bottle up and took a long drink.

"Cheers" The Mayor said and took a drink from his bottle.

"What's on your mind Mayor?" Malik asked as he put down the bottle and picked up the file and piece of metal again.

"You'll be heading back to Founder's Rock soon?"

"In a little while yes, there are some questions that I need answered"

"We were all hoping you both would stay, Torkle feels safe again since you both came"

"I'd really like to, this place reminds me of Halton my home town"

Malik started to work on the small piece of metal again. He then took it and placed it against a long metal rod. He picked up the Blacksmith's welding pen and fused the two pieces of metal together.

"We would gladly give you both a large home here" The Mayor continued.

"Sorry but I just couldn't accept that" Malik said putting down the pen and blowing on the metal before he continued.

"But I might be prepared to buy a property and some land here"

"Buy?" The Mayor nearly choked on the beer.

"Certainly! I have money I've never really used and recently there have been... developments so I'm looking to buy a place in the country. Besides this town needs the money to rebuild itself"

"What exactly did you have in mind?" The Mayor asked.

"I noticed that there was a very nice looking estate on the outskirts of Torkle when we were coming here"

"Vindrel Manor? That place has been abandoned and not been used since our last Lord buggered… Oh"

Malik carefully opened the door and quietly walked into Aris's room. He carefully put the box he was carrying by the side of the bed.

Aris was asleep on the far side of the bed. With great care Malik climbed onto the bed and lay down beside her, Aris murmured and rolled over. She put her arm around him and settled back to sleep.

Malik gently lifted her head and put his arm under and around her so her head rested on his chest then fell asleep and slept peacefully until the morning light shone through the window and woke him.

He turned his head to look at Aris. She was quietly watching him.

"Good morning" She whispered and smiled.

"Good morning to you" He replied.

"I have something here for you"

"For me?"

Malik picked up the box and handed it to her.

"Here you are. Sorry, I had to break your last one as you were trying to kill me with it"

Aris sat up in the bed and unwrapped the box before she opened it, when she saw what was inside her eyes opened wide.

"It's beautiful" She said taking a silver rod out of the box.

The rod was a foot long and was decorated with runes and crystals that ran across its surface.

"It's a very special staff. It's one of a kind just like you" Malik said.

"Not that I'm ungrateful but it is a bit short to call it a staff"

Malik smiled and leaned over.

"Press the little jewel by your thumb there"

Aris did so and the rod extended to over four times its original length. It then returned to its original length when she pressed the jewel again.

"That's amazing! You made this for me?"

"Of course! I also made this as well"

He reached into a pocket and pulled out a small silver ring, which he held out to her.

"After all we have been through together I don't want to be without you ever again. So would you marry me... Please!" He said smiling nervously.

Aris put her hand across her mouth in surprise and then she took her hand away.

"Malik there is something you should know. Before you can marry me you have to first complete a trial"

"Why?"

"It's one of the rules set out by the Council of Mages"

"Alright so I pass a trial"

"Even if it could cost you your life?"

"Of course! I had to let you go once before and I'm not doing that ever again"

Aris held out her hand and smiled. Tears started to form in her eyes as Malik slipped the ring onto her finger.

"Malik, promise me you will pass the trial and not die" She cried.

Malik placed a hand on her cheek and gently wiped the tear away from her eye with his thumb.

"I promise you here and now, I will marry you and nothing is going to stop me"

Aris flung her arms around Malik and kissed him as he put his arms around her holding her tightly.

"Come on I've got to show you something!" Malik said.

"There's more?"

"Just one other thing. Come on get dressed"

"What's the rush" Aris giggled and pulled the covers back.

"Nothing that cannot wait"

Malik pulled his shirt over the top of his head and jumped as Aris placed a cold hand on his chest.

"That's cold" He said as he lay beside her and ran his hand up and down her body.

"Well come here and warm me up then!"

Aris pulled the covers back over them.

Much later that morning Malik sat in the kitchen with a mug of tea in his hand while Aris was talking with a group of her new friends she had made. Malik recognised some of them as captives from the compound. They were all crowding around Aris looking at her ring that she wore on her finger.

Malik took a drink from the mug when he felt a slight tug on his arm. He looked down into a small young boy's face.

"Hello, you are one of the Mayor's grandchildren aren't you!"

"Yes Sir" The small child said.

"What can I do for you?"

"Granddad Brian said you can make your eyes glow! Is that true!"

"Err" Malik said looking around in case anybody had heard.

"Please show me"

"I can't do that" Malik said desperately.

"Yes you can granddad Brian said you could and he is always right!" the little boy said jumping up and down.

Malik sighed and crouched down by the little boy then he looked around again to make sure no one was watching.

"Alright but if you have nightmares about it don't say I didn't warn you!" Malik whispered.

He gently increased his power so his eyes slowly turned brighter. The little boy's eyes widened and he broke out into a huge grin then clapped his hands together.

"Make them brighter!" The little boy laughed.

"Alright how's this!"

Malik smiled and made a large increase in his power so his eyes shone brightly. Unfortunately this also made the room vibrate as well, the table rattled across the floor followed by a chair.

Malik quickly dropped his power back to normal and stood up straight rather more quickly than he intended.

Aris was standing looking at him. She had her arms crossed and was tapping the floor with her foot, the stern look on her face said all Malik needed to know.

The little boy was excitedly jumping up and down behind Malik and laughing.

"Do it again! Do it again!" He said excitedly.

"Err... I think I'm just going outside to get some fresh air!"

Malik sheepishly and quickly ushered the small boy out of the door. When he had quickly departed out of the door Aris burst into laughter followed by the rest of the women.

Outside the little boy pulled Malik along by the hand to the market building outside of the town hall.

The rest of the Mayor's grandchildren were sat under the roof of the market square. The little boy ran up to them and with a triumphant look on his face pointed at Malik.

"He can make his eyes glow!" The little boy laughed.

"And he made the house shake!"

"No he didn't" One of the boys said.

"You're making it up"

"Yes he did! I saw him do it!" the little boy protested.

"Prove it, make him do it again!"

"Oh Gods" Malik said.

The little boy looked up at Malik.

"Please!" He pleaded.

"Alright one last time then that's it!"

Malik kneeled down and changed again to make his eyes glow. This time though he was careful to avoid pushing his power too far.

The little boy stood proudly by Malik as if showing off a new toy.

The other children's jaws dropped.

"That is so amazing!" The eldest grandchild said excitedly.

"What else can you do?"

Malik looked around and saw a weathercock on top of a building at the other end of the street.

"Alright boys, see that weathercock on the building other there"

Malik pointed and the boys all strained to see it. He then looked around the ground.

"Yes" They all chorused together.

Malik reached down and picked up a small stone he tossed it up and down in his hand testing its weight. He concentrated on the weathercock and his vision zoomed in on it.

"Ready?" Malik said and when they nodded he threw the stone.

There was a whizzing sound as the stone flew through the air at an extraordinary speed.

The stone connected with the weathercock and made a loud clanging sound. That rang out over the town. It also made the weathercock spin around incredibly quickly for several minutes. Several miles away a red hot stone landed in a small pool of water with a large plop and a large cloud of steam.

A large Carnitoad jumped out of the pool and hopped around wildly croaking until it cooled down.

The boys all cheered and clapped.

"Having fun darling?" Aris said from behind Malik.

He cringed slightly as if waiting for her to yell at him.

"Err I was just I…" Malik said as he walked over to her, Aris smiled at him.

"Do you see now that you are no monster" She said putting her arms around him.

"Those boys think you are wonderful, and so do I. You know, I actually find them attractive!" She said and looked into Malik's brightly glowing eyes.

He waggled his eyebrows at her, she laughed and kissed him.

They both tactfully ignored the sound of the boys behind Malik as they made vomiting noises and stuck fingers in there mouths.

"What did you want to show me?"

"Oh yes, I'd forgotten all about that" Malik said as his eyes returned to their normal colour.

He held her hand and gently led her down the steps of the Town hall.

"Come with me!" He said and led her down the street toward the outskirts of the town.

"Can we come too?" The boys shouted from behind.

"Come on then" Malik said and waved his other hand.

The boys jumped up and followed them down the street.

When they reached the outskirts of town, Malik pointed to a spire that appeared over the top of some trees in the distance.

"Do you see the spire over there?" He asked Aris.

"Yes"

"That is the high tower of a manor house. The lands surrounding it also belong to the house.

"So?"

"Well it's mine now"

"Your's"

"Yes, I bought it"

"Bloody hell!" Aris paused for a moment then asked.

"Why?"

"Well I like it here, and I always wanted a home away from the city"

"And?" She said.

"What do you mean?"

"There's more, I can tell by your face"

"Well…"

"Go on!"

"I thought your parents would be more accepting of a land owner and…"

"Yes"

"I don't want to raise our children in the city"

Aris looked side long at Malik he was blushing and looking down at the ground.

"Malik" She said softly.

"Yes" He said dreading what was coming next.

"You really are sweet aren't you! It's beautiful, can we go see it?" She said taking his hand.

"Of course" Malik said and let out a sigh of relief.

A coach rolled up beside them and the Mayor leaned down.

"Can I give you both a lift? I was just going to unlock the manor house for your Lordship"

"Lordship?" Aris asked.

"Oh yes you see whoever owns the manor is also granted the title of Lord"

"But you're the Mayor!"

"Oh yes I run the place but the Lord owns the lands that the town is built on and has the final say"

"What do you think? Would you like to be a Lady?" Malik asked.

"Yes please!" Aris said still slightly shocked.

Malik jumped aboard and held out his hand, which Aris took and he pulled her up into the carriage. The coach pulled away and rattled down the lane with the boys running along side it. Two voices could be heard from within.

"Malik, how much did it cost"

"Err Three hundred thousand gold pieces give or take" Malik said scratching his head.

"Bloody hell, how much money do you actually have?"

"Well I haven't really spent much money over the years, and I got paid a lot last year for making new weapons for the whole of the Royal Guard. That was when I wasn't sleeping at night, before I met you"

"So how much do you have? Come on you know it doesn't matter to me!"

"Well nearly five hundred thousand at the moment give or take"

"Malik"

"Yes Sweetheart"

"I love you!"

"I know you do"

"Can I have some new shoes?"

The coach rattled on down the lane and disappeared from view followed by the group of children.

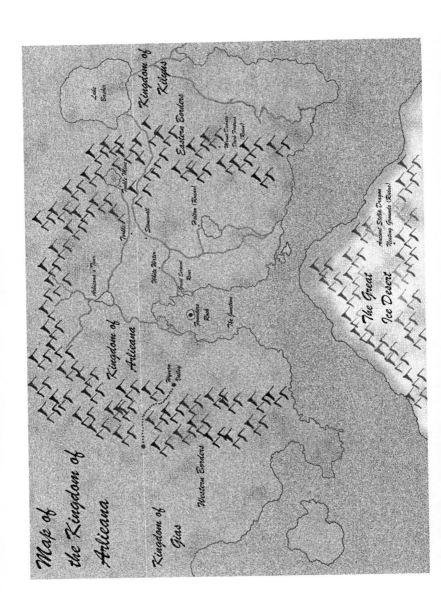

Appendix:

A

Arlieana & the City of Founders Rock

*The kingdom of Arlieana lies between two other kingdoms.
The entire country is ringed by a vast mountain range which
stretches from the Western borders to the Northlands and
round to the Eastern borders. The mountains cease to the
south. There lies the Great Sea and many of Arlieana's
trading ports.*

*Flowing from the mountains in the north down to the sea
is the River of Storms. The River of Storms varies from
being small individual rivers and streams in places to the
body of water called "The Junction" on its journey from the
Northland Mountains to the Great Sea.*

*The capital city of Arlieana is Founders Rock a city built in
the middle of the Junction. Legend has it that first King of
Arlieana made a pact with the Dragonlord of the Western
Mountain range. The deal was that the Dragonlord would*

aid him to build a city in the Junction, in return for letting the Dragonlord and his brood live in Arlieana. The foundations of the city Founders Rock was provided by the Dragonlord and his brood. Legend claims that they sunk a mountaintop from their homelands into the Junction.

Founders Rock has docks built all around it providing shipbuilding and cargo transport. As the River of Storms covers most of Arlieana and converges at the Junction, Founders Rock is the trade centre of Arlieana. Ships are a common sight moored or sailing around Founders Rock.

After the docks the outer wall provides the city's first line of defence. Market stalls line the interior and exterior of the outer wall and provides visitors with anything they need for a price. There are four gateways that allow entrance to the city through the Outer Wall into the Outer Rim. Each of the gateways can be sealed with a massive steel door that drops into place. Four Guardians are stationed at each of the gates, two above on top of the gate and two below on either side at ground level.

The Outer Rim of Founders Rock provides the city's Industrial, Storage and Commerce sectors. The foundries process ores brought down on the barges and River Runners from the mountains. The warehouses store the processed materials, before being transported all over Arlieana by the Guild of Merchants.

Beyond the Outer Rim is the Second Wall and is linked to the centre of Founders Rock by the Master Gateway. The Master

Gateway is the largest of the gates and provides the last line of defence if the Outer Wall is breached during an invasion.

The Centre of Founder's Rock contains the city's most valuable buildings. The Guild Houses line the inside of the Outer wall along with the Headquarters and Training Grounds of the Crimson Guardians. Moving further towards the centre of the city the Library, Treasury, City Guardians Barracks and Elemental Mages College are spread around the base of a high hill upon which stands the Royal Palace.

The Palace is raised above the Outer Wall so from the highest tower of the palace (also known as Dragon Roost Tower) it is possible to see the whole of Founders Rock and surrounding waters.

B

Borug

Borug is an abnormally huge and powerful Orc in Tethis's army of darkness. Taller than a house Borug is used primarily as a siege weapon to remove any outer defence a town might have before letting in the rest of the Orc raiders.

Battlemages

The Battlemages are the main combat force of the Elemental Mages College and have been the only means of defence against the Shades that the Dark God commands. Shades are only vulnerable to attacks by magic making them almost impossible to kill by none magic users. For this reason the Battlemages are one of the most important parts of the Elemental Mages College.

C

Calgar, Aris

Youngest Daughter of Marcus and Helena Calgar Aris is a powerful Elemental Mage. Trained from a young age in the arts of magic the same as her older siblings she is more than a match for any adversary at a distance.

Having spent much of her youth in Founders Rock and the College of magic she hadn't experienced some of the dangers in the outside world. On a trip to the town of Halton she had an encounter with a Carnitoad, a large carnivorous and generally bad tempered toad.

She was rescued by a young boy called Malik. She spent the summer with him. Over the course of the time they spent together the two became close friends and set about causing mischief in Halton. Before she had to leave Halton she and Malik cast a powerful spell to bring them back together.

It took fourteen years to reunite them but they are and they are very much in love with each other. Their bond is so strong that when the Dark Shade Tethis hurt Aris her scream triggered Malik's own 'Awakening' allowing him to overpower and seriously injure the Dark Shade.

Aris has learned much from Malik after being reunited. She is more self confident and has become adept at close combat fighting under Malik's expert tutorage. She has managed to combine her spell casting with some of the combat techniques taught her by Malik to lethal effect.

She is overjoyed that Malik has asked her marry him but is worried about the trial that Malik has to undertake as she knows it will test him to his limits.

Calgar, Danier / Aston, Danier

Danier is the second of Marcus Snr & Helena's three children. Danier has found the Arcane Library to be very much to her taste. She has taken on the role of Chief Historical Researcher for the Elemental Mages College. She is an expert in ancient languages and is one of the few people to be granted access to the Draconis Records kept in the Royal Palace. She has recently gotten married to Lieutenant Phillip Aston a Battlemage in the 'Red Ravens' unit. They met when Marcus Jr introduced them at a formal dinner event held at the Royal Palace. They are both currently away on their honeymoon.

Calgar, Helena

Helena is a senior member of the Council of Magic and wife to Marcus Calgar. She has been with her husband since they were children and like her husband has been friends with James Heald and Tiber Owen for many years.

A protective mother she and her husband have three children. Marcus Calgar Jr the eldest son. Followed by Danier Calgar the first of their daughters and finally the youngest is Aris Calgar.

She is proud of all her family and dotes on her grandchildren from her son's marriage and is eagerly hoping for more from Danier's recent marriage.

Calgar, Justin & Marie

*The twin brother and sister are the children of Marcus Jr &
Faith Calgar. They are doted upon by their grandparents
Marcus Snr and Helena Calgar. The twins love spending
their time with their youngest Auntie, Aris who teaches
them Arial Acrobatics. Both Children have great magical
potential but it is Marie who has an uncanny ability to sense
a person's character. So much so that her father makes a point
of never trusting anyone that his daughter doesn't like (He
'arranged' for her to meet Phillip Aston before Marcus would
promote him to Lieutenant. After the meeting Marcus then
introduced him to his younger sister Danier – the two have
since gotten married).*

Calgar, Marcus Snr

*Arch Mage of Founders Rock Elemental Mages College of
Magic and husband to Helena Calgar a member of the
Council of Magic. He is a long term friend of James Heald
and Tiber Owen as they all served together in the Royal
Guard.*

*He often visits his friend James Heald and is one of the few
people to know the true identity of May's mother.*

*Under his guidance and with the backing of his wife the
Elemental Mages College has become more involved in the
protection of Arileana. He spearheaded the creation of the
Battlemages, a group of Elemental Mages trained in combat
tactics. When used in conjunction with Crimson Guardians
they form a very effective combat unit that is difficult to
defeat.*

Calgar, Marcus Jr

A senior member of the Elemental Mages and commander of the 'Red Ravens' a special unit of Battlemages. He is known to be reliable and level headed for this reason he is usually deployed to deal with delicate situations. He is married to Faith and they have two children Marie and Justin. He is fiercely loyal to family and is mistrustful of people that his daughter doesn't like.

Crimson Guardians

The Crimson Guardians are the elite Guardians of Arlieana. They were founded by Captain James Heald twenty years prior to the events at Torkle. Only a handful of people become Crimson Guardians and uniquely they are not all soldiers. The Crimson Guardians include many disciplines from Forest Rangers to Scouts and Heavy Calvary. The only people who know why this is the king of Arlieana and a few select other individuals. It has been speculated by other parties that bloodlines have something to do with it but it is only speculation after all.

D

Dark Gates

Dark Gates are used to transport people or items to or from the Chaos realm of the Dark God to the various Dark Worlds spread over the universe. They work by folding the fabric of space between two gates making travel between them instantaneous. Dark Gates vary in design from world to world as they are constructed on each world by the Dark God's influence. Once the gate is complete a small army marches through the gate and spread out. More gates are built to bring more troops and equipment through to the world to be conquered.

D

Draconis

The Draconis are a race of Human/ Dragon hybrids. After the Dark God's defeat at The Dark Fortress the Dragon Riders returned home. The Dragonlord ordered that the Dragons would return to their lands and they would hide away from the world. Some of the Dragons and their Riders had formed tight bonds that couldn't be broken including the Dragonlord's own daughter Fara. In an act of defiance the Dragons cast off their physical forms and took on human forms instead. Although they were now human they still carried Dragon's blood in their veins. This was passed on down through the generations.

All Draconis have the increased speed, agility, strength and healing abilities. Some Draconis gain the ability to 'Awaken'. When this occurs the individual gains a massive increase in all their abilities and power. It is unknown why this happens – some speculate that as each new generation is born they are evolving as they become more in tune with the Dragon's blood inside them.

Some Draconis are born with the ability to 'Awaken' from birth while others will 'Awaken' as a reflex to a dangerous situation or to protect another. One thing is common though. Once a Draconis has 'Awoken' they can change at will.

When in an awoken state all Draconis's eyes glow with the colour of their original dominant Dragons colour. Female Draconis also take on the hair colour of the dominant gene, for example the female members of the Royal Family all have golden blonde hair from the link to the golden Dragon Fara.

Over the generations though two types of Draconis have appeared those known as 'Casters' and those known as 'Alterers'

'Casters' are Draconis who can cast spells without the need for Elemental Crystals. Usually when identified 'Casters' are inducted into The Elemental Mages College where they train to harness their magical abilities.

'Alterers' are Draconis who cannot cast spells but instead use magic to bend the laws of physics to their advantage. This allows 'Alterers' to move incredibly fast and have unnatural strength. A good example of how 'Alterers' can use their abilities is this example. If a person stood on a raft that was floating untied beside a riverbank tried to jump onto the riverbank they would end up in the river.

This is because physics says that for every action there is an equal an opposite reaction. So the force being used to jump forward toward the riverbank is also pushing the raft away from the riverbank at the same time.

If a Draconis 'Alterer' tried the same experiment the raft would remain where it was while the 'Alterer' would land on the riverbank nice and dry (not that a Draconis would bother too much with a raft, they would just jump the river in a single bound).

Draconis 'Alterers' can mostly be found in the Crimson Guardians. The Crimson Guardians are the defenders of Arlieana and while they cannot fight Shades they are more than a match for anything else that threatens the Kingdom. The units made up of both 'Casters' and 'Alterers' are a very powerful combination that is not to be taken lightly in combat.

E

Elemental Crystals

Elemental Crystals are a special type of crystal that grows naturally in the mountains of Vishante. They are special as they can take on and retain certain elemental properties. These properties have been explored and technologies developed to take advantage of them. For example Ice crystals are used to refrigerate food and run large cold rooms. The most used crystals are the Fire crystals, which are used to create endless amounts of steam to power engines on ships and more recently the engines on the new powered coaches.

Elemental Mages

The Elemental Mages are an organisation of individuals dedicated to the practice of elemental magic. Elemental Magic was taught to humans by the Stella Dragon of Vishante five centuries ago during the Dark Age of Vishante. They are based in the Elemental Mages College in Founders Rock and are responsible for the development of technologies based on the elemental crystals that are found in the mountains of Vishante.

H

Heald, Captain James

Captain and founder of the Crimson Guardians unit James Heald answers only to the King of Arlieana himself. Captain Heald was rapidly promoted to Captain twenty years ago for saving the Princess Tia. Despite him being only a Royal Guard at the time the Princess fell in love with him. During the time he and the Princess spent trying to return to Arlieana from Gias they both came across a Spirit stone in a cave. The Captain later used half of the stone to create a pendant for the Princess. The other he fused with his family sword.

When they returned to Arlieana James Heald asked the King for the Princess's hand in marriage. The King could not allow a public marriage to someone who wasn't born of high nobility.

The Princess's Royal suitor did not take kindly to James Heald's proposal and challenged him to single combat for the hand of the Princess. The Royal suitor was certainly more powerful than James and easily beat the guard but it wasn't until he was about to deliver the fatal blow that the tables turned.

There were no witnesses to the combat but somehow James overpowered the Royal Suitor and beat him but did not kill him. The outraged Royal suitor accused James of attempting to murder him and had the guards arrest him.

James would have been executed if it were not for the Princess. She confessed to her father the love she has for James and had in fact known about the combat. She had witnessed what had happened there. The Princess attributed James's victory to his sudden 'Awakening' a fact that surprised the King.

The King summoned James to his quarters and confronted him about his love for the Princess. The King offered James a challenge. If he could match the King's power he would acknowledge there love and consent to it.

James accepted without thinking it was only then that the King revealed a secret held in the Royal Bloodline. The Royal bloodline held Dragons blood in its ancestry that dated back to the beginnings of Arlieana. This gave the Royal Bloodline incredible power and only one who could match it would be allowed to marry into the family.

James held his ground against the King and in doing so revealed much to his own surprise the Dragons blood in his own family line. It was revealed that there were a number of families that also held Dragons blood in its ancestry but no official records were made.

The King was impressed with James and consented to there love but decreed that they could only marry in secret. This was so the secret of the bloodlines could be preserved. They agreed and were married in secret in the palace chapel.

They have a daughter called May and the princess takes on the guise of the Captain's housekeeper to be with her family each night.

James was promoted to Captain and convinced the King to allow him to form a new unit called the Crimson Guardians. They were made up of similar people who had also 'Awakened' or were known to carry Dragons blood in the family. They now serve as the elite guardians of Arlieana.

It causes him so much pain that he cannot tell May the truth about her mother and that he cannot be with his wife in public.

Heald, May

She is the secret daughter of James Heald and Princess Tia Heald. May is a very strong willed and intelligent young woman who cares for her friends and family. She doesn't know who her mother is but does not believe that she is dead, as her father has told her. May was raised by the Captain and his housekeeper (the secret guise of Princess Tia so she could be with her family). She has a very strong bond with Malik and Charleston and the three have been inseparable ever since they joined the Crimson Guardians.

The second eldest of the trio next to Charleston (although there is only a matter of months between the three of them) she often looks out for Malik like a big sister.

May is the Chief Administrator of the Crimson Guardians and given her father's lack of organisational skills it is a very good job too. She looks after the day to day running of the Crimson Guardians and is the one to talk to if you have a problem. Though she is the Chief Administrator she is an expert marksman and can handle a sword as well as any of men in the Crimson Guardians.

Heald, Tia

Princess Tia Heald is the eldest daughter of King Liyon the second and the secret wife of Captain James Heald. She is an incredibly beautiful woman whose beauty masks a very quick and intelligent mind. In order to be with her family she dons the disguise of the Captain's housekeeper each afternoon and leaves early in the morning to resume her original identity. Along with May she has looked after Charleston and Malik as they were all brought into the Heald household by the Captain.

She takes pride in her daughter's achievements and is glad that May keeps an eye on James and looks after him while she is not around.

She loves to travel and often does on royal business. Travelling also gives her time to spend with her husband as Captain Heald is officially the Princess's personal bodyguard and she will not travel without him being close by.

She always wears a pendant made by her husband, which contains half of the Spirit Stone that they found. The pendant glows when she is in danger and allows the Captain to know exactly where she is at any time.

K

King, Charleston

Malik's best friend since Malik first came to Founders Rock with Captain Heald.

Charleston is a quick-witted young man and is fiercely loyal to his friends. Charleston grew up with both Malik and May and the three have always stuck together. Though he may have a laid back approach to life he is an excellent Crimson Guardian and will do whatever is needed to protect the people and his friends. In Malik's absence both He and May have grown closer than before.

Never afraid to protect his friends Charleston has gotten into several altercations over the years with various people. The most notable was his and Malik's encounter with Baron Richardson who was harassing May. The result of which was the Baron's armed private guards being beaten black and blue and left hanging upside down after being tied to a lamppost.

O

Orcs

Orcs form the backbone of the Dark Army. They were the first race that the Dark God enslaved. They are strong and resilient creatures that can survive in the harshest of conditions (in all probability this is the reason they were enslaved as they can adapt to any world that the Dark God wants to conquer).

All of the Orcs in the Dark Army have been bread for viciousness and aggressiveness. They are totally loyal to their master (whether due to magical control or breeding is unknown) and have limited regenerative abilities that are the main reason for their incredible adaptivness to other environments. In single combat they are little challenge to an 'Awakened' Draconis but when they attack as a pack they become a very dangerous enemy capable of even overwhelming a Draconis by sheer weight of numbers.

Owen, Darcy

Darcy is the mother of Malik Owen and Wife to Tiber Owen. A long time friend of Helena Calgar, Darcy Firestaff was introduced to Tiber Owen by Marcus Calgar when he was made the Archmage of the Elemental Mages College. The two felt an instant attraction and quickly fell in love. Darcy began to help Tiber with his experiments. They both discovered the existence of 'Male' and 'Female' Elemental crystals and how to breed 'hybrid' crystals. Hybrid Crystals were Elemental Crystals that combined elements from both parent crystals into a single crystal with new properties. After the discovery Tiber's workshop was destroyed by an unknown attacker. Darcy was seriously hurt in the attack and reported that the attacker had used Black magic. After she had recovered both her and Tiber were ordered by the King to rebuild the work they had lost in a secret location. They selected the quiet town of Halton in the east of Arlieana to be their new base.

After several years they decided to marry and returned to Founders Rock for the ceremony. Darcy was heartbroken when her father refused to take part in the ceremony as he saw Tiber as unsuitable for his daughter. Although Tiber was a fully awakened Draconis he was not a mage. Darcy's father saw this as a disgrace to the Firestaff's long Draconis Bloodline, which had always been made up of Casters.

Darcy rejected her father's views and was walked down the isle by Marcus Calgar the Archmage with Helena as her Bridesmaid. The ceremony took place in the Royal Palace and was performed by Princess Tia.

The following year Malik was born and the family lived happily together. Darcy always took pleasure in watching Malik with his father as they went out exploring or fishing (which Malik loved too do). She loved the little ways her son acted like his father and saw the same strength in his young body.

After six years of work Darcy and Tiber managed to complete their great work. The creation of a Spirit Stone that would allow a Draconis to destroy a shade with a physical weapon. She sent word to Marcus Calgar the Archmage and a short time later he arrived with Darcy and His youngest Daughter Aris.

During the weeks that Marcus & Helena spent in Halton, Darcy had seen Malik playing with Aris. There was one horrible night when they both disappeared but Tiber went out and found them Camping and brought them back safely.

After they returned to Founders Rock, Darcy noticed a strange mark on Malik's shoulder and recognised what it meant. She quietly told Tiber about it and the two decided to leave it at that knowing full well the choice Malik had made was the right one.

Several weeks later when the Mayor had called Tiber to a meeting the Town was attacked by Black Orcs. Darcy was unable to defend her family with her magic as she had discovered he was pregnant with a baby girl a few months before. Instead she hid Malik under a bed in their home and tried to hide herself. Unfortunately it proved useless as she was killed by a Black Orc champion who also found Malik and seriously injured him giving him the large scar that runs across his chest.

Captain Heald arrived with a squad of Crimson Guardians a day too late to help. He found Malik instantly recognising him and brought him back too Founders Rock where he grew up with May Heald & Charleston King. Malik eventually joined the Crimson Guardians.

Owen, Malik

Malik Owen is the orphaned son of Tiber and Darcy Owen. He is the sole survivor of the town of Halton, which was destroyed overnight by a mysterious army when he was six years old. Malik found a rare elemental spirit stone hidden in a secret cavern underneath his parent's house. Rescued by Captain Heald of the Crimson Guardians a trusted friend of his parents Malik was taken to Founders Rock where he met May Heald and Charleston King and became the best of friends.

Years later he began to suffer from nightmares that prevented him from sleeping. He occupied himself with studying and crafting. As a result he is widely regarded as the finest weapons craftsman in the Crimson Guardians.

He was commissioned by the King (on the recommendation of Captain Heald) to produce new weapons for the Palace Guard. Upon doing so he was rewarded with a substantial amount of money from the King himself.

While doing some reading he came across some text written by his father in the Crimson Guardian library. He learned what the stone he had found years before was. Using the text as a guide he began experimenting and finally fused the stone into a sword he had made for himself. The effort of fusing the stone took a strain on him and he was bed ridden for two days afterwards.

Shortly afterwards he was ordered to go to Torkle and investigate a series of incidents that had been occurring. He was partnered with a young Elemental Mage call Aris Calgar, daughter of Marcus and Helena Calgar.

Though at first they didn't exactly see eye too eye they later discovered they were close friends years before. The dark curse placed on Malik had blocked many of his memories as well as stopping him from sleeping.

Aris's parents had stayed in Halton on important business the year before it was destroyed.

Aris had been playing by herself when she was cornered by a Carnitoad. She was rescued by Malik and the two spent the summer months playing together, having adventures and generally giving Darcy Owen a headache and getting into trouble (The worst was when they got lost and had to spend the night camping).

Before Aris had to leave with her parents she and Malik performed a spell that would bring them back together and keep them together. The spell required them to mark each other with a unique symbol. Malik's symbol is on his right shoulder while Aris's is on the underside of her right arm.

They were parted for fourteen years until they were brought back together by the spell. After the events at Torkle he has proposed to Aris but first needs to complete a trial before he can actually marry her...

Owen, Tiber

The father of Malik and Husband to Darcy Owen Tiber was a member of the Royal Guard for many years. He had a talent for metal work and crystal work that led to him often repairing or modifying his fellow guards armour and weapons. He became friends with a Royal Guardsman called James Heald who he had worked with on several missions for King Liyons. The pair also met and became friends with an Elemental Mage Marcus Calgar and his wife Helena at the battle for Wyvern Valley. The four remained good friends for many years. Tiber met a young Elemental Mage called Darcy Firestaff a classmate and friend of Helena's. The two instantly connected and spent much time with each other. After James Healed returned with Princess Tia and was promoted to Captain he enlisted Tiber to help him form the Crimson Guardians. While helping to create the Crimson Guardians Tiber was also continuing his work with Elemental Crystals, aided by Darcy his research grew in leaps and bounds.

They jointly discovered that there were 'Male' and 'female' crystals and that under certain circumstances they could mate to produce hybrid crystals. After the discovery Tiber's workshop was attacked and destroyed while Darcy was seriously hurt.

After she had recovered from her injuries they were ordered to restart there work in a secret location known only to the James Heald and Marcus Calgar. Darcy was ordered to serve as Tiber's Magical Guardian and protect him from any Black magic.

The pair made there way to Halton where they spent several years rebuilding the lost work. During this time the two got married and risking being detected returned to Founders Rock for the ceremony. Darcy was walked down the isle by Marcus with Helena as her bridesmaid. Captain Heald was the best man and the ceremony was performed and blessed by Princess Tia herself in a secret ceremony performed at the palace. The two returned to Halton where they continued their work. The following year Malik was born and the family lived in peace. After six years of work Tiber sent urgent word back to Marcus in Founders Rock that he had finally accomplished what he had set out to do.

Marcus and Helena went to Halton with their youngest daughter under the cover that they were going on holiday. While they were there Tiber revealed his and Darcy's greatest achievement. A Spirit Stone that reacted with the energy of an awakened Draconis to produce a type of energy that would allow physical weapons to kill a Shade.

Impressed Marcus and Helena along with a very upset Aris returned to Founders Rock to report on the success.

Several weeks later Halton was attacked while Tiber and Darcy were separated. A Shade had taken on the guise of

Tethis the Mayor of Halton and had timed the attack for this very reason.

Tiber was killed by the Shade who crushed his heart with Black magic.

R

Reapers

Vicious insect creatures used as a terror weapons by the Dark Army. A Reaper has no will of its own instead it is controlled by a Dark Army commander (usually a Shade or other strong magical user). The Reaper can perform two functions.

Firstly it is a very effective torture device. A Reaper lave is placed upon the back of the torture victim. The lave proceeds to bury itself under the victims skin causing intense pain as it rapidly grows and starts consuming the victim from within.

The victim is then usually released where upon they will seek aid. Sometimes if a soldier is implanted with a Reaper lave they will be left on purpose where they can be found by other soldiers and brought back to base for medical aid.

This is where the Reapers second function becomes apparent. After the victim has been brought back to base, the lave upon command from its master will burst from the victims body in a shower of blood and gore and viciously attack those around them causing mass panic and terror.

A fully-grown Reaper has two sickle shaped claws, which are covered in a lethal poison the Reaper exudes from pores on each claw. The poison when inside a victim's body will quickly spread and breakdown the body's structure giving the effect that the body melts.

The poison is not lethal to Draconis (Awakened or not) but it does stop the rapid healing ability of the Draconis body. This can make even the most powerful Draconis vulnerable for a period of time until either their body clears the poison or they receive magical healing.

Red Ravens

The Red Ravens are a special unit of the Battlemages that specialise in aerial attacks from above. They usually fly above the target in their specially converted Airship and glide down on top of the enemy and attack them by surprise. They are under the command of Marcus Calgar Jr and are deployed to help deal with delicate operations.

River Runners

River Runners are a type of boat or ship. They are widely used all over Arlieana for the transport of people and light goods.

The basic layout of a River Runner is three decks. The lower deck houses the engines of the craft as well a cargo hold. The engines are mounted at the front of the River Runner. The engines work by sucking in water from the front of the vessel. The water flows into a chamber where a special crystal superheats the water and produces lots of steam. The steam turns a turbine, which turns a propeller and moves the River Runner through the water.

The middle deck has basic living accommodation. The rear of the middle deck is usually unenclosed and allows access to the cargo hold. The bridge deck is usually located above the living accommodation.

River Runners all have a flat bottom to their hulls. This allows them to travel up shallow rivers that are inaccessible to other types of craft. As they sit quite high in the water River Runners are also equipped with pontoons which are attached to an outrigger assembly.

When in dock the outriggers retract pulling the pontoons next to the hull. When in open water the pontoons are extended out and provide a wider base for the River Runner keeping it stable in the water.

S

Shades

A Shade is a creature from the Dark God's Realm of Chaos. Capable of taking over another being's physical body a Shade is a form of parasitic Shadow.

The Shade has no physical form making it completely immune to normal weapons. Magic is the only way to effectively fight and kill a shade but this is not always an easy task. Shades can cast powerful Black Magic spells that both attack and defend making a Shade a foe not to be underestimated.

Spirit Stones

Spirit Stones are the rarest type of Elemental Crystal. They have the ability to dramatically increase a person's physical abilities far beyond what they are naturally capable of. But it can only do so if it is integrated into an item or weapon and bonded to the individual. The crystal needs to be bonded to an individual's blood for any effect to occur.

Stonewall

The town of stonewall is a small port town surrounded by a large wall that runs around the exterior of the town. Stonewall is often called the gateway to the Northeast as most of the land traffic to the other surrounding areas run from Stonewall and vice versa.

T

Tethis

Tethis is a powerful Shade from the Dark God's realm of Chaos. Shades are best described as Shadows without a physical body of their own. They exist on Vishante by taking over a creature or a person's body and controlling it. The only real tell tale sign that a person has been infected by a Shade is the colour of their eyes which turn completely black when under a shades influence.

Tethis's main goal is to reopen as many of the buried Dark Gates as possible to bring reinforcements into Vishante and bring about a second Dark Age.

Tethis has a personal interest in Malik Owen, Tethis has cursed Malik with Black Magic causing him to loose many of his memories and suffer from nightmares. Malik is the only survivor of Tethis's attack on Halton where Tiber and Darcy Owen were killed fourteen years ago.

W

Waterwraiths

A Waterwraith is a native creature of Vishante and is found in the large mountain lakes and rivers where the water is very cold.

The Waterwraith is a very large breed of carnivorous fish that has evolved the ability to hunt on land as well as in the water by dragging itself along with two large claws it has evolved from the fins on its side. They breathe air and do not have gills so they have to surface to take a breath of air before they can return underwater.

They have been known to be washed downstream in the spring floods where they come into contact with, and pose a serious danger to fishermen.

Due to the danger they pose to local fishermen the Kingdom has placed a bounty of 500 gold pieces on any Waterwraith that has been washed downstream.

This has created a new type of fisherman who can make a good (and very dangerous!) living by specialising in hunting Waterwraiths. They use a special type of fishing spear which has an Electrical Elemental Crystal embedded in the spear tip (the fishermen refer to these as 'Shockers') which they use to spear and stun a Waterwraith after they have drawn one in close using chopped up bait.

Lightning Source UK Ltd.
Milton Keynes UK
04 September 2010
159416UK00001B/4/P